The Cru

Simon McCann

Crescit sub · Simon McCann · pondere virtus

The Conrad Press

The Crucian Case
Published by The Conrad Press in the United Kingdom 2025
Tel: +44(0)1227 472 874
www.theconradpress.com
info@theconradpress.com
ISBN 9781917673556
Copyright ©Simon McCann 2025
All rights reserved.
Typesetting and Cover Design by: Levellers
The Conrad Press logo was designed by Maria Priestley.
Printed and bound in Great Britain by Clays Ltd, Elcograf S.p.A.

Dedication
This book is dedicated to my wonderful wife, Jane,
who is and always will be the love of my life.

Foreword

I wrote this book while in hospital receiving a bone marrow transplant for myelofibrosis, a type of blood cancer.

I want to pay tribute to the amazing team of doctors, nurses and carers in the Bone Marrow Transplant unit at University Hospital of Wales, Cardiff, as well as the specialists in haematology, neurology, radiotherapy, occupational therapy, diet and physiotherapy who also cared for me. Not only is their clinical skill and professionalism absolutely world-class, all of them in BMT went the extra mile to support my mental and emotional wellbeing, which sometimes included a shoulder to cry on in the night. I cannot praise or thank them highly enough.

I must also give huge thanks to the anonymous donor of the stem cells that I received. He literally saved my life. Hopefully, I will get to thank him in person one day.

The stem cell donation and transplant were made possible by the amazing charity, Anthony Nolan. They make life-saving connections between patients and donors, as well as funding ground-breaking research that could transform the future for patients with blood cancers and blood disorders. I would strongly urge anyone aged 16 to 30, to consider joining the stem cell register via Anthony Nolan, at https://www.anthonynolan.org/help-save-a-life/join-stem-cell-register

or have a look at their website to see other ways of helping,

www.anthonynolan.org.

One day, you too may save someone's life.

Then there is the amazing network of family, friends and neighbours who sprang into action to give lifts, do shopping, gardening, dog-sitting, read and comment on early drafts of this story, and provide all kinds of help and support for me and my wife, as well as all those who prayed for me, had Masses said for me and sent me messages of hope, jokes, photographs and news. Special mentions must go to the chaplains of the UHW Catholic Chaplaincy and our parish priest, who have provided me with great hope and spiritual care; and also to a close family member who is an outstanding clinician and gave me much valuable advice and help to explain what was going on and allay my fears. One truly sees the very best of humanity at times like this and I thank each and every one of them.

There are two messages I would like to give to anyone suffering from myelofibrosis or other cancers, particularly those who are newly diagnosed.

The first is, *never give up*. Fight it with every fibre of your being, and treat every achievement whether big or small, at home, work or in exercise or pastimes, as a personal victory. I was first diagnosed nearly 20 years ago and until last year, when it became clear I needed the transplant, was able to enjoy a full family life, work a full time job and indulge my passion for running. This was, in large part, thanks to the excellent support I have received from the Haematology team at Cardiff over the years, and one absolutely brilliant professor/consultant in particular. While the diagnosis is a huge shock, it isn't the end – you can live a full, happy, active life with the right support. There is also a great deal of useful information and support available, both from Anthony Nolan and the excellent charity MPN Voice, at www.mpnvoice.org.uk.

The second message is, *do whatever exercise you can*. To quote one leading cancer expert, Professor Prue Cormie of the Australian Catholic University, '*Exercise is the best medicine someone with cancer can take in addition to their standard cancer treatments. That's because we know now that people who exercise regularly experience fewer and less severe treatment side effects; cancer-related fatigue, mental distress, [better] quality of life'*. There is also a lower risk of the cancer coming back and ultimately, of dying from the disease. The old approach of wrapping cancer patients in cotton wool is gone, and it is now recommended that people with cancer be as physically active as their current ability and conditions allow. I can personally attest to the fact that exercise has kept me going for much longer before requiring serious treatment, has improved my quality of life and meant I was fitter going into the transplant process and therefore, much better able to deal with it. So please, please, do whatever exercise you can.

I must also particularly mention and thank a trio who, although unknown to each other, greatly influenced this book: an old friend who got me into the highly-addictive world of carp fishing, which gave me the idea for the story; another old friend and former boss who very kindly gave a lot of himself to the book; and a certain grumpy, but very precise, Yorkshireman who spent a huge amount of time helping me with the editing.

Finally, and most of all, I must thank my wonderful wife, Jane, without whom I could not have got through this process.

Anthony Nolan –

Saving Lives Through Stem Cells

Anthony Nolan was a young boy who tragically died at the age of seven due to Wiskott-Aldrich syndrome, a rare blood disorder, without finding a matching donor for a bone marrow transplant. His mother, Shirley Nolan, founded the world's first stem cell register in 1974, named in his honour, to help others with similar conditions find compatible donors. Today, the charity Anthony Nolan continues her work, saving lives through stem cell transplants for people with blood cancer and blood disorders.

Anthony Nolan makes lifesaving connections between people with blood cancer and blood disorders, and incredible strangers ready to donate their stem cells. They're giving four patients another chance at life every day.

By growing the stem cell register, carrying out groundbreaking research and providing the best post-transplant care, they're giving families a future.

There are many ways you can help, for example -

• If you're aged 16–30, join the register at https://www.anthonynolan.org/help-save-a-life/join-stem-cell-register, and become a potential lifesaver;

• Give money or raise money to help fund Anthony Nolan's vital work, from adding new donors to the register to enabling further research;

- Volunteer your time to help raise awareness, support patients and donors, or even deliver the lifesaving cells.

To find out more, please visit their website at https://www.anthonynolan.org.

You too could save someone's life, as an amazing and generous donor did mine.

Disclaimer

THE CRUCIAN CASE

Chapter 1 –

Paradise Lost

Farewell happy fields,
Where joy forever dwells;
Hail horrors, hail!
John Milton, *Paradise Lost*

Dai Jonas drove his builder's van carefully along the winding country lane in the pre-dawn darkness.

It was 6.20 am, on a wintry February morning in the Vale of Glamorgan. After about half a mile, he saw what he was looking for in the dead white wash of the headlights – a narrow opening in the high hedge on his left.

He turned into the entrance, switched off the engine, got out and fumbled in his pocket for his keys. A high steel gate, set into an industrial-type eight-foot high spiked steel fence, barred the entrance.

Wincing at the icy touch of the metal, Jonas reached under the cover and pulled out the padlock on its chain. He unlocked the gate and swung it wide with a ghostly screech that seemed to echo in the pre-dawn stillness. He got back in the van, drove through the open gate, then carefully closed and re-locked it behind him, as per the rules.

He got back in the van, drove sixty or seventy yards further along a short unsurfaced track, then parked up by the lakeside. With a grunt of disappointment, Jonas saw another vehicle – a glossy black Kia Sportage, this year's registration – was already parked there. He liked to have the first couple of hours to himself. A double disappointment was that he knew who the car belonged to. There would be no friendly chat or jokes with the owner – the best he'd get would be a surly grunt, if he was lucky. Anyway, on the plus side, his favourite spot, next to an overhanging willow tree, was unoccupied.

Jonas lifted his gear out of the van – rod bag, tackle box, landing net, bait and a padded folding chair. He dipped his nets and the padded unhooking mat in the large vat of disinfectant, for he was a man who always followed the rules. He quickly tackled up, having tied his rigs at home to avoid fumbling with cold fingers on the bank.

There was enough light now to distinguish the outline features of the lake. He cast one rod out long distance, close to the big bed of lily pads in the centre. It was baited with sweetcorn, for bream, carp, or anything else that might come along. The other rod he cast sideways, under the willow tree, only a few yards out, baited with a nice smelly fishmeal pellet for – well, the same thing everyone else was after at the moment, although he hardly dared admit the possibility to himself. He threw in a couple of handfuls of groundbait laced with a strong attractant, over where his bait had landed, then settled down to wait.

The first rays of sunlight started to shine through the trees on the far bank. It was a clear, cloudless day, and Jonas would be facing the sunrise, but he had sunglasses and his long-brimmed cap.

He settled deeper in his comfortable padded chair to enjoy the peace; and a nice cup of tea. He preferred to brew it fresh, rather than let it go stale in the flask, and as he poured the hot water onto the teabag in his insulated mug, he became aware of the birdsong.

This was the time he loved. The robins, of course, had been singing all through the winter, but a couple of song thrushes had now joined them, as the spring approached. Occasionally, there was the harsh, staccato call of a green woodpecker. As it got lighter, he would probably see a few kingfishers and a heron or two. Having grown up in the industrial Valleys, and now semi-retired, Jonas loved seeing and hearing the birds, and sitting in this circle of woodland, cut off from the world. You would never guess you were almost on the outskirts of Bridgend and only a mile or two from the M4. It was a place full of peace and, even if he caught nothing, Jonas loved coming here.

As the sun rose, the details of the lake started to emerge. It was a smallish lake, about three hundred and fifty yards long and a hundred and fifty wide, surrounded by trees which mostly hid the high steel fence. In the middle was an island, originally formed of the spoil dug out when the lake had been a quarry, but now covered in small trees and scrub, providing a haven for ducks and moorhens. A small solar panel and storage battery stood semi-hidden in the scrub, providing a power source for the aerator pumps that kept the water oxygenated.

As the water warmed after the night's frost, tendrils of vapour rose and twisted slowly a few inches above the still surface, creating an ethereal, almost mystical effect. Jonas couldn't see the other fisherman, and so guessed he was on the far bank, hidden by the island. He thought to himself he'd walk over and say hello in an hour or two – perhaps the guy was just shy, or lonely, and might appreciate a word.

As the light grew stronger, Jonas could see something unfamiliar in the water between him and the lily bank which bordered the island. A clump of weed that had come loose and floated away? A branch?

It didn't quite look like either – a wide, low, smooth hump projecting only an inch or two above the surface. He was perplexed, but thought that the prevailing current from the aerator pumps would eventually bring it closer to him, so he could get a better look. He reeled in the furthest-out bait, so that the line would not snag on the object as it drifted leftwards and towards the bank, and then re-cast to the other side of it. For some reason he couldn't explain, he started to feel uneasy.

A high-pitched shriek overhead startled him. A black-headed gull, in winter plumage, circled round several times, as if inspecting the thing in the water, and then descended and landed on it with an audible thump of webbed feet. Ripples spread outwards from the object, disturbing the calm of the water.

Slowly, not wanting to believe what he thought he saw, Jonas reached for the small pair of binoculars he kept in his bag and focused them. His mind recoiled as the binoculars confirmed what he had feared – the back of a man, clad in a camouflaged jacket, floating face-down in the water with his legs trailing beneath the surface. After a few seconds' frozen incomprehension, Jonas leapt to his feet with a wild yell, waving his arms to drive the gull away. Then, with shaking hands, he took out his phone and began to dial.

Chapter 2

A wound of hate

Never can true reconcilement grow where wounds of deadly hate have pierced so deep ...
John Milton, *Paradise Lost*

It was 8.30 that same morning when Detective Inspector Tomos Hopkins walked into the Major Crime Investigations Team room at Bridgend Police Headquarters.

Hopkins was a small, slightly-built man in his mid-fifties, with wispy hair that showed signs of having once been red, but was now losing a battle with the winter snows. Gold-rimmed spectacles gave him the air of a scholar, rather than a policeman. He walked slowly over to the small kitchen, trying to shake off the weight of tiredness, for he had slept badly the night before.

As he filled the coffee-maker with ground coffee and switched it on, he became aware of someone leaning on the doorframe behind him.

'Morning, sir', came the not-so-dulcet tones of Detective Sergeant Reilly, Hopkins' assistant. 'Better not get too comfortable – just had a report of a possible suspicious death out at a lake called' - he paused to look down at the scrap of paper in his hand – 'Yr Hen Chwarel'.

Reilly's flat Lancastrian vowels, which he had not lost despite twenty years of living in Wales, mangled the Welsh pronunciation.

"Possible suspicious'? How can it be possible suspicious? It's either suspicious or it isn't.' Hopkins could be annoyingly pedantic at times.

Reilly unpeeled his lanky frame slowly from the doorway.

'The body's been reported floating in the water, sir. Diving team are there now recovering it.'

'And?'

'The lake's in a locked compound sir. No way in or out except to the members of the fishing club that run it. So I'm thinking, he either had some kind of heart attack or fit and fell in, or else committed suicide, or ...'

'... Someone who had a key put him in there.'

'Exactly, sir.'

'Where is this place, John?'

'East side of town sir. Just past the Enterprise Gateway industrial estate, in amongst some fields. Near the village of' – again Reilly consulted his notes – 'Rhyd yr Afon.'

Hopkins hid his wince at the pronunciation. He looked around the MCIT office. MCIT was the team of specialist detectives within the Criminal Investigation Department of South Wales Police, tasked with investigating serious or complex crimes such as murder, manslaughter, extortion, violent robberies and so on. A couple of junior ranks were in, but no-one else at Hopkins' level.

'Well, as I'm the only one in at the moment who's qualified to act as Senior Investigating Officer, I suppose we could go and take a look. Jeffries can allocate a different SIO later if he wants. How far is it?'

'No more than 20 minutes, sir. We could go in my car?', Reilly added hopefully.

'No, thank you, John.' Hopkins had seen from the car park that Reilly had driven in today in his pride and joy, a 1980s Ford Capri that he had lovingly restored. Hopkins had ridden in it once before and found it noisy, uncomfortable and lacking adequate heating. 'I'll drive.'

...

Hopkins drove his Volvo carefully out of the carpark, waving courteously to the security guard on the gate. Once on the road, he asked,

'So what do we know about this place?'

Reilly was consulting his smartphone.

'According to the club's webpage, it used to be a quarry, closed in the 1950s. It flooded over time, and then the club leased it in 1992, stocked it with fish, and have maintained it since.'

'How many members?'

'70, it says here. Very exclusive. You have to apply and wait for a vacancy.'

'God, so we've got to interview that many keyholders?'

'Let's hope not sir. There may be some way of telling who was there at the relevant time.'

Reilly thought for a minute.

'Funny sport, though.'

'What do you mean?'

'Well, it says here, fish welfare is paramount, only barbless hooks allowed, nets to be disinfected, blah-

blah, all fish to be returned to the water. I mean, what's the point if you can't take it home and eat it?'

'Well, I suppose it's no stranger than you running up mountains, John.'

'Sport of kings, sir' grinned Reilly, 'You should give it a go. Can't beat the feeling of running along a hilltop with ...'

'... The rain lashing down, freezing cold, and dressed in a vest and skimpy shorts? No thanks John, I'll stick to my poetry.'

'You know what they say about Welsh mountains and poets[1], sir – it might make you even better.'

'Or it might make me madder than some of my colleagues already think I am.'

'I couldn't possibly comment, sir. Ah, here we are, turn right at the next roundabout into the industrial estate.'

As they entered the industrial estate on a wide dual carriageway, passing several large boards advertising the businesses based there, both of them simultaneously saw the tall white pole on the grass central reservation.

'CCTV! I wonder if it's on all the time and who has the records? Find out for me when we get back, would you John? Also check if this is the only way in or out.'

'Will do, sir. Take the next right at the end of the main road through the estate.'

They turned off the wide dual carriageway onto a narrow country lane, only wide enough for one car, with occasional passing places.

---

[1] An old saying has it that a person who spends too long on a Welsh mountain, comes down either mad, or a poet.

'Should be another quarter of a mile, sir. Gateway in the hedge on your left.'

As they reached the gate, they saw it was standing open. A marked police car and a van were parked across the end of the short drive. Hopkins blew his horn and a uniformed officer appeared, waved at them in recognition and moved the car back to let them in.

Once in the small parking area, Hopkins looked around. Besides the police vehicles, there was a small white van with DJ Builders written in black and red on the side, as well as a battered old Land Rover Defender, and a new-looking Kia Sportage. Two uniformed officers stood by the van talking with two men, whilst two other uniforms watched the lake, presumably keeping an eye on the divers. Hopkins could see the outline of a third man, sitting hunched in the front seat of the police van.

There were shouts from the officers on the banking, so Hopkins and Reilly hurried over. As they got to the edge, they could see the two divers, anonymously hooded in neoprene, gently wading forward pulling the body with an arm under each shoulder. The gentleness was not just out of respect – they didn't want anything important falling out of the pockets.

The strange cortege moved along the shore, to a small concrete ramp that Hopkins guessed was used for launching boats to get to the island for maintenance. Then, the divers' efforts became more strenuous, as they moved step by step up the ramp and had to bear the weight of the corpse with its water-sodden clothes. At last, they pulled the body free of the water and laid it on its back. Rivulets of murky water ran out of the folds of clothing, combined to form streams, and ran down the ramp back into the lake. The two men standing with the uniforms by the police van started to come over, but Hopkins waved them back and the two officers with them placed restraining hands on their shoulders and gently turned them towards the van again.

Hopkins and Reilly leaned in over the body. It was clear the body was male, but beyond that, it was hard to distinguish much in the way of features, as his face was swollen and puffy from being so long in the water. He wore a waterproof camouflage jacket, dark waterproof trousers and green wellingtons.

'We'll struggle to identify him unless he's carrying some ID', said Reilly.

'Oh no, sir' said one of the uniforms. 'They' – he gestured towards the men standing by the van – 'think they know who it is. They recognised his car.'

'So who do they think it is?' asked Hopkins.

'Name of Jason Reynolds. Mid thirties. Lives in Maesteg. Been a member for just over a year – apparently joined when his father passed away and took his place.'

Hopkins leaned forwards to slide a hand inside the jacket, to look for a wallet or other form of ID, but suddenly froze.

'What is it, sir?' asked Reilly.

'How long until the pathologist gets here?'

'He's on his way, sir.'

'Call him and tell him to get a move on.'

'Why?'

24

Hopkins placed his hand on the man's chest, his long, bony fingers either side of a small rent in the camouflage jacket, just over the heart. He carefully spread the fabric, to reveal a small, neat, slit-like puncture in the pale flesh, less than an inch long, slightly puffy and purple around the edges, but long since bled dry.

'Because this looks like murder.'

Chapter 3

The scale turns

Justice turns the scale, bringing to some learning through suffering.
Aeschylus

Plastic screens had been erected around the body by the uniformed officers. Reilly was on his phone trying to arrange for a Scenes of Crime team to attend, as well as trying to chivvy along the pathologist.

Hopkins spoke to the divers.

'See anything else while you were down there?'

'No, but we didn't carry out a full search. We don't know where the body entered the water or how far it drifted. We don't have the equipment for a full search – we'd need to come back with a full team. We just looked in the area where the body was floating and nearby. Nothing.'

'Some bloody big fish, though', said the second diver.

Hopkins gave him a withering look.

'Well, you'd better get in the van and get warm and changed. We may have to come back for a full search later.'

The divers shouldered their air tanks and, carrying fins in hand, trudged off towards the van, and the promise of dry clothes and hot coffee.

Hopkins walked over to Reilly, who was just finishing leaving another message on the pathologist's answering service.

'Any update on when he'll be here?'

'No sir, but I guess he must be driving, as I can only get his voicemail.'

'Mortimer should have been here by now – he only lives a short way away.'

'It's not old Morty, sir. He's away at a conference. It's someone called Dr A Madhvani, from Cardiff.'

'Well, we may as well talk to the witnesses then, while we're waiting.'

They walked over to the small group where the vehicles were parked.

Hopkins addressed the two men standing outside the van first.

'Hello gentlemen, I'm Detective Inspector Hopkins and this is Detective Sergeant Reilly. Could I ask your names please?'

'Bryn Richards, Club Chairman', said the first, a small, balding, anxious-looking man with a moustache, wearing a well-worn, but clearly expensive, tweed sports jacket.

'Craig Walters, Chief Bailiff.' This man was a completely different proposition. Over six feet tall, with a thick neck and bulging shoulders that strained his waxed jacket, he looked like he could have played prop forward. He appeared to be in his sixties, with close-cropped iron-grey hair. There was a certain stillness, a watchfulness about him that seemed to convey a warning.

'And were you two present when the body was found?'

Walters seemed to elect himself the spokesman of the two.

'No. I'm listed as the emergency contact for the club and so the police rang me as soon as the call came in about the body.' He gestured at the Land Rover. 'I picked Bryn up on the way here.'

'Very well', said Hopkins, 'Then I think we'd better speak to the man who found the body first. Where is he?'

'In the van, sir' said one of the uniforms. 'Name's Dai Jonas. We think he might be in shock.'

Hopkins knocked gently on the window of the van, then opened the passenger door. Jonas jumped, as if waking from a dream, and blinked at him.

'Mr Jonas? Would it be OK to ask you a few questions? I realise you've had a terrible shock, but the sooner we get this over with, the sooner you can get home.'

Jonas nodded, and Hopkins climbed up to sit on the bench seat next to him. Reilly slid into the driver's seat.

'*A fyddai'n well gennych siarad Cymraeg?*' asked Hopkins gently. Would you rather speak Welsh?

Jonas shook his head.

'No, I don't speak much Welsh. They didn't teach it in the schools much, when I was growing up. Or I didn't pay attention.' He had a distinct Valleys lilt, as opposed to the harsher Cardiff accent.

'That's alright. I understand you found the body and raised the alarm. Could you tell me what happened?'

'Well, not much to tell really. I'd just arrived and set up my gear, and as it got lighter, I could see

28

something in the water. I couldn't see what it was, but after about half an hour, it drifted closer to me. Then a seagull landed on it and I could tell it was something solid, so I got my binoculars, and – I saw it was a man, floating in the water.'

He seemed to shiver at the memory.

'I feel terrible I didn't do anything more, like try to rescue him or something, but he was face down in the water and hadn't moved the whole time I was there. And I can't go jumping in freezing water, at my age.'

He looked pleadingly at Hopkins.

'Don't worry, Mr Jonas. We think he was already dead when he entered the water. There was nothing you could have done.'

'So you think he was – '

'I'm afraid we can't tell at this stage, Mr Jonas. What can you tell me about Mr Reynolds – if we assume that's who it is?'

'Well, I shouldn't say this, but he could be a bit of a funny bugger.'

'That's OK, Mr Jonas, we need to know everything about him and his background. Don't worry about speaking ill of the dead. In what way?'

'Well, he was just unfriendly, never wanted a chat or anything. Just grunted or gave one-word answers. Most of the guys here like a chat and a laugh, share tips, that sort of thing. And I'm not sure he ever really liked fishing that much. I knew his Dad well before he passed away, old Greg, and he was always sad Jason wouldn't come fishing with him. Everyone was a bit surprised when he took his Dad's place in the club.'

'But Jason was a regular at the lake?'

'Oh yeah. Two or three times a week. Mostly at nights.'

'Nights?'

'Yeah. I'd be packing up, 5 or 6 o'clock, and he'd turn up. The other lads who night-fish saw him a lot, too. I assumed it was because he was working during the day, or something.'

'Anything else you can think of?'

Jonas furrowed his brow and thought for a few seconds.

'He was always on his phone a lot. I mean, we all make one or two calls or read stuff on our phones, like, but most of the time we're focusing on fishing or just enjoying the peace.'

'Do you know if he was making calls or just scrolling?'

'No, as I say, I didn't tend to overlap with him much. This is what the other guys told me.'

'That's great, thanks Mr Jonas, you've been really helpful. And please don't worry – you couldn't have done anything to save him. Now, do you want someone to drive you home and you can pick your van up later, or do you think you're OK to drive?'

'I'm OK thanks. And I need the van tomorrow for work.'

'Very well. DS Reilly will get them to let you out. We might need to speak to you again, so would you mind giving him your contact details?'

Hopkins got out of the van, while Reilly noted down Jonas' details. The two of them then walked over to Jonas' van and, after a few more words, Jonas got in and drove out of the gate. Reilly came back to

Hopkins, who was staring out at the lake, rubbing his temples tiredly.

'You OK, sir?'

'Yes, thanks, John. Just tired. Bad night. Shall we go and talk to the other two?'

They walked over to where Richards and Walters were standing.

'Sorry to keep you waiting, gentlemen', said Hopkins. 'Do you mind if we ask you a few questions?'

Both shook their heads.

'Did either of you know Mr Reynolds?'

'Not well' replied Walters, who again seemed to have appointed himself the spokesman for the two. 'His Dad was a member for years. When he died, we offered the place to the family, as we usually do, before we go to the waiting list. We were a bit surprised when Jason took it up, as we'd never seen him here with his Dad.'

'And he's been a member just over a year?'

'That's right.'

'I gather he was a regular night fisherman, though?'

'Yes', Walters answered again. 'Strange he was here last night, though.'

'Why's that?'

'Fish don't feed much when it's freezing cold. You might get lucky occasionally, but most anglers stay home when it's so cold overnight. The fish might get a bit more active once the sun comes up, particularly where the sun's shining on the water, but not much tends to happen on cold nights.'

'I see. Any idea why he might have been fishing last night?'

'Not – ' began Walters, but Richards, perhaps feeling he should say something, broke in nervously.

'Maybe he was after the Lady of the Lake?'

Walters gave him a sideways glance.

'The what?' asked Hopkins.

'A possible British record Crucian carp we have here', said Walters, with the hint of a resigned sigh. 'Caught last summer weighing just under the record – 4 pounds 12 ounces. The current record's 4 pounds 14. Then someone hooked and lost it in November and reckoned it looked bigger. So quite a few of the members have been coming here more often, to try and catch it.'

'I thought carp were much bigger than that?', asked Reilly.

'Oh yes, common and mirror carp can get up to 50, even 60 pounds. We've got a few 20 pounders and above in this lake. But Crucians are much smaller.'

'And people are very motivated by catching a record, are they?' asked Hopkins.

'Well, some of the members are. The specialist carp anglers. There's quite a bit of publicity involved – reports in the angling magazines and online forums, possible sponsorship deals with tackle companies, and so on. But most of the members, who just fish for fun, aren't too bothered.'

'And would you have thought Jason Reynolds would be motivated by that?'

Richards and Walters looked at each other.

'Well, not really. But I can't think of any other reason anyone would sit up through a freezing cold night', replied Walters.

'Do you know where he was fishing last night?'

'I would guess over the other side, behind the island.'

'Can you show us?'

'No problem.'

The four men set off to the left, walking clockwise around the lake's shore.

'So, does anyone else outside the club know about this – possible record fish?' asked Hopkins.

'We don't think so,' answered Richards.

'We're trying to keep it under wraps', said Walters. 'We don't issue day tickets, and we're only a small club, so we don't want tons of pressure from people asking for day tickets, or poachers trying to sneak in.'

'What's that?' asked Reilly, pointing to a shipping container with a large, open, corrugated-roofed lean-to adjoining it.

'Toilet and equipment store', said Walters. 'Members can get in with their keys. There's some picnic tables and chairs under the lean-to if anglers want to get out of the rain or sit and have a chat.'

'And only members with keys can get in or out of the gate?'

'Yes. Except for the farmer who leases us the land. He installed the septic tank for us a couple of years back, and he sometimes needs access to clear the drainage channels onto his land, so he has a key as well.'

'What's his name?'

'Jimmy Lewis. He lives in the farmhouse a few hundred yards down the lane after you turn left out of the gate.'

'Does the lane go anywhere else?'

'No, dead end just after the farm.'

'So anyone coming to the lake needs to come through the industrial estate first?'

'That's right.'

'This is a pretty serious fence you've got around the lake. How come it's so secure?'

'Occupier's liability. Parts of the lake are pretty deep, and if a kid fell in and drowned, the club might be liable. Also, we have had problems with poachers in the past.'

Richards seemed to be about to say something, then thought better of it.

'Yes, Mr Richards?', prompted Hopkins.

'Well, I was just about to say, there's sometimes strange characters around at night on quad bikes or off-road bikes.'

'On the farmer's land?'

'Yes.'

'What do you think they're up to?'

Hopkins could have sworn Walters shot Richards a warning glance.

'Oh, I don't know, maybe lamping rabbits, or just kids from the village messing around. I don't know.'

They were now rounding the corner of the lake.

'Were either of you here over the weekend?' asked Hopkins.

'Saturday, not Sunday', said Richards, quickly.

'I was working here on Sunday', said Walters. 'Clearing brush and overhanging branches.' He pointed to a pile of fresh-cut branches up against the metal fence, and waved to indicate several other piles around the lake.

'What time were you here?' asked Reilly.

'Between about 2 and 5 o'clock.'

'Did you see Jason Reynolds then?'

'No, there was maybe 5 or 6 people fishing when I left, but I guess they would have cleared off once it started getting cold.'

Something about Walters' bearing, the natural way he took the lead, and the precise way he gave his answers, prompted Hopkins to ask, 'If you don't mind my asking, sir, have you ever been in the services?'

There was a distinct hesitation, then Walters reluctantly answered, 'Yes, Royal Marines. 1983 to 1997. Why?'

'No reason', said Hopkins. 'Just wondered.'

Walters stopped walking and pointed. 'There's his gear.'

About twenty yards in front of them was a small green dome-shaped bivouac tent, a sort of black tubular metal cradle holding two fishing rods, a large landing net on a long pole, and a tripod with an instrument hanging below it, connected to a canvas sling. The line from one rod still stretched into the water, whereas the other lay on the bank.

'Looks like he caught something worth weighing', piped up Richards, as they walked closer.

'How do you mean?' asked Hopkins.

'Well, one rod's lying on the bank, and he's set up his scales – that tripod there. They don't usually do that unless they've got something worth weighing.'

'Is it electronic? Would it give us an indication of when he last used it?'

'Oh, I think so. Do you want me to have a look?'

'Stay back, please sir. This may be a crime scene. John, would you mind?'

'No problem, sir.'

Reilly took blue plastic overshoes out of his pocket and slipped them on, followed by blue nitrile gloves and an evidence bag. He walked carefully forwards, watching the ground so as not to disturb any possible footprints or other evidence, then reached under the tripod, unhooking the device and detaching it from its sling. He then placed it in a clear plastic evidence bag and walked back to the other three.

Reilly held the device towards Richards and Walters. It had a grey LCD screen and several buttons. 'What do I do to turn it on?'

'On/off switch to the right of the screen', said Walters, taking the lead again.

Reilly pressed the button through the clear plastic of the evidence bag. Black numerals appeared with the date and time, and a series of zeros for the weight.

'Now press the back arrow. That should show the last activity.'

The time and date changed, showing 23:03 the previous night.

The weight showed five pounds and one ounce.

Chapter 4

Riddles and truths

With these words from her shrine the Sybil of Cumae sang her fearful riddling prophecies, her voice booming in the cave as she wrapped the truth in darkness...
Virgil, *The Aeneid*

'So that's our motive? Someone stabbed him so he wouldn't get the glory of catching a record fish?' asked Hopkins, disbelievingly. They were sitting in Hopkins' car. Richards and Walters had returned to Walters' Land Rover.

'It's a possibility, sir, isn't it? We haven't anything else to go on, at the moment. And fishermen – well, the carp specialists anyway – do seem to get a bit fanatical about these things. I mean, staying up all night in tents in the middle of winter. You'd have to be a bit crazy to do that.'

'Would you stab someone who beat you in a fell race?'

'Course not. But that's mostly about finishing, not winning.' Reilly pondered a moment. 'I might do one of the Les Montagniers lot if they overtook me, though. Flash bastards. Why do they have to have a fancy French name when they're from Cardiff?'

'Getting back to the point, John, it seems a bit thin for a motive to me. Also, the weighing scales only told us the weight, not the species. We don't know that it was this record Crucian carp.'

'But he wouldn't have bothered weighing anything else, would he? I mean, 5 pounds is pretty small for the other types of carp they've got here.'

'I don't know, John. Hello, I wonder what he wants, now?'

Richards, the club chairman was coming over to their car. Hopkins got out.

'We were wondering, er, if you still need us, or whether we could be, er, going?' ventured Richards.

Hopkins looked at Reilly, who shook his head.

'No, I don't think we need detain you any longer, sir', replied Hopkins. 'Have you left a key for the gate with the uniformed officers?'

'Yes.'

'Sir?' asked Reilly. 'Just wondered if it would be a good idea to get a message out to the members. Let them know we want to speak to whoever was here over the weekend.'

'Good point, John. Mr Richards, do you have an e-mail group or something that you can use to contact all members?'

'We do.'

'Please could you tell them the lake will be closed until further notice. We'll need to get a forensics team in. Don't tell them about anything else – particularly the scales. Also don't tell them the identity of the body. We need to inform Mr Reynolds' next of kin and do a formal identification. Then could you ask the members, which of them was here on Sunday, at any time, and send me their details. Here's my card.'

Richards nodded nervously and hurried away. A few moments later, the Land Rover reversed, turned round, then drove out of the gates.

'So, sir, if everyone who drives here has to come through the industrial estate, they're going to get picked up on that CCTV camera we saw. We know Reynolds was here from some time after 5pm yesterday and went into the water some time after 11:03. If we check the responses to the e-mail against the footage, we'll be able to tell pretty quickly if anyone's lying.'

'Yes, John, assuming we can get the CCTV footage. Also, if someone approached from the farm direction, they wouldn't get picked up by the camera.'

'But that's a dead end, sir, according to the map. Only the farmer, Jimmy Lewis, could come from that direction.'

'That seems so. Well, we'll just have to wait and see what comes back. Ah, this seems to be our pathologist at last.'

A pristine black Mercedes was pulling into the car park. Once parked, a slim Indian woman got out, very smartly dressed in a stylish dark trouser suit. She came over to them, carrying her bag, a black holdall.

'Doctor Amrita Madhvani' she introduced herself. 'Sorry I'm late. Crash on the M4 outside Cardiff.'

Hopkins introduced himself and Reilly. 'I've not seen you around before, Doctor.'

'I've just transferred from West Midlands.' And indeed, her otherwise educated accent held a trace of Brummie.

'Ambulance on its way?' she asked, briskly. Hopkins nodded. 'Right, I'd better get on with it, then.'

She walked close to the plastic sheeting erected around the body and peered over the top. She unzipped her bag and started pulling on a disposable white suit, overshoes and gloves.

'I'd better observe the niceties, even though it looks as though you've been trampling all over the crime scene.' She indicated the wet, muddy footprints from the divers and others surrounding the body.

Reilly bristled.

'That's not the crime scene. We pulled him out of the water and just laid him there.'

'Well, hopefully you've not done too much damage.'

Reilly opened his mouth to speak again, but Hopkins touched his arm.

'Perhaps, Doctor, you could play nicely with my sergeant? Like all Northerners, he has a somewhat sensitive disposition.'

Reilly glared, and Madhvani's eyes crinkled in amusement above her mask. She took a small digital camera out of her bag and clipped a microphone to the front of her suit, slipping the recorder into a pocket of the oversuit. She then unclipped one of the plastic sheets from its pole and approached the body, squatting down beside it.

'Subject is a white male, approximately mid-thirties. Recovered from the water. Some distension of features due to water absorption.' She gently rotated his head from side to side. 'No visible marks on face or neck.'

Madhvani began unzipping the jacket. She reached inside and felt in the inner pockets. 'iPhone, probably waterlogged.' She retrieved and bagged it. 'Wallet.' She opened the canvas wallet with a velcro fastening. 'Driver's licence in the name of Jason Reynolds.' She placed the wallet in another bag.

Then she started unbuttoning the shirt and lifting up the thermal base layer underneath. 'Puncture wound between fourth and fifth rib, on the left side, probably going directly into the heart. Some bruising around the wound, indicating impact of the weapon handle or crosspiece. The blow appears to have been delivered with some force.'

She looked up.

'That looks like your cause of death, Inspector. And someone either knew what they were doing, or got very lucky.'

'How's that?'

'Single stab wound, straight between the ribs into the heart. Didn't glance off a rib, no frenzied multiple stab wounds. Looks like a long, narrow, very sharp weapon, like a fish-filleting knife or similar.'

She reached across the body to the opposite shoulder and hip.

'Turning the body over now.'

'Do you want a hand?' asked Hopkins. Reilly ostentatiously stood back.

'No need. I know the technique.' Madhvani deftly rolled the heavy, water-sodden corpse over onto its front. She lifted up the layers of clothing on his back.

'No sign of an exit wound, so I'm guessing the knife was around eight inches or less in length.'

She took more pictures of the corpse lying on its front.

'I'll bag the hands just in case. However, I think it likely that the water will have washed away any DNA or other residue that might be under the fingernails.'

She placed elasticated evidence bags over the hands, then stood up.

'Right, that's all I can do for now. You can move the body to the morgue. I'll do a full autopsy and send you my report in the next couple of days.'

'Could you run toxicology tests as well?' asked Hopkins.

'Standard practice in a case like this, but I'll remind the lab. Don't you want to ask me the time of death or how long he's been in the water?'

'I didn't think you could tell that without a full autopsy.'

'I can't. But you'd be amazed by how many officers think I can, just from looking at a body. Too many TV crime shows. Ah, here's the ambulance now.'

A black, windowless van with 'Private Ambulance' on the side was just pulling into the car park. Two undertakers dressed in dark overalls got out, one of them unrolling and unzipping a black plastic body bag as he walked.

Reilly's phone rang and he walked away from the group to take it, cupping one hand over his other ear to muffle the slight breeze that had sprung up.

Hopkins hesitated, then asked Madhvani, 'I wonder Doctor – we're going to have to bring the next of kin in to do a formal identification. Will his face still – look like that?' He gestured towards the body.

Madvhani's severe expression softened a little.

'It will look a little better. The distension will subside as the fluids drain out of the body at the morgue. But you had better prepare them.'

'Well, thank you Doctor. No doubt we'll speak soon.'

'We certainly shall, Inspector.' Madhvani flashed him a smile, got into her Mercedes and drove away.

The uniformed officers were just returning from erecting blue and white tape around the area where Reynolds' fishing gear had been found.

'Thanks' said Hopkins. 'I need one of you to stay and guard the gate and let the forensics team in when they get here. The rest of you can go.'

The uniforms conferred among themselves, then three got into the van and drove away. The other went to sit in the remaining patrol car, parked facing the gate.

Reilly came back.

'What was that about?' asked Hopkins.

'I asked Davy Lane and Sue Wilshaw back at HQ to check his background, once we thought we had an ID. They've just come back. Mother died a few years before the father. Jason's not married, but there is a woman registered to the same address – a Lisa Hughes. Maybe a girlfriend?'

'We'd better go and see her. We can leave forensics to do a search of the area. When can the divers get back here to do a full search?'

'Not until tomorrow, sir. But they said that, as it's still water and no-one's fishing or disturbing the bed, anything that's there will still be there tomorrow.'

'Oh well, I suppose it's the best we can do. Let's go and break the news to Ms Hughes. Could you get a Family Liaison officer to meet us there?'

'Will do. There's something else sir. Jason Reynolds has got a record. As in a criminal one – not a fishing one.'

'Really? What for?'

'Cautioned for possession of ketamine and cocaine three years ago. Suspected of dealing, but the quantities weren't quite enough to charge him. His fingerprints and DNA are on the system, so we can check them against the body.'

'How's his DNA on the system? They don't normally take that for minor drug offences, do they?'

'No sir. He voluntarily answered a call for local men to come forward for screening, to do with a sexual assault, as he knew the victim. He was ruled out.'

'But they shouldn't have kept his DNA on record afterwards.'

'No sir. I can only guess Drugs Team wanted it kept, if they suspected him of something bigger. But yes, shouldn't have happened.'

As they drove out of the car park, Hopkins said, 'Nice lady, our new pathologist.'

'If there's any pike in that lake, she could give them a run for their money', grunted Reilly.

Chapter 5

Grief and anger

Everyone can master a grief but he who has it.
Shakespeare, *Much Ado About Nothing*

The two policemen kept relative silence during the drive to Maesteg, other than Reilly giving directions. The Volvo crossed over the M4, then headed up an A road running north and west. After about 20 minutes, they came to the small high street of Maesteg, then turned off into a street of terraces. After a couple more turns, Hopkins pulled up outside a small well-kept stone terrace. Flower baskets with winter pansies and dwarf conifers hung either side of the door. The windows and door looked new.

As Hopkins was locking the car, a woman got out of a car parked along the street. She was early forties, casually dressed with short dark hair, and had a motherly air.

'Janet Ellis, Family Liaison', she introduced herself.

'Thanks for meeting us here' said Hopkins. 'Well, we'd better get on with it. Worst part of the job.'

Reilly knocked, and the door was opened by a young woman in her thirties, with long mousy hair and wearing an apron.

'Ms Hughes?'

'Yes, that's me. Can I help?'

Hopkins showed his warrant card.

'South Wales Police ma'am. I'm Detective Inspector Hopkins and this is Detective Sergeant Reilly. This is Janet Ellis from Family Liaison. May we come in?'

'Oh my God, what's happened?'

'It would be better if we spoke inside. Can we go in?'

She stepped back wordlessly and gestured them in.

The officers crossed a thick, cream-coloured carpet in the hallway and waited by what looked like the living room door. Lisa Hughes opened the door and waved them in. The living room was also covered in the same thick, cream carpet and there was an enormous leather corner sofa and matching armchairs taking up most of the room, facing a gigantic wall-mounted plasma TV.

'You're lucky to get me at home', Lisa ventured. 'It's my day off. I usually work on reception in the solicitor's office on the High Street. What's all this about – is Jason OK?'

'Ms Hughes, I think you'd better sit down.'

'Oh my God', she said again. 'It's bad, isn't it?'

Hopkins knew from experience it was better to get it over with quickly.

'I'm afraid Jason is dead. We found his body at the fishing lake this morning.'

Wordlessly, Lisa hunched forward, her head in her hands and shoulders shaking with sobs. Janet sat next to her and tentatively put an arm round her shoulders. When Lisa leaned into her, she gave her a full on hug, the younger woman frantically sobbing into her shoulder.

The two policemen sat in embarrassed silence for a few minutes, until Lisa calmed somewhat and, sniffing, lifted her tear-stained face and looked at Hopkins.

'What – what happened?'

'We're not sure at this stage, Ms Hughes. But he had a knife wound, so we're treating it as a suspicious death. I know it's an awful time, but would you be up to answering a few questions? We can always come back later if you'd rather.'

Shakily, she nodded her head.

'Should I make you a cup of tea, love?' asked Janet. Lisa nodded again. 'Through here, is it? I'll be back in a minute.' Janet headed towards the kitchen.

'How long have you and Jason been together?' asked Hopkins.

'About three years, a bit more. We met in a club in town. I was on a works do and he was out with some of his mates.'

'What job did he do?' The past tense, used for the first time, caused her to start sobbing again.

'I'm sorry' said Hopkins, cursing himself for his insensitivity.

'It's – it's alright', she said. 'He worked at the parcel distribution centre on the estate near Sarn – forklift driver. He was trying to start his own business though.'

'And what was that?'

'An online fishing tackle shop. He thought he could buy in bulk and sell on, but I thought he was mad. There's too many big companies in the market. I couldn't see him making a go of it.'

'How far had he got with his plans?'

'Not far. He'd got a lease on part of an old mill building in Bridgend. He took me to see it when he got it. All derelict and shuttered up. But he had no time between work and fishing to take it much further.'

Janet came back into the room and placed a large mug of tea on the coffee table in front of Lisa. She hadn't asked how Lisa took it, but had just made it sweet and milky, the universal treatment for shock. Lisa nodded her thanks, took a sip and grimaced at the taste, but said nothing. Janet sat protectively close to her on the sofa.

'Ah yes, the fishing', said Hopkins. 'We gather he was out two or three nights a week. That must have been hard on you.'

'It was. He wasn't much interested in it until after his Dad died. Then he said it made him feel closer to his Dad, helped him cope with the grief. At least ...' Her voice trailed off.

'What, Ms Hughes?'

'Call me Lisa. No, I shouldn't say.'

'Lisa, we want to find out what happened to Jason. We need to know everything about him to help us do that. Nothing you say can hurt him now, and it can all be totally confidential, I promise you that.'

'I'm not sure he was always fishing when he said he was.' There was anger in her voice now, through the tears. 'I think he was seeing another woman. I was working up to confronting him about it, but the time was never right.'

'Why do you think that, Lisa?'

48

'Well, sometimes when he came back, he smelled clean, you know? Like he'd had a shower. Not like he'd been camped out all night in a tent.'

'I see. Anything else you noticed?'

'No, that was it, really. He was just the same, didn't seem distant or anything. I did hear him talking to some woman on his mobile once. Out the back – he didn't think I could hear him.'

'How did you know it was a woman?'

'I heard him call her Sandra, I think. I asked him about it afterwards, but he said it was just business. I wanted to believe him.' She laughed, bitterly.

Hopkins seemed to have no more questions, so Reilly changed tack.

'Very nice place you have here, Lisa. You've obviously worked hard on it.'

'Well, Jason had quite a bit of money left him when his Dad died. His parents' house and that. He was the only child.'

'I see. Anything else, sir?'

'No, I think that's it for the moment. Lisa, here's my card. We may need to talk to you again, but in the meantime, if anything occurs to you, doesn't matter whether you think it's important or not, give me a call. Is there anything you want to ask me?'

'When can I see him?'

'Tomorrow, if you feel strong enough. I'm afraid we'll need to ask you to make a formal identification.' Hopkins hesitated, then went on. 'Look, you need to be prepared. He was in the water for quite a few hours. His face will be quite swollen and pale-looking.'

Lisa nodded, but he wasn't sure if she understood. The numbness of shock seemed to be setting in.

'Well, Janet will be able to explain more, when you're ready. She's going to stay with you for a while now, to make sure you're alright. She can help you contact relatives and so on, if you want. Thanks for all your help – we really appreciate it.'

Lisa remained silent, so the two detectives got up, said their goodbyes, and left her with Janet.

Hopkins and Reilly got back into the car.

'Where to now, sir?'

'Back to HQ, I think, drop the phone off in the lab. It's probably beyond repair, but hopefully they can get something off it. We can see how the forensics team are getting on, searching the place where he was sitting.'

As it was just after 2 pm, they stopped at a motorway service station on the way back and bought sandwiches. They sat in the car in silence, munching away, while the steam from their coffee gradually obscured the windscreen.

'So what did you make of that, sir?' ventured Reilly, as he folded his sandwich wrapper and picked up his coffee.

'Well, seeing another woman seems more likely to me than sitting by a lakeside in a tent two or three times a week, particularly given that other club members seem to think he wasn't actually that keen on fishing. But I don't know where it takes us.'

'Jealous husband, maybe, sir?'

'Could be. But we've got nothing until we can track this Sandra down. If the phone's too damaged, maybe we can get his call records off his provider?'

'I'll get someone on it, sir.'

'Yes, and one more thing, John. See if you can get onto the Probate Registry and HMRC and find out what his Dad's estate was really worth. Wills are lodged as a public record and there should be tax records.'

'You don't buy the story that that's where the money came from?'

'I don't know, but I don't see how they can live like that on a fork-lift driver's and a receptionist's salary. I know the house is modest, but everything in it was top-notch. And his car's a new model, top of the range by the look of it.'

'So you think there's more to this than meets the eye, sir?'

'Well, I'm certain that it doesn't all come down to a bloody fish.'

Chapter 6

Hidden serpents

...be ye therefore wise as serpents, and harmless as doves.
Matthew 10:16

Back at the office, Reilly busied himself with the various research tasks Hopkins had set him. Hopkins started trying to catch up with his interminable paperwork, but was struggling to concentrate, a combination of his sleepless night and the events of the day. As he sat in a reverie, gazing into space, he became aware of someone at his shoulder and saw a young detective, newly promoted to MCIT, standing there. Hopkins struggled to remember his name.

'Sir? The Hanger told me he wanted to see you as soon as you got back in.'

'That's Detective Chief Superintendent Jeffries to you, constable', Hopkins gently reprimanded him.

'Yes sir. Sorry sir.' The constable reddened and headed back to his desk.

Detective Chief Superintendent Mike Jeffries, head of CID, Queen's Police Medal, president of the golf club and all-round pillar of the local community, was generally an affable, easy-going boss, who ruled his dominion with a light touch, combined with a sharp eye for detail. However, that hadn't stopped his underlings from nicknaming him 'the Hanger', after the notorious hanging judge, Judge Jeffries of the Bloody Assizes. Hopkins wasn't sure whether or not Jeffries knew about the nickname.

Hopkins went up the corridor to Jeffries' office and knocked.

'Come in! Ah Tom, thanks for dropping by. Hell, man, you look knackered.'

'Bad night, sir, nothing more.'

'Yes, well, try and get home early tonight and get some rest. How's that fishing club case going?'

Hopkins filled him in on the details.

'Hmm. So it looks like homicide, but the only motive so far appears to be a record fish?'

'I know, sir. Seems far-fetched, so we're digging around Reynolds' background, to see what falls out. He was suspected of drug-dealing, so that seems one line to try.'

'Yes, have a word with the Drugs Team about that. They may have some more recent information on him.'

'Will I continue as SIO on this one, then, sir?'

'I think so, Tom. We'd normally have at least a Detective Chief Inspector leading a murder inquiry, but you've done the SIO training, you've done this sort of thing before, and you're one of our best. So, as you've started, you may as well carry on. I take it you'll want Reilly as your deputy?'

'Yes sir. And Lane and Wilshaw, if you can spare them. They've already helped with some of the background stuff.'

'Very well, let's start on that basis and review it as we go on.'

Jeffries hesitated a moment, then said, 'Look, Tom, you may need to tread a little carefully with this one.'

'Why's that, sir?'

'Bryn Richards, the chairman. He can be a nasty piece of work.'

'What, him? He looked like he wouldn't say boo to a goose.'

'I know. But he was a senior partner in one of the big accountancy firms in London, and you don't get there by hiding in a corner. When he came back from London, about twenty-odd years ago, he bought a medium-sized local practice, turned it around and made it super-profitable within a few years.'

'Sounds impressive, sir.'

'Yes. Although he seems to have done it by kicking out most of the old guard who were there when he took over, and bringing in friends from his London days. He can be quite ruthless. And he's well-connected, politically. He's put his money into a network of property companies. Specialises in buying up derelict industrial land, getting grants to tart it up, then promoting it to the government for housing or new industrial units. Nothing dodgy – all strictly above board. Never suspected of anything criminal. But he's well in with local MPs, Senedd members, civil servants, local planning committee, the lot. A few of them are in the fishing club too.'

'How does this affect the investigation, sir?'

'Well, not directly. But he's already been on the phone to me trying to find out what he can, and putting pressure on to get it wrapped up as soon as possible. Worried about his reputation, I suppose.

CBE for services to enterprise and all that. Of course I didn't tell him anything.'

'I see, sir.'

'Just tread carefully, Tom. He can be a nasty bugger and he's well-connected. Don't rub him up the wrong way.'

'I'll try not to, sir.'

'OK, well, lecture over. How's Mair?'

'Very well, thanks sir.'

'We must all get together for dinner some time.'

'We certainly must, sir.' The Hanger had been making the same suggestion for years, and they had never met for dinner.

As Hopkins turned to leave, Jeffries called out, 'Oh by the way, what did you think of the new pathologist?'

'Tough cookie sir, but seemed very good at her job.'

'Good, good. West Midlands asked me to keep them posted on how she's working out. Well, mustn't keep you.'

As he walked back to his desk, even in his tired state, it occurred to Hopkins that the last exchange had been decidedly odd. Since when did a head of CID concern himself with a pathologist employed by the Home Office, and report back on them to senior officers in another force?

Chapter 7

Different treasures

For where your treasure is, there will your heart be also.
The Sermon on the Mount, Matthew 6:21

Hopkins sank down wearily into his chair. He stared morosely at the pile of paperwork and tried to force his brain to concentrate. But after a few minutes, he found that he had re-read the same line several times, while his mind wandered off. He looked at his watch. Nearly 5 o'clock. He got up, went over to Reilly's desk and tapped him on the shoulder.

'Do you want to see if you can get us a conference room, John, so we can have a catch up on the day? I'll go and make us some coffees.'

'OK sir.'

A few minutes later, Hopkins shouldered open the door to a tiny conference room, just big enough for four people if they sat closely around the small table. He put down the mugs on the table. Reilly's mug bore the crest of Bolton Wanderers over a red Lancashire rose. Hopkins' was bright red, with 'Llanelli RFC – the Scarlets' in Celtic lettering. Reilly was spreading out papers from a slim file.

'So, what do we have?'

'Looks like we may be lucky with the CCTV, sir. Security manager for the industrial estate says the camera would have been on all through the night and they should have the video. He's checking now and says he'll get it over to us on memory sticks in the morning.'

'Great. As it was a Sunday night, hopefully there won't be too many cars to check. We can rule out any large commercial vehicles – lorries and big vans. Just look at private cars and smaller vans.'

'OK sir. Forensics team finished looking at the taped off site. Nothing really of any note. All the usual fishing paraphernalia, camp bed, shelter, etc. Bag of sandwiches, partly eaten, flask of coffee, two empty cans of low-strength beer. They've taken a few fingerprints off his rods, cup, etc., but they think it likely that Jason's will be the only fingerprints.'

'Footprints?'

'None, sir. The path was gravel, and led directly onto the wooden fishing platform where he was sitting. There's some mud either side, but no recent prints. Some old ones, mostly eroded by the rain, but nothing they could use.'

'Damn. I was hoping footprints would give us something. No sign of the murder weapon?'

'No sir. And apparently, from looking at fishing shop websites, most of these filleting type knives have hollow handles, so if you drop them in the water, they're designed to float. So I don't think the divers are going to find it either.'

'They're coming back tomorrow?'

'Yes sir.'

'See if you can get a team to do a search all around the lake as well, tomorrow, John. There's lots of bushes and piles of cut brushwood, as well as the drainage channels running out under the fence into the field. Tell them to have a good ground search, turn everything over, you know the drill.'

'OK sir.'

'What about the phone?'

'Again, no good sir. Lab says an iPhone lasts half an hour, tops in water. They've tried, but it's damaged beyond repair. I've asked his provider to supply call records. They're complying and we should have them tomorrow or the day after.'

'Anything from pathology?'

'Dr Madhvani e-mailed', said Reilly, his tone carefully non-committal. 'She's going to do the autopsy first thing tomorrow morning, and get her report to us asap afterwards.'

'That's quick.'

'She's only just arrived here – I suppose she hasn't got a full workload yet. And I spoke to Janet, the Family Liaison lady. She says Lisa is willing to do the formal I.D. tomorrow. Says she wants to get it over with.'

'OK – let's see if we can get her in tomorrow afternoon, after the autopsy.'

'Will do, sir.'

'Well, not much to go on at the moment.' Both detectives fell silent, knowing well that the first 48 hours in a murder investigation were usually crucial. Lose the impetus, and the trail could go cold very quickly.

'Let's try and be positive though, John. I think we need another couple of bods in the team to speed up all the background enquiries you're running. Can you bring in Lane and Wilshaw, subject to their other commitments, seeing as they've done some work on this already? And see if you can get us a permanent room for this case, with a whiteboard and a bit more room to breathe.'

'Yes sir.'

'Right, John, there's nothing more we can do tonight. I'm going to take our fearless leader's advice and head off early. I suggest you do, too.'

'Makes a change, sir. Have a good night.'

'You too, John.'

...

It was 6.30pm when Reilly pulled up outside his house, a modern semi-detached on the outskirts of Cardiff. He negotiated his Capri, with its wide turning circle and lack of power steering, through a many-pointed turn until it faced into his drive. Then he drove it carefully into the garage, using the fob on his key to open and close the automatic roller door. The family's main conveyance, an elderly VW Passat estate, sat outside on the road.

He went through the connecting door into the kitchen. Immediately, he braced himself for the impact of two small, fast-moving, blonde-haired blurs, which resolved themselves into his twin seven-year old girls, Beca and Eli.

'Daddy!!'

He picked one up on each side and stood, grunting a little with the effort.

'Did you catch any bad men?'

'Hundreds!'

'Did you get in a car chase?'

'Yes! 200 miles an hour, in my Capri.'

Reilly's wife, Catrin, came into the kitchen. 'I think your Daddy might be telling you a few fibs, girls'. Like her daughters, she was small, blonde-haired and blue-eyed.

'Noooo!' said Reilly, a look of mock seriousness on his face. 'Daddy never fibs, does he girls?'

The twins giggled. He hugged them once more, then set them down on the floor with a groan of relief. 'I swear you two get bigger every day.'

'Right girls', said Catrin. She switched to Welsh. 'You can finish watching Peppa Pig, then bathtime. Then Daddy will read you a story before bed.'

The twins scampered off, gabbling away in a mixture of English and Welsh. Reilly had tried to learn Welsh, but although he could read and understand a fair bit, he struggled to follow conversation, particularly at the speed his girls spoke. He and Catrin had met at Manchester University and immediately after finishing their degrees, he had moved to Wales to be with her. They had been married for just over fifteen years and had struggled to start a family, with round after round of fertility treatments unsuccessful. Then, seven years ago, when they had almost given up hope, the miracle had happened.

'How was your day, love?' Reilly asked Catrin, kissing the top of her head. She was a teacher at a Welsh-medium high school.

'Well, I wish you'd come in and put the fear of God into the Year 11s. Some of the boys were absolute pigs today. How about you?'

'Spent most of the day talking to old men about fishing.'

'Oh no! I heard about that body in the fishing lake on the local news. They didn't say anything – just that a body had been found – was that what you were doing?'

'Yeah. Looks like it might be a murder. We don't know too much yet, though.'

She shuddered. 'I wish you didn't have to deal with stuff like that, John.'

'It's the job, love. Someone has to do it.'

She was about to ask, why him? But they'd had this conversation before, and she knew he loved his job, and would never change.

Instead, she said, 'Come on through. The girls will be finishing Peppa Pig soon. You grab some food while I give them a bath, then you can read them a story. There's some lasagne just needs warming up.'

Reilly heated the food in the microwave while he made a cup of tea. Then he wolfed down the lasagne one-handed, while reading the news on his phone. Half way down the local news, there it was – 'Body of man found in lake', but with no further details yet. He guessed that would change once the media became aware the police were treating it as a suspicious death.

As he finished his food, he became aware from the noises upstairs that bathtime was ending. He made a fresh cup of tea for Catrin and went upstairs.

A few minutes later, Reilly was sitting between Beca and Eli's beds, reading Roald Dahl's 'Fantastic Mr Fox'. As he immersed himself in the story and his children's rapt attention, he felt the tension of the day slipping away. He reached the end of the chapter, then said 'Right! That's enough for tonight. Prayers, and then bed.'

Immediate howls of protest. 'But we can't sleep now! We don't know if Mr Fox will tunnel fast enough to save his family!'

'I'm sure you'll manage. And anyway, if I tell you now, what'll be left for tomorrow?'

'Awreet, Daddy' said Beca, in a slow, exaggerated Northern accent. He growled at her, and both girls giggled.

They quietened down and said prayers together. Reilly had been brought up a Catholic, a remnant of his Irish ancestry, and often wasn't sure whether he believed or not, but felt he had the duty to pass it on to his kids, then they could decide for themselves one day. He kissed both girls, turned off the light and went out. He waited a few minutes outside the bedroom door. There were a few minutes of whispered chatter, then silence. He tiptoed carefully downstairs.

As he came into the living room, Catrin was pouring herself a glass of wine. She handed him an opened beer and a glass.

'Want to watch 'Lincoln Lawyer'?'

'Go on, then.'

They both enjoyed American crime and courtroom shows, although he mainly liked laughing at the inaccuracies in investigative procedure and wild plot leaps.

As he settled down on the sofa, one arm around Catrin and the other holding his beer, he suddenly thought that he was as happy as a man could possibly be.

...

Tomos Hopkins sat looking at his laptop in the large, open kitchen of a converted farmhouse near

Bonvilston in the Vale of Glamorgan. The Aga kept the large room nice and warm, although he occasionally muttered about the cost of fuel and servicing. Mair, his wife, was folding a pile of clothes and lying them on top of one of the closed Aga hob lids to dry.

'What are you looking at, *cariad*?' she asked, in Welsh. 'Not work, again?'

'No, I'm reading these submissions for the University poetry magazine. It's my turn to edit it this quarter.'

'Any good?'

'Awful, most of them. Like a bunch of sixth formers trying too hard. Why can't they just write what they really feel, instead of having to hint at some sort of existential crisis to make themselves seem more interesting?'

'That's a bit harsh, Twm', Mair said, and came over to look.

After reading a few lines, she said, 'I see what you mean, though. This one's really cheery. About her life being like an unheard song on a jukebox, or the empty glass in her hand as she stands at the bar.'

'Well, the poor thing is from Blaenau Ffestiniog. All that grey slate and rain – bound to have an effect. The children's competition's always more cheerful – lots of sheep grazing in green valleys, birds singing and flowers.'

'Well, pack it up for now. You need a good night's sleep. And don't forget, you've got the consultant at the hospital first thing Wednesday morning.'

'I hadn't forgotten. Although I was trying to. Heard from the kids at all?'

'Cai's enjoying his course. They've got a reading week next week, so he might come back.'

'Might?'

'I think there might be a young lady influencing that decision.'

'Hmm. How about Eirlys?'

'She's out on a works do with her department. Apparently, they got judgment in on a big case today – they won. So they're all off out celebrating.'

It had been nearly six months since the youngest child, Cai had left to go to college in London. Eirlys, the eldest, had moved out several years ago and had a flat in the centre of Cardiff, near the law firm where she worked. But the house still felt empty and quiet to Hopkins. The case, the melancholy poetry, and his other worries, the ones that recently never went away, swirled around him like a cold wind, giving him an uncomfortable, tight feeling in the pit of his stomach.

He got up, went over to the drinks cabinet, and poured himself a generous measure of Penderyn Welsh whisky, the extra smooth one matured in bourbon casks, as endorsed by Bryn Terfel, the velvety smooth Welsh baritone.

'That won't help you sleep, Twm' said Mair, concerned.

'It's just the one. While I read something more cheerful. You go on up to bed. I'll be there in a minute.'

On a whim, he Googled Crucian carp. He was quickly engrossed in the minutiae of their origins, how to distinguish the true Crucian from hybrids, their diet, habits and how and where to catch them. He found some pictures of prize specimens being held as gently as new-born babies by grinning anglers. The fish looked like overgrown goldfish, but more bronze-coloured than gold, with deeper bellies and high, humped backs sporting long dorsal fins. He saw a picture of the current record, four pounds fourteen ounces, and read the story of its capture in an online magazine.

Then he sipped the last of his whisky, turned out the lights, and went upstairs.

Chapter 8

Pit of evil

There's hell, there's darkness, there is the sulphurous pit; burning, scalding, stench, consumption!
Shakespeare, *King Lear*

Hopkins and Reilly arrived into the car park at about the same time, just after 8, the next morning. As they converged on the main entrance, a group of bleary-eyed officers were on the way out. One stopped to talk to Reilly, their heads bowed together, then Reilly patted him consolingly on the shoulder and he walked out with the others.

'Drugs bust last night' said Reilly, in answer to Hopkins' questioning glance. 'Shadows night club, you know, that place that opened up in town a couple of years back. Fancy cocktail bar during the day and early evening, nightclub at night.'

They started up the stairs to the MCIT room.

'I take it they were unsuccessful?'

'Yep. Undercover officers had seen some small-scale dealing going on there and they had a tip the club was being used as a major distribution centre for a county lines operation. So they went in after hours, searched the place from top to bottom – nothing. You're looking better today, sir.'

They entered the MCIT room, Hopkins slightly out of breath from the stairs.

'Yes John. Seems there's nothing like reading about fishing to send you off to sleep.'

'Ah, researching the case?'

'Not really, just aimlessly looking at some background. Didn't really get me anywhere, other than to sleep, so that's something.'

'Anyway, the Scenes of Crime Team are down at the lake already sir. I've asked them to do a full search all round the lake, right up to the perimeter fence, and have a good poke around with their poles in any undergrowth. Diving team should be there to start their sweep about 9 – 9.30ish.'

'Good, anything else?'

'I've started looking into the background of all the people we've spoken to so far. You remember how Craig Walters, the bailiff, was a bit hesitant when you asked him about being in the Services?'

Hopkins nodded.

'I think I may have found the reason. According to the system, he hasn't got a record, but he is being investigated by the Ministry of Defence's Historic Investigations Team for something that happened in Northern Ireland. I've requested the details from them.'

'Interesting. Anything else?'

'I think we can definitely rule out Dai Jonas. Wasn't there at the likely time of death, no connection to Reynolds other than they were members of the same club, no convictions and, as you saw, completely shocked by the whole thing.'

'Yes, I think you're right. Rule him out. What about friend Richards?'

'Nothing more than what the Super told you yesterday. Made it big in London in the boom of the '90s, came back here and took over a local firm, put all his money in property. Awarded a CBE two years ago, won loads of business awards, does lots of fund-raising for charity.'

'Has he got back to us with the responses to his e-mail yet? I mean about who was at the lake on Sunday?'

'Not yet. I think he said he'll get it to us this morning. Oh, and the security manager from the industrial estate has just dropped off the footage on a flash drive. Dave and Sue are looking through it now, to identify cars and small vans. We can then cross-check the list against the responses from the club and see if anyone's lying.'

'OK, I'll just grab us both a coffee and then I'd better start getting through this bloody paperwork. We'll go down to the lake about lunchtime – the SOC team should be finishing up by then.'

'Righto, sir.'

A few minutes later, Hopkins was ensconced at his desk in a cubicle a few feet away from Reilly and other colleagues. He forced himself to look at the screen and concentrate. Why was it so hard these days? His mind seemed to slide off sideways every time he tried to force it onto the mundane but necessary. He used to be able to plough through this stuff, reports, forms, etc. with a few hours of focused effort. Was it age? Or was he just getting lazy?

With a huge effort, he forced himself to concentrate, and managed to have a reasonably productive couple of hours. He was relieved, however, when Reilly came over and tapped him on the shoulder.

'Sir? SOC have found something. I think we should go there now.'

...

It was about 11.30am when they drove through the gate to the lake. To their right, a team of four officers with long, white poles was carefully pacing clockwise around the edge of the lake and the surrounding bushes and trees, in a more or less even line. It looked as though they had nearly completed their circuit, assuming they had started from the car park. On the left hand side of the lake, two members of the diving team walked slowly along the banking, holding yellow ropes that trailed into the water and were presumably attached to the two submerged divers.

The officer in charge of the search hurried over to meet them.

'Morning sir. We thought you'd better see this, as soon as possible.'

They walked quickly around the lakeside, in the direction of where Reynolds' fishing gear had been stationed. As they got near to where he had been sitting, the officer turned off the path, towards the metal fence, which was set a few yards back. One of the large piles of brushwood, a result of Craig Walters' work over the weekend, had been loosely stacked against the fence, but was now pulled apart, revealing a bare area of grass and weeds.

'What's this?' asked Reilly.

'One of the team poked his pole through the brushwood and heard a hollow thump. So we pulled the branches back and – well, have a look.'

The officer reached into what had been the middle of the pile of brush and poked around with his pole. After a few seconds, he located a ring hidden in the grass. With a heave, he levered upwards and a two-foot square section of the turf came up. On closer inspection, it appeared to be a trapdoor, disguised by a layer of turf let into it.

'Come and have a look inside.' The officer shone his torch down into the chamber below.

Hopkins and Reilly stepped forward and peered in. It appeared to be a small plastic cubed chamber, like a septic tank, about six or seven feet wide and deep. On one side was a stack of brick-sized bales wrapped in plastic. On another were cardboard trays of plastic pill bottles, also wrapped in plastic.

'We'd better get the Drugs Team here', said Hopkins. 'Nobody touch anything. Secure the site around here.'

'Yes sir', said the SOC officer, and Reilly got on his phone.

Hopkins stepped away and stared morosely at the lake. This was where it always seemed to lead. The legacy of industrial collapse, the fragmentation of the old communities, a life that seemed to hold few prospects for the young. Thus creating a demand that predators were quick to exploit. The tentacles of the evil trade were everywhere, reaching into and destroying young lives.

'I suppose it's an ideal spot, sir.' Reilly, breaking into his thoughts.

'Hmm?'

'Well, it's a secure site, limited access, pretty secluded in amongst all these trees, and not too far from the M4. Probably using it as a storage site before transferring smaller quantities into town to sell. That would tie in with the off-road bikes and so on driving around at night. Maybe they're the couriers.'

'Maybe, John. God, why does everything have to come down to drugs?'

'You know the Valleys and the old industrial towns are rotten with it, sir.'

'Yes, I know' said Hopkins, heavily. 'Come on, let's sit down over there.' He gestured to the lean-to, next to the shipping container that served as storage and a toilet. Both sank down onto plastic garden chairs.

'Well, at least we've got something to go on, now', said Reilly. 'It could be county lines – you know, Reynolds drives up the M4 when his girlfriend thinks he's out fishing, meets the suppliers from London somewhere nice and dark off the motorway, comes back and stashes it here when no-one else is around, then hands small quantities through the fence to the couriers who come through the fields.'

'Maybe – but who could install something that size without anyone else in the club noticing?'

'Well, the bailiff's in charge of all works, I think. And he said the farmer installed the other septic tank, under there' – he gestured with his thumb to the shipping container.

'We'd better interview them both then. But first I want to find out about that tank.' Hopkins pointed to the area currently being taped off. 'Let's see if there's a make, or a brand, or a serial number on it. See if we can trace where it came from and who bought it. These things are fairly environmentally sensitive, so whoever supplied it might have a record.'

'OK sir. I'll get them to stick a camera down and see if they can find any identifying marks.'

The two divers were now climbing out of the lake, at the side nearest to where Reilly and Hopkins were sitting. The two detectives got up and went over to them.

'Find anything?'

'No, nothing. No weapon or anything like that. The only strange thing was a load of fish heads on the bottom over there.' The lead diver motioned towards an area about ten yards from where Reynolds' gear had been.

'Fish heads?'

'Yeah, small silvery ones. Looked like mackerel or herring. Neatly sliced with what looked like a sharp knife.'

'What on earth would they be doing there?' wondered Hopkins, bewildered. 'Some weird kind of sacrifice?'

'Might be an idea to give Bryn Richards a call, sir', suggested Reilly. 'Perhaps he can shed light on who carries out works and what the fish heads mean?'

'Good idea, John. Let's go to the car and see if we can get him on speaker.'

They got into Hopkins' car and Reilly dialled Richards' number. After only three rings, he picked up. 'Yes?'

'Mr Richards? Detective Sergeant Reilly here, sir. Could I put you on speaker to talk to me and Inspector Hopkins?'

'Well... yes, I suppose so.'

'Many thanks, sir' Hopkins switched to speaker. 'Can you hear us, sir?'

'Yes, yes.'

'Inspector Hopkins here, Mr Richards. I was just wondering, could you tell us who in the club is authorised to carry out works? You know, digging, drainage, maintenance, that kind of thing.'

'Oh, that would be Craig, Craig Walters. The Committee pretty much leaves everything to him. He's very efficient, you see. Gets quotes in, manages the contractors when necessary, sorts out the accounts, etc. Over the years, we've come to rely on him and we just let him get on with it, unless it's something unusually expensive.'

'I see, sir. And when would be the last time any major works were done?'

'That would be the septic tank by the container. About two years ago. Craig sourced the tank and fittings online, then got quotes. As it turned out, the farmer, Mr Lewis, was cheapest as he was hiring a mini-digger at that time for the renovation work on his barn. He got it done in the course of a day, as I recall.'

'And no other significant works since then?'

'No, or we'd have seen invoices and receipts to sign off on. What's this about, Inspector?'

'Oh nothing, just getting background. One more thing, sir. The divers found a load of fish heads at the bottom of the lake near to where Mr Reynolds' gear was found. Have you any idea why that might be, sir?'

'Probably someone pre-baiting for pike, Inspector.'

'Pre-baiting? Could you explain that, sir?'

'Yes, when we took over the lake, there were a number of pike there already. We don't know how many or how big. They don't seem to take too many of our stock fish, so we leave them be. Some of the members like to fish for them, and they sometimes come the night before and throw fish heads and other tasty bits in the water, to attract the pike for when they come the next day to fish.'

'I see, sir. So someone could have been at the lake on Sunday night, chucking fish heads in with the intention of fishing Monday?'

'Yes, Inspector.'

'Wouldn't the pike have eaten them all by now?'

'Not necessarily. It depends where they are, how hungry they are, water temperature, weather. Very fickle things, pike. They may have taken a few and left the rest, then the divers would have scared them away.'

'And who fishes for pike in the club?'

'Not many. It's a lot of effort for not much reward. Three or four, including myself occasionally, but only one goes regularly after pike.'

'And who's that?'

'Rob – Robert Locke. Retired – lives in the village near the lake.'

'Rhyd yr Afon?'

'That's it.'

'Well, thank you Mr Richards. I think that's all for now.'

'One thing Inspector, if you don't mind.'

'Go ahead, Mr Richards.'

'When can we re-open the lake for fishing?'

Hopkins looked across at Reilly, who held up two fingers.

'Probably the day after tomorrow, Mr Richards. One area may still be cordoned off.'

'And sir?' broke in Reilly. 'Have you managed to send that list of names yet? The people who were here Sunday?'

'Yes, it should be in your inbox now.'

'Thanks very much, sir, goodbye for now.'

Hopkins ended the call.

Reilly had his phone open.

'Let's see ... five names on the list from Richards, plus Walters, of course. Interesting – Locke's not on the list.'

'So he wasn't here on Sunday throwing bait in the water – or he's not admitting it. That is interesting.'

'What should we do now, sir?'

'Back to the office, I think. Have a word with the uniforms before we go. No-one to be let in or out of the gate until the Drugs Team have finished. Not a word of what we've found to anyone outside the team and particularly no-one in the club. When the Drugs Team have finished, I want them to put that brush wood back over the tank and seal it off. I don't want anyone having a look at it when the club re-opens the lake.'

'OK, sir. I'll get them to put a sheet over it and pile the branches back.'

'Have you got the details of the investigation into Walters yet from the Ministry of Defence?'

'Not yet. They promised it this afternoon.'

'OK. Let's see if we can get Walters in for interview tomorrow afternoon. I'm out in the morning – just a personal matter.'

'What shall I tell him, sir?'

'Tell him it's just a few questions. If he pushes, say we're not charging him with anything – we'd just appreciate it if he cleared a few matters up for us.'

'Will do, sir. How about the farmer, Lewis?'

'Let's wait until we have some more details on the tank.'

...

At 5pm, Hopkins called them together in what they were now calling the Murder Room. Reilly had got them a larger, air-conditioned conference room that seated six comfortably. A whiteboard at the front displayed pictures of Reynolds, Lisa, Jonas, Richards and Walters, together with a map of the lake and markings showing where the body, Reynolds' gear and the second septic tank had been found. Someone, presumably Reilly, had drawn a red cross over Jonas' picture. There was also a blank square with 'R. Locke' inked in.

The two detectives Reilly had brought in to assist the investigation entered. Dave Lane was in his thirties; tall, prematurely balding with a serious air. He was reckoned by other MCIT officers to be hard-working and diligent. Sue Wilshaw was a similar age, with short blond hair, a strong build and steely-looking eyes. Women's rugby and tae-kwon-do were her pastimes.

Once mugs, pads, papers and pens had been set out, Hopkins cleared his throat.

'OK, so you know the SOC team found what looks like a fairly sizeable haul of drugs in a disguised pit by the lake. That puts a different complexion on things and gives us a potential motive for the murder. Reynolds was arrested for possession in the past and suspected of dealing. There's also evidence of him and his girlfriend spending a lot of money recently – car, home improvements and so on. We don't know how or when the tank holding the drugs was installed – but Craig Walters, the Chief Bailiff, is apparently the only person responsible for carrying out that kind of work. Seems unlikely he could have done it on his own, though. What else do we know about Walters?'

'MOD records came through this afternoon, sir.' said Reilly. 'He was in the Royal Marines during the years he said, highest rank attained, sergeant.' He paused.

'And what was the investigation into him about?'

'He did a tour in Northern Ireland, in 1992. His platoon were manning a vehicle checkpoint at night on a country road in South Armagh. A car tried to drive through, Walters opened fire and killed the driver. Turned out to be a fifteen-year old kid. The MOD team think that, as he fired after the car had already passed, the shooting wasn't justified, as his men weren't in danger. He's contesting it. No charges brought so far.'

'He should know how to use a knife, sir', said Lane.

'Why's that, Lane?'

'I'm pretty sure it would have been part of Commandos' training, sir, back when Walters served. And the dagger is on the badge they're awarded when they pass training.'

'So he could be our man', said Reilly. 'He's killed before, and probably knows how to use a knife. And he's the only one responsible for works, and the tank was covered up by brushwood that he cut.'

'Yes, but what's his motive, John? And we've got nothing to connect him directly to Reynolds or the crime scene. He says he left about 5pm, before Reynolds, remember.'

'He could have sneaked back, somehow. No CCTV on the gates, sir.'

'Possibly, but we've still got nothing to really tie him in.'

Hopkins thought a moment.

'What do the Drugs Team say?'

Sue Wilshaw spoke. 'Looks like cocaine in the bundles. Could be cut with ketamine – that's been turning up a lot on the streets recently. Nasty mix. The pills could be MDMA or Es. The lab's checking it out now. Street value could be fifty, sixty thousand. The stash might only have been half full – there was room for much more. No way of telling how much has gone through there.'

'Any info on Reynolds?'

'No. He's on their watchlist as a possible dealer, but he's not done anything recently to come up on their radar. But I've been checking traffic cameras on the M4, asking the system to look for his number. So far, we've got his car going eastbound at night three times in the last month. Last camera that picked him up was Magor services, but nothing the other side of the Severn bridge. So if he was going to a pick up, it was somewhere in the Magor area.'

'OK. How have we got on with the CCTV at the entrance to the estate?'

'Still checking it' said Lane. 'But so far, no vehicles belonging to club members other than the five, plus Walters, who've said they were there.'

'Call records?'

Sue Wilshaw answered. 'Not many calls in the last month or so, according to the provider's records. We've not found any unregistered numbers yet. They all seem to be family or friends, but we'll keep on checking it out.'

'Hmm. That doesn't tie with Jonas' account, that he spent a lot of time on his phone when he was fishing. Anyone called Sandra in the list?'

'No sir, but we'll keep working on it.'

'Right, well tomorrow morning, Dr Madhvani's doing the autopsy and should get her report to us by lunchtime. I've got to be somewhere else tomorrow morning. John, could you pick up Lisa and take her to do the formal identification at the hospital, say about 12 o'clock? I'll try and meet you there. Then, let's see if we can get Walters in for about 3pm.'

The meeting broke up, but Reilly held back. From his awkward demeanour, Hopkins could tell he had something on his mind. 'What's the matter, John?'

'Oh, nothing sir. Just wondered ... is everything OK? I mean, you've seemed a bit worried for a while and you look like you could do with more sleep. And your appointment tomorrow – you never take time off.'

'No, everything's fine, John. Just a routine medical check-up. The rewards of getting older. Don't worry, honestly.'

'OK, if you say so, sir.'

Chapter 9

Invictus

In the fell clutch of circumstance,
I have not winced nor cried aloud.
Under the bludgeonings of chance,
My head is bloody, but unbowed.
William Ernest Henley, *Invictus*

Hopkins sat in the waiting room of a small private hospital just outside Cardiff, nursing a paper cup of surprisingly good coffee from the complimentary machine. He hadn't wanted to go private, but the GP had strongly advised him to use the work private healthcare scheme in the interests of speed.

That was when he had started to worry.

The waiting room was modern, carpeted, with tasteful prints of Impressionists on the walls. Art wasn't Hopkins' strong suit, but he recognised a couple of them. He thought they looked insipid and washed-out, but guessed the intention was to be as bland and calming as possible, for the patients' benefit. He much preferred the Kyffin Williams prints that Mair had chosen for their house; the bold, stark style, and blacks, whites, dark greens and greys, to him conveying the savage beauty of the Welsh mountains; and the sturdy, rugged figures, the indomitable spirit of its miners and farmworkers.

The receptionist picked up a phone, listened, nodded and then said, 'Certainly Dr Bradley, I'll send him through now.' She put the phone down, called out to Hopkins, then said 'Down the corridor, second door on your left.' She returned to her computer screen.

Hopkins walked down the bright, white corridor with its blue skirting boards and blue-framed pictures. He came to the second door and knocked.

'Come in!' boomed a cheerful voice.

Dr Bradley more closely resembled an ascetic monk, than a physician. He was slim, austere, with a bald domed crown surrounded by a thin circle of white hair.

'How are you feeling?'

'Well, OK I suppose. Bit worried.'

'In that case, the quicker we get to it, the better. I've seen your blood results and the MRI scan from two weeks ago. Are you feeling a lot of fatigue? Loss of mental concentration?'

'Yes, quite a bit of both.'

'Itching? Like a deep, fiery itch you can't scratch, when you come out of the shower, or if you get cold?'

'Yes, that too.'

'Let's have a look at you. Get up on the couch there, lift up your shirt and loosen the waist of your trousers, if you wouldn't mind.'

Hopkins, slightly embarrassed by his middle-aged body, complied. The doctor ran his fingers from the bottom of his ribcage on the left side, towards the navel and then the stomach area. He palpated gently, seemingly looking for something, then suddenly pressed in a little harder.

Hopkins grunted.

'Sore?'

'Just a little tender.'

Bradley took a marker pen out of his pocket, made a small mark on the abdomen, then produced a tape measure and measured from the ribcage to the mark. He then placed his hand flat on Hopkins' abdomen and tapped the back of it with the other, moving around and tapping, like Basil Fawlty looking for hollow spots in a bedroom wall, thought Hopkins.

'OK, you can sit up and get dressed now.'

Hopkins rebuttoned his shirt, fastened his belt and sat in the chair again.

'It will take a bone marrow test to be a hundred per cent sure, but I'm pretty certain you have myelofibrosis.'

Hopkins felt numb. 'That doesn't sound good.'

'It's nothing to panic about. We appear to have caught it early. And there are some good treatments around now, not like a decade or so ago.'

'What exactly is it?'

'It's a blood disorder, genetic in origin. A gene, we call it JAK-2, mutates and sends messages to your bone marrow, causing it to become fibrous and stop producing blood.'

Hopkins felt numbed, in shock.

'So, what's producing my blood?'

'Well, this is where the spleen comes in. It produces blood in babies in the womb, but normally stops after that. However, in this case, it's fired up again and is merrily producing red blood cells for you. That's why it's growing and you have that slight bulge in your abdomen.'

'I thought it was just middle-aged spread.'

'No, you're in good shape, as regards body mass index, for your age. But the problem with the spleen taking over blood production is, it's not very good at it. Not efficient. So it grows bigger and bigger, but becomes less efficient and eventually produces less and less blood.'

Hopkins swallowed, hard. He was starting to feel sick at the thought of this rogue organ, growing inside him, working against him. 'So, what can be done?' he asked.

'Well, as I said, the good thing is, we've caught it early. Your haemoglobin levels are good – on the low side of the normal range, but not abnormal. Plenty of men your age have lower levels just through stress, bad diet, lack of exercise, etc. Also, there's no evidence of blasts – cancerous cells.'

'Cancer?'

'Left untreated, myelofibrosis can turn into leukaemia. But we're nowhere near that stage. And last of all, your spleen, although enlarged, isn't at a level where we need to think about doing anything drastic. Now, as I said, there are some good treatments around nowadays. In particular, there's a drug called ruxolitinib, came on the scene in about 2012, so we've a lot of data on it now. It works by blocking the messages from the JAK-2 gene and it can stop the condition progressing, or even reverse it a little. I'll need to get you in for a bone marrow test to confirm, but that would almost certainly be the first step.'

'How do I take this drug? Injections?'

'Oh no, pills. I'd start you on quite a high dose – twenty milligrammes twice daily. You might feel rough for the first four or five weeks and your blood counts might drop, so we'll need to monitor you regularly. You might even need a blood transfusion to tide you over. Then, things should start getting back to normal and we can gradually reduce the dose to see what level keeps you on an even keel. You should notice a reduction in the size of the spleen – you might even have a little concave hollow on the left side of your abdomen, until your other organs move to fill the gap.'

Hopkins felt queasy again.

'And how long will I be taking this drug for?'

'Oh, indefinitely. The data we have shows that it's effective for about ten years, maybe a year or two longer. Then the JAK-2 gene seems to figure out a way to get around it.'

'And what happens then?'

'There are other drugs, other combinations we can try. And ultimately, there's the option of a bone marrow transplant. But I would stress, we're nowhere near that stage yet.'

Bradley paused, eyeing Hopkins keenly.

'Look, I know it's easy to say, but try not to worry. This is a very slow-moving condition. I've got patients on my books who were diagnosed twenty years ago and are still living normal, healthy lives. We've caught it early and with rux, we have an excellent chance of stopping it.'

'For ten years.'

'Maybe longer. And treatments are developing all the time. And I know you're a detective and it's your instinct to investigate things, but don't Google myelofibrosis, whatever you do – you'll scare yourself to death.'

'Thanks a lot.'

'Look, Mr Hopkins, it's a huge shock, I know, but this condition isn't necessarily life-limiting. There are lots of people with it who manage to live full, happy lives. And there are a few things you can do to take control of it. Diet, for one – I'll get our dietician to send you a leaflet. And exercise – exercise is shown to improve outcomes and quality of life in this and many similar conditions.'

'My sergeant's going to be glad to hear that. That's what he's always advising me to do.'

'Well, on this occasion, I concur with his learned medical opinion. No need to go mad. Go for some nice walks in the country. Do some light work in the gym. It'll help boost your blood production, and you'll feel better.'

'OK.'

'See my receptionist on the way out, and book in for a bone marrow test in the next week or so. Once it's confirmed, I'll write you a prescription for rux. I'll see you in my NHS clinic after the test, then you can take it to the hospital pharmacy and collect it for free.'

Hopkins realised the consultation was at an end.

'Well, thanks Doctor. I appreciate your time.'

'Not at all. And look, if you have any questions, you can always e-mail me. And there's lots of information and support available from a couple of charities, for patients with similar conditions. Anthony Nolan and MPN Voice – I'll get the receptionist to send you the details.'

Hopkins walked out of the room, down the blue and white corridor with its blue and white carpet, past the bland, dreamlike blue and white paintings. He paused to book the next appointment with the receptionist then walked out into the carpark. He leaned against his car, unsure what to do next. Weak sunshine from a pale blue sky with wispy white clouds washed over him. He felt weak, nauseous, empty of all hope.

Suddenly, he shook himself like a dog emerging from a stream, unlocked the car and got in, staring determinedly ahead.

He preferred Kyffin Williams. He wanted black and white.

He wanted certainty.

Chapter 10

Descent into the Underworld

The gates of hell are open night and day;
Smooth the descent and easy is the way;
But to return and view the cheerful skies;
In this the task and mighty labour lies.
Virgil, *The Aeneid*

It was 12.45 when Hopkins arrived in the car park of the hospital. He looked around the reserved car park spaces and saw that Reilly, presumably in deference to the solemnity of the occasion, had collected Lisa in the family Passat.

The route to the morgue was unfortunately familiar to Hopkins, having had to attend a number of formal identifications in cases of suspicious death. As always, when he reached the small, grey waiting room with its worn, grey plastic chairs, Hopkins wondered why they couldn't do something to make it a little less grim and institutionalised for relatives. But maybe nothing would improve things for someone torn apart by grief and waiting to confirm the worst.

Reilly was sitting in a corner with Lisa and Janet, the Family Liaison Officer. Lisa's eyes were red-rimmed, as though she had been crying, but she looked resolute and determined.

'Hello sir', began Reilly, doubtless glad to have someone else to talk to in the sombre atmosphere. 'Everything go OK with the – '

'Fine, John, talk about it later' Hopkins cut him off. 'Ms Hughes, sorry, Lisa, so sorry once again for your loss. And thank you for being here. We know how difficult it will be, and we really appreciate it.'

Lisa sniffed and wiped her nose with a tissue. 'Have you any idea yet who killed him?'

'We're working on it. There are one or two leads, but it's early days yet.'

Lisa shrugged and looked down. Clearly, she thought the answer an empty platitude. But there was nothing else Hopkins could say.

More to fill in time, than in the hope of eliciting any information, Hopkins asked, 'Did Jason have any quarrel with anyone that you know of? Anyone who might have wished him harm?'

Lisa, head still down, shook her head.

'Was there anyone he associated with, met up with regularly?'

'Not really. A couple of mates from school he used to see from time to time, and his uncle. His Mam and Dad of course, when they were alive. But mostly, when he wasn't out fishing or working, he was with me.'

'Would you be able to e-mail the names of his friends and his uncle to us?'

'The friends I could. I never met his uncle, don't know his name. Jason mentioned him a few times recently, and said he was going to see him. I don't think he was a real uncle though – I got the feeling he was someone more distant, like a relative by marriage or a family friend. I don't remember seeing him at his Dad's funeral.'

'Thanks, Lisa.' Hopkins was about to ask something else, when the door to the room opened, and Dr Madvhani and a mortuary assistant, both in scrubs, entered. After introductions, Madhvani led them down a corridor.

'Jason is in a separate room down here.' She paused. 'I am sure the officers will have explained this to you, but he will look a little different, because of his time in the water.'

Lisa nodded, but kept her composure.

Madhvani held open a door and they filed inside. Jason lay on a trolley, under a pale green sheet, his feet, knees, chest and nose raising contours, like a barren mountain range.

'Are you ready?' asked Madhvani gently, then raised the sheet from his head and carefully folded it away from his face. Hopkins was relieved to see that much of the bloating had subsided. The top of the head was covered in a cotton stretch bandage, Hopkins assumed to cover the scars left by the autopsy.

'Lisa, can you confirm for the record that this is Jason Reynolds?' asked Reilly, formally.

Lisa half nodded, then said in a whisper 'Yes.' Then, 'Could I see his left arm?'

Madhvani raised the sheet again. Just above the left wrist was a tattoo, an ornate heart with the letters 'J' and 'L' inside it.

'Yes, that's definitely him', said Lisa, and then at last broke down in tears. Janet put her arm around her and led her outside. The mortuary assistant replaced the sheet and started releasing the brakes on the trolley, preparing to take the body back to the morgue.

'So Doctor,' began Hopkins, 'What did you find in the autopsy?'

'Haven't you read my report? I sent it to you this morning.'

'We've both been out of the office' said Hopkins, quickly, before Reilly could jump in.

'Well, nothing much more than we surmised at the lakeside. The stab wound we observed was clearly the cause of death – a long, thin blade penetrating directly into the heart. He would have died very quickly. There was hardly any water in his lungs, so he was almost certainly dead when he entered the water. Given the angle of the blow, the person who struck it was probably standing in front of him, quite close. There were no other wounds or signs of struggle.'

'Seems likely to be someone he knew, then?' said Reilly. 'As he was taken completely by surprise, no time to defend himself?'

'That would appear to be the obvious conclusion, yes, Sergeant.'

'What about toxicology?' Hopkins asked.

'Nothing unusual. Small amount of alcohol in his system, well below the drink-drive limit.'

'Yes, we found a couple of empty cans of low-strength beer. Any evidence of drugs?'

'Nothing in his system. No residue under his fingernails or in the pockets or folds of his clothing. But any residue would have been likely to be washed away by the water. One interesting thing, though – he had the beginning of Dupuytren syndrome.'

'What's that?'

'Hereditary condition, mostly in people of Scandinavian ancestry. It causes thickening and tightening of the tissues in one or both hands, so the fingers start to curl. Often mistakenly called rower's syndrome, but it's got nothing to do with rowing. Just genes.'

'Interesting. But we still haven't got very much to go on', said Hopkins morosely.

'Well, maybe you'll have some luck with the phone', answered Madhvani.

'No good', said Reilly. 'His iPhone was completely dead from the water.'

'Oh, didn't I mention?' said Madhvani, with the air of a magician about to produce a rabbit from a hat. 'Of course, you haven't seen my report yet.' She reached into a pocket and pulled out an evidence bag. It contained a small, basic Nokia.

'He had this, wrapped in a plastic sandwich bag, in an inner pocket. There's still power in the battery. Came on as soon as I pressed the button.'

...

Hopkins and Madhvani walked down the main hospital corridor. Reilly had driven back to HQ to give the phone to the tech team and prepare for the interview, and Janet was giving Lisa a lift home.

'I'm going for lunch' Madhvani offered, 'If you want to join me? Just something from the concourse.'

Hopkins wasn't really in the mood, but couldn't think of a convincing excuse.

Later, they sat at a small round vinyl table, she eating pasta elegantly out of a foam tray and somehow managing not to drop any on her blouse or suit; he desperately trying to eat a panini without looking like Ed Miliband eating a bacon sandwich.

His precise mind objected to having had to order 'a panini', when the singular should have been 'panino', but he had been met with looks of incomprehension when he had tried to order correctly in the past. He consoled himself with the thought that, at least the blackboard outside the café hadn't advertised 'Panini's', with a misplaced apostrophe.

'So, any leads on the case?' she asked.

Hopkins, surprised, looked around. The concourse was crowded with diners, but the level of noise reverberating off the fake marbled floor and high windows made the likelihood of being overheard small. Nonetheless, he still leaned forward and lowered his voice.

'Well, one or two things. Looks like it may be connected with drugs.'

'That's a surprise. Got a suspect in mind yet?'

Again, Hopkins was surprised at her directness. But, he guessed she could always access the file anyway.

'We're interviewing one guy this afternoon. Right sort of profile and background. But so far, nothing to tie him to the crime. So it's just questioning at this stage, not an arrest.'

'And who is it?'

'No offence, but I'm not comfortable discussing the details here, if that's OK. It's a bit public.'

'No, that's fine, I understand.'

Effortlessly, she switched the flow. 'So tell me about yourself. I gather you're a poet in your spare time.'

'You've done your homework.'

'The wonders of Google and LinkedIn.'

'Well, I don't know if I'd call myself a poet, really. I dabble a bit. Helps me relax.'

'I read that you won a Bardic Crown and you judge competitions. Sounds pretty impressive to me.'

'Flattery will get you everywhere.'

'I'm serious. Not usual to come across a cop with intellectual interests.'

'You sound like you speak from experience.'

'Hmm. Maybe. Could I read some of your poetry sometime?'

'I doubt it would make much sense to you. I write nearly everything in Welsh.'

'Ah. Anything in English?'

'Not much. Only silly little things, satires, wordplays, that sort of thing. Just stuff I share with like-minded friends.'

She correctly interpreted that to mean he wasn't comfortable sharing with her, and changed tack again.

'So how did someone like you end up in the police?'

'We're not all knuckle-dragging gorillas, you know.' He paused. 'OK, my Dad was a criminal defence lawyer. Duty solicitor. I used to help him out in the holidays, carry his bags to court, do the photocopying, that kind of thing. Back then, there was a lot of rough justice, particularly during the miners' strike. Cases getting rushed through without proper scrutiny, officers getting together to agree their evidence beforehand and, in some cases, making it up. He wanted me to follow in his footsteps, but I guess I naively thought I could change the system from the inside.'

'So do you think things are still as bad?'

'Well, to some extent, but in different ways now. Look, sorry, I've got to rush. I've got to call my wife about something important. Thanks for lunch.'

If she was surprised by his abruptness, she hid it. 'Not at all. We must do it again sometime.'

'Erm, yes. Thanks again.' He waved vaguely in her direction and got up, pulling his mobile from his pocket as he walked towards the exit to the car park. He was now feeling guilty for not having rung Mair sooner to tell her about the outcome of the morning's appointment. But he didn't think he'd have been able to tell her calmly straight afterwards, and then he'd been busy driving and at the mortuary.

As he dialled her number, he thought, why on earth is the pathologist so interested in this case? And apparently, in me?

Chapter 11

Wounded sergeants

This is the sergeant
Who like a good and hardy soldier fought...
Shakespeare, *Macbeth*

It was just before 3pm when Hopkins got back to HQ. The call with Mair had taken longer than expected. She'd been worried, of course, and he had been grateful that he'd been able to control his voice and sound unworried, matter of fact.

However, as she asked him more and more questions, he realised there was a lot he hadn't asked the doctor, due to his numbed state. All his mumbled 'don't knows' and surmises seemed to increase her worry. Then, he had suddenly remembered that he needed to be back at HQ for Craig Walters' interview, and so he had cut the call short with an apology and a promise to be back home on time.

He had a nagging feeling of guilt for ending the call so suddenly.

Hopkins went straight over to Reilly's desk. 'Is he in, yet?'

'Not yet, sir. I was thinking.'

'Yes, John?'

'He's an ex-Marine, sir. He'll have had training on interrogation techniques and what to do in the event of capture. He's going to be difficult to crack – he'll be used to pressure being put on.'

'I think you're right. He'll probably just clam up if we're too tough on him. We need to make him want to talk. Any ideas on lines to take?'

'Well, I thought we could start with getting him to admit he's the only person responsible for works, but not let him know we know about the second tank. Then, if he does know about it, that should get him worried and off balance. Then we change tack, ask him what he was doing on Sunday night.'

'Should we ask him about the historic incident investigation, do you think?'

'I wasn't going to, unless it seems relevant. I thought it might get his back up. And he'll have all his answers ready, having already been grilled by the MOD lawyers.'

Reilly's desk phone buzzed. He picked it up. 'OK, thanks, we'll be right through to get him.' He put the phone down and looked up at Hopkins. 'He's here now sir.'

...

Walters looked even bigger in the confines of the cramped interview room.

Reilly gave the time and date, details of those present and asked Walters to confirm his identity for the tape. Walters just sat impassively, apart from confirming his name. He had refused to engage in any small talk during the walk from the waiting room to the interview room. Now he sat upright, with that same still watchfulness Hopkins had noticed earlier.

Reilly began.

'Mr Walters, could you confirm how long you've been employed by the fishing club?'

'Just over ten years.'

'As Chief Bailiff?'

'Yes.'

'And what does that involve?'

'Looking after the lake. Checking water quality, maintaining the pumps and aerators. Stocking fish. Clearing vegetation. Checking permits and making sure that everyone's complying with the rules.'

Hopkins stepped in.

'A very responsible job. Does anyone else help you?'

'Not at the moment. In the summer, we sometimes get work experience kids in for a few weeks to help. But mostly it's just me.'

'And do you do the heavier stuff as well? Digging ditches, drainage, that kind of thing?'

'Some. If it's drainage onto the farmer's land, he comes in to do it. He's got his own key. And if it's major, we'll get a contractor in.'

'What sort of major works do you do?'

'Sometimes a tree needs felling. Installing the concrete base for the shipping container and the lean-to. And there was the septic tank a couple of years ago.'

'And who's responsible for major works?'

'Me.'

'Just you?'

'Yes. I get quotes, get the contractors in, report to the committee, get the bills paid.'

'So, no one else is involved?'

Hopkins saw a shadow of suspicion cross Walters' face.

'No, why's all this important? I thought this was all about Jason Reynolds' death?'

Reilly took over. Change of tack. Let him think he'd got away with that one.

'Quite right, sir. Now, as you know, we need to eliminate people from our enquiries. Could you tell us about what you were doing on Sunday?'

'I went to Chapel in the morning with my wife.' Some surprise must have registered on the detectives' faces, for Walters added, 'I'm not really a believer. I go for my wife's sake. And I like the singing. The old Welsh hymns.'

'And then what?'

'We had lunch. Then just after one, I set off for the lake. There was some brambles, overhanging tree branches and so on, needed cutting. I got there around two-ish. I walked around, had a word with the guys who were there, unloaded my gear, and started work.'

'So you cut the brushwood – what did you do with it?'

'Stacked it in piles around the fence. The small stuff rots away and I shred the bigger bits once the leaves have died and dropped off. Sometimes the farmer takes some for firewood.'

'So all the piles around the fence – you put them there?'

'Yes.' Again, the look of suspicion.

'And what did you do next?'

'Got the little boat out of the container. Went over to the island to check on the solar panels and pumps, and reset the timers. Then I packed up about five and went home.'

Hopkins asked, 'And Jason wasn't there when you left?'

'No.'

'What did you do when you got home?'

'Had supper, then a couple of beers. Watched TV. Went to bed about 11.'

'Can anyone confirm that?'

'Just my wife.'

Reilly stepped in again. 'I'm still interested in the works side of things, if you'll bear with me a moment, sir. If some work needed doing, say an extra septic tank, would it have to go through you?'

'Of course, I've just told you. No-one else has the authority.'

'Has anything like that been done in the last year or so?'

'No, nothing.'

'You're sure?'

'Of course I'm sure! Look, why is this important?'

Hopkins decided to try to take advantage of Walters' irritation.

'In your training, in the Marines, Mr Walters, did you learn how to use a knife?'

The reaction was the opposite of what he expected. Flatly and calmly, Walters replied,

'Yes, it was part of close combat training back then. Never used one in anger. And I didn't kill Reynolds, if that's what you're asking.'

'I wasn't, but thanks for clearing that up. But you have killed someone, haven't you?'

100

'I don't have to answer that. It's not relevant to this case. And unless you're charging me, I'm leaving now. I don't think there's anything more I can usefully add.'

'Of course, you're free to go, sir' said Hopkins. 'You're not under arrest.'

Walters stood and picked up his coat from the chair next to him. Then he looked straight at Hopkins and said, quietly and fiercely,

'It was war. We were on a country lane in the middle of South Armagh. There could have been a terrorist hiding behind every hedgerow. Then we get a car coming towards us. At first it slows down, then we hear the engine revving and it comes straight at us. We only just had time to jump out of the way. My men were in danger, so I opened fire.'

'But the car was past the checkpoint when you fired,' said Hopkins.

'Yes, but I had two men stationed further down the road to guard our backs from ambush. The car was heading straight at where I thought they were. So I fired through the back windscreen to protect them. I'd do the same again, even if I knew it was a 15 year-old kid. I wanted to get all those lads home safe. They meant more to me than some kid I'd never met.'

...

Reilly came back into the MCIT room after showing Walters out. He puffed his cheeks and breathed out heavily to release the tension.

'Well, what do you make of that, sir?'

'I'm not sure. We need to check his alibi, but I'm sure his wife will confirm it, whether it's true or not. Get one of the others to give her a call.'

'OK sir.'

'We know that only Walters can carry out or authorise works. He confirmed that. We also know he has the training to kill someone with a knife, and that he has the capability to kill someone, in the right circumstances. To protect someone else, say. Maybe to stop Reynolds peddling drugs to someone he cared about?'

'But we still have nothing to link him to the scene at the relevant time. And if his wife backs up his alibi, that's it.'

'Exactly, John. Whoever rolled him into the water after killing him was very clever. It would wash away any DNA or fibres from the attacker, any traces of drugs, and wipe the data from the phone, apart from call records held by the provider.'

'But he didn't know about the second phone, sir.'

'No, and that was obviously the important one to Jason. He must have wrapped it in plastic to keep it safe in case it rained, or he dropped it. How are the tech guys getting on with it?'

'They've unlocked it, sir. Mixture of Jason's and Lisa's birth dates. Easy enough for them to guess after trying a few different combinations. They should be sending the list of calls soon.'

'Good. And how have you got on with the probate stuff while I was out?'

'Interesting, sir. His parents' house did sell for a tidy sum – about £200,000. But according to the Land Registry, it was mortgaged up to the hilt. Equity release, probably to pay for care at home fees and a couple of cruises, stuff like that, then a second charge to the council for social care when that money ran out. Jason would have only got a few grand at best.'

'So that wouldn't fund a new car, house renovations, and so on. It seems likely his income was coming from the drugs.'

'One last thing, sir. Greg Reynolds wasn't his Dad.'

'What?'

'I called up his birth certificate, to check against the tax and Land Registry records. Name of father was left blank.'

'Doesn't necessarily mean he wasn't the father. Perhaps she had her reasons for not putting him on.'

'Possibly sir. But why? They were married at the time. Seems very strange.'

'Nothing about this case is simple, John. Everything seems to be spreading outwards, in different directions, rather than leading us to the answer.'

They sat in silence for a few minutes.

'So how did your doctor appointment go this morning?' asked Reilly.

Hopkins didn't know what to say. Reilly was one of his closest, maybe his best, friend, but he didn't know how to process it yet, even to himself.

More sharply than he intended, he said, 'Just leave it, OK, John?'

'OK sir', said Reilly stiffly, and started to walk away.

'John?' Hopkins called after him. 'I'm sorry. We will talk about it. But – I'm not ready yet.'

'That's OK. And look – anything I can do, just say? I mean that.'

Hopkins nodded, too full of emotion to speak.

Reilly went back to his desk. After a few minutes' decent interval, he called over, 'We've got the call list from the tech guys. The first five contacts are just numbers. #1, #2, #3, #4 and #9. Multiple calls to numbers 1 to 4, usually several per night, two or three nights a week, over the course of the last month and before.'

'Probably the couriers on quadbikes. Makes sense not to have their names. What about 9?'

'Very few. One a month or less.'

'I wonder what significance '9' has, and why it's out of sync?'

'Don't know. The last one is 'Alex.' A few calls per month – two or three.'

'I wonder' said Hopkins, 'Could that be Alexandra – Sandra? The name Lisa thought she heard? See if you can trace the number – see if it's registered to anyone of that name. And ask our friends in the Drugs Team about the names of any known associates of Jason's.'

'OK sir.'

'I'm also thinking about the logistics, though. The amounts you could carry on a bike, presumably in a rucksack, would be quite small. And the couriers wouldn't march straight into a pub or club, spattered in mud from the fields, and start breaking open bundles like the ones we saw. They'd need to split it into smaller packets for street sale. Could there have been a staging post somewhere closer to town, so bundles could be broken up and shared out to the street dealers?'

'The only place Drugs Team have had their eye on recently was the club – Shadows. They drew a blank on that one.'

'Well, ask them anyway? This whole thing seems to revolve around drugs – despite the interesting fish theory – so I'd like to know a bit more about any background info the Drugs Team may have.'

'On it, sir.'

'See you tomorrow, John. And – well, thanks.'

Chapter 12

Sins of the fathers

*The sins of the father are to be laid upon the children.*Shakespeare, *The Merchant of Venice*

The next day was a Thursday, and Hopkins was called away to attend a court hearing in Swansea Crown Court in a fraud and false accounting case, where Hopkins had led the investigation. The defence barrister had raised a technical issue about whether some of the evidence was admissible, alleging improper search procedures, and so Hopkins had been summoned for an urgent hearing before the judge in chambers, without the jury present.

As expected, after hearing from both the respective Counsel and Hopkins, the judge had dismissed what was clearly a speculative application by the defence, and ruled that the evidence should go before the jury. Nonetheless, it felt like a wasted morning, plus the 30-minute drive each way. Consequently, Hopkins was in a distinctly frustrated mood when he strode into the MCIT room.

He threw his coat angrily at his chair then watched as it slowly, and seemingly mockingly, slid off onto the ground. He turned, saw Reilly's quizzical expression, and burst out laughing, his mood lifting.

'Tough morning, sir?' enquired Reilly, with one lifted eyebrow.

'A waste of time. But at least the judge ruled our search evidence in, on old Slimy Stevens' case. Hopefully he'll change his plea to guilty now and save us all some grief.'

'That would be a plus. Guess what – we've traced the septic tank, sir. Came from an agricultural engineering company up in Machynlleth.'

'You pronounced that really well, John' said Hopkins, surprised.

'Did I, sir? Catrin's parents are from there, so I've sort of learnt it by ear. Anyway, the make and serial number checked out to this company. I rang them this morning, and they do keep records. Have to, under environmental regulations, like you said.'

'And?' Hopkins sensed Reilly was enjoying drawing this out.

'It was sold and delivered to the farmer, sir. Jimmy Lewis. He said it was for installation on his farm and gave details of the location. Of course, the location he gave wasn't the lake.'

'This looks like the break we needed. Well done, John.'

Reilly looked pleased. 'Should we get him in, sir?'

'No, let's wait. I want to interview the others who were there on Sunday, get the full picture. Also, Lewis will know by now what we've found. All he has to do is look through the fence to see the roped off area. Let's leave him to sweat for a bit.'

'When do you want to see the other members, sir? The ones who were there on Sunday?'

'Well, seeing as the lake's open for fishing again, it might be easiest to ask if they can all get together there late this afternoon or early evening after work.

Plus Robert Locke, even though he says he wasn't there. I don't think any of them are likely to have much to add, so we can get through them quickly. Was there anyone on CCTV who hasn't admitted to being there?'

'No sir. And all their cars were gone by about 8pm at the latest.'

'Right. Well, ask Bryn Richards to put out the word. I appreciate it's short notice, but if he wants this cleared up quickly, hopefully he'll put pressure on them to attend.'

'OK sir. What about Jason's parentage? Should we try and do a bit more digging?'

'Don't waste too much time on it, John. See if you can find a relative, an aunt or an uncle or something, who might have known what went on. Actually, I've got a better idea. Why don't I speak to Janet, the Family Liaison lady? She helped Lisa to call Jason's relatives – she might remember if there was anyone the right age. Might save us a bit of time.'

Reilly nodded and went off to his desk.

Hopkins sat down, retrieved his coat and slung it on the back of his chair. He picked up his phone and dialled. Reilly could see him speaking, listening, nodding, then reaching for a pen and scrawling something down on a yellow Post-It. After a few minutes, he thanked Janet, put down the phone, and came over.

'Reynolds' mother has a sister, living just this side of Maesteg. In her seventies, but sounded on the ball when Janet spoke to her. A Mrs Moira Griffiths. I think I'll go over and see her now – fill in the time before we go to the lake.'

'Do you want me to come along?'

'No, you carry on here, John. I'm not sure this is all that important, and I don't want to spook her by turning up mob-handed.'

'I'll have you know, I'm always very kind to old ladies, sir.'

'I know, you're one of Nature's gentlemen, John. A sort of noble savage, if you will. But I think it's a better use of your time to crack on here.'

...

Hopkins knocked at the door of another stone terrace in Maesteg, remarkably similar to the one lived in by Jason and Lisa, save that this one still had its wooden window frames and front door.

The door was opened by a small, elderly lady with a head of tight, grey curls and alert, bright eyes. In fact, the immediate adjective that sprang to Hopkins' mind was 'birdlike.'

'Mrs Griffiths? I'm Detective Inspector Hopkins, South Wales Police. I'm really sorry for your loss. I wondered if I could ask you some questions, if you're up to it?'

'Come in, Inspector. I'm afraid the house is a bit of a mess. I wasn't expecting anybody.'

As Hopkins suspected, when he entered the small front room, it was immaculate. Mrs Griffiths was clearly very house proud. Old china and crystal sparkled from behind the glass door of an antique Welsh corner cupboard, showing not a speck of dust. Numerous little ornaments, mostly lifelike depictions of blackbirds, robins and thrushes, covered the mantelpiece. The only surprising thing was a number of lurid, violent-looking thrillers on a small bookshelf under the television.

'Can I get you a cup of tea, Inspector?'

'That would be lovely, thanks Mrs Griffiths. Milk but no sugar, please.'

As she busied herself in the small kitchen, Hopkins looked at the family photos. There was a much younger, but instantly recognisable, Moira in a flowery dress with her husband, wearing Army uniform. Graduation pictures of a girl and a boy, grinning awkwardly and self-consciously. A wedding picture of the same girl a few years later with her husband, and then a picture of her holding a baby. Then, a picture of Jason, in his late teens, with two adults, presumably his parents, on a beach somewhere.

Moira came back into the room, carrying a tray with two delicate china cups and a plate of biscuits.

'Ah, yes' she said, seeing him looking at the photo. 'That was the year we all went down to Tenby for a week. Me, my Ted and our two, and Gwen, Greg and Jason. We had a lovely time. But I think Jason was a bit bored.'

'I'm so sorry again, Mrs Griffiths' said Hopkins.

'Well, it sounds terrible, but at my age you've got to speak the truth, haven't you? I've been fearing something like this would happen for years. I hoped he'd settled down, once he met Lisa and got a house, but, well, you know.' Her voice trailed off.

'Why did you think something like this was going to happen?', Hopkins asked.

'Gwen and Greg worried terribly about him. He started going off the rails from about 16, 17. Just little

110

things at first, shoplifting, vandalism, stealing bikes. He got in with the wrong crowd, you see. He was such a nice boy before that, doing well at school. Mind you, he was always nice to me, even after. Still came to see me once a week to help me get my shopping and check on me, after Ted died.'

'And what happened after he left school?'

'Well, it was round about then he got into drugs. I don't think he ever took much himself, he was clever enough to see that he could make money selling them. But Gwen and Greg found out, and they were worried sick. They did everything they could to stop him, but they couldn't. It was so sad.'

'Mrs Griffiths, I'm really sorry to have to ask you this, but we found out that Greg wasn't on Jason's birth certificate, and ...'

'You wondered who his real father was?'

'Yes, Mrs Griffiths. I'm sorry to ask, but anything that helps build up a picture of his life could help us to find out what happened to him.'

'Well, everyone's dead and gone, now, so I don't suppose it matters any more. Gwen was engaged to someone else before she married Greg. A solicitor. But he went off to London, and she didn't want to go, so they split up.'

'Can you remember his name, Mrs Griffiths?'

'Arthur, Arthur Copeland, I think. It was a long time ago, though.'

'And what happened after Gwen married Greg?'

'Well, they seemed very happy together for a couple of years. Then Arthur came back for a visit. Gwen told me everything after. She didn't mean to, but she fell for him again and they had an affair for a few weeks. Then he went back to London, and she found out she was pregnant. She came clean to Greg and he was devastated, but once he got over it, he said he still loved her and would bring the baby up as his own. The only condition was, he didn't want his name on the birth certificate, because he didn't want to lie. He said they would tell the child when he reached sixteen. So that's what they did. But that's when the trouble started with Jason.'

'Did she ever tell Arthur?'

'I don't know for sure. I don't think she did.'

'Was Greg a good father?'

'So far as I could tell, yes. But they never seemed really close. Greg would try to do things with him, take him fishing or to the rugby, but he never really wanted to go. Maybe Jason could sense something in Greg, some sort of distance, I don't know. In the end, Greg started going fishing on his own, maybe to escape what was going on with Jason.'

'Do you know if Arthur is still alive?'

'No, sorry, he never came back after the affair, so far as I know.'

'Well, I think that's all I wanted to know for now, Mrs Griffiths. Thank you so much for the tea.'

'You're welcome, Inspector.' She paused. 'I do hope you catch whoever did this to Jason, but it won't make any difference, not really. It won't bring him back, and he won't be the last poor young man to die for drugs.' She wiped away a tear. 'And you be careful too, Inspector. You seem like a kind man, and these are evil people.'

'I will, Mrs Griffiths. Goodbye.'

Chapter 13

Of lakes and monsters

Grendel's mother,
monstrous hell-bride, brooded on her wrongs.
She had been forced down into fearful waters,
the cold depths, after Cain had killed
his father's son, felled his own
brother with a sword.
Seamus Heaney (trans.), *Beowulf*

Hopkins called Reilly to say he'd meet him at the lake. He wanted some time on his own to think. He drove south, back across the M4, then down towards the coast. He parked on the bluffs at Ogmore, looking across the estuary of the river Ogwr, spreading out across the sands as it met the sea.

He bought a takeaway coffee from a van, then went and sat on a bench overlooking the beach. The tide was far out, so he could barely hear the waves. A few oystercatchers and other wading birds pottered about in the margins of the river, while gulls kept a beady eye on them, hoping to steal their catch.

The weather was pleasant, warm for the end of February, although it was still frosty at nights. In the grass verges of the car park, clumps of daffodils, heads still tightly closed, bobbed in the light breeze.

Hopkins stared out to sea and let his mind wander. He found that was usually the most productive way of making progress on cases. He had been on various courses advocating drawing mind-maps, spider diagrams, linking suspects and evidence with different coloured arrows, and so on. This had never worked for him. He found it too rigid, too regimented. If he cudgelled his mind to work in a particular way, it immediately rebelled and slid off somewhere else. Reilly on the other hand, was a great lover of such techniques, and indeed, the whiteboard in the Murder Room was starting to look like a variation on the London Tube Map.

Walters' angry face swam into his mind's eye. 'It was war', 'I'd do the same again.' Would he kill, to protect someone? But Walters hadn't been at the lake at the time, or at least they couldn't prove it, if the wife's alibi held up. And about the second septic tank, Hopkins' gut feeling was that he believed Walters' apparent lack of knowledge. He had seemed more irritated at the apparent pointlessness of the questions, than worried about where they were going.

So someone other than Walters had to have done the work. Jimmy Lewis looked likely, given the trail back to the tank supplier. But how could he have done it without Walters knowing? Who could have authorised it, and made sure no-one was there to see?

What about Richards? But he was wealthy, owned many properties, was a respected businessman. What could possibly justify the risk for someone like that? And if he was trying to cover something up, why had he raised the matter of the off-road bikers riding around at night, which Walters apparently didn't want him to mention? And he hadn't been at the lake at the right time either.

Jimmy Lewis? He had yet to be interviewed, and that ought to prove interesting. He was also the only potential suspect who could have approached by road from the opposite direction, thus avoiding the CCTV camera at the entrance to the industrial estate. However, Hopkins' instinct was that he was probably only a bit-part player. A professional wouldn't leave such a trail to the tank supplier – he would have left someone else to take the rap, which currently looked to be Jimmy. So, someone standing behind Jimmy, pulling the strings?

Or was the motive not drugs after all, but plain old jealousy? Who was Sandra? Even Lisa had to be at least notionally in the frame. She had suspected an affair, although her grief seemed real, but again, she had not, so far as they could tell, been at the scene.

With a linkage to his previous train of thought that made him feel slightly guilty, Dr Madhvani then strode, both elegantly and unbidden, into the foreground of his thoughts. There was clearly some kind of agenda going on there. Why were West Midlands keeping tabs on her through the Hanger? And why was she so interested in the case and, apparently, keen to get on his good side?

And how did the Crucian carp fit into all this, if at all? Hopkins did not believe for a moment that it could be a motive, but there seemed to be some kind of link that he didn't understand.

And who, if not Robert Locke, had been at the lake on Sunday evening to throw fish heads in the water?

Last of all, was it at all relevant that Jason's apparent father, Greg, wasn't his real father? Was there any point in trying to trace the real father, assuming he was still alive? Hopkins initially hadn't been convinced it was a lead worth following, but having spoken to Moira Griffiths, he now felt there might be something in it.

Or was he just clutching at straws? With most homicides, there was an obvious suspect or a clear direction of travel within the first few days. But with this case, there didn't seem to be any such indication.

As he moodily watched a large container ship plodding laboriously up-Channel towards Bristol, it occurred to him that it was a good metaphor for this case; a large number of boxes, with unknowable contents, waiting to be unlocked.

...

It was 4.30pm when Hopkins pulled into the car park. The sun was just dipping below the trees and the evening chill was starting to gather. Several cars and vans were parked in the car park, including Reilly's.

Hopkins parked, then walked over to the lean-to where several men were sitting on the plastic garden chairs. Hopkins saw Reilly, Richards, who apparently hadn't been able to resist coming along to orchestrate things, and two others he didn't recognise.

After saying hello, he asked, 'Where are the others? We should have six, including Robert Locke.'

Reilly waved to the other side of the lake, where a small clump of tents had sprung up, and one solitary shelter, fifty or so yards closer to where they stood.

'They said, as the lake was open, they might as well do a bit of fishing while they waited for us. I couldn't think of a good reason to say no.'

'OK, then. I'll speak to these gentlemen here, and maybe you could walk around the bank and speak to the others?'

Reilly went to his car to collect notepad and recorder, then walked off around the lake to the small encampment.

'Right then, Mr Richards, if you could wait in your car while I speak to these two gentlemen, then I'd be grateful for a few words after, if that's OK?'

'Of course, Inspector.'

Hopkins sat down across the picnic table from the first individual and took his details, while the second wandered off for a smoke. As Hopkins suspected, there wasn't a lot that he could add. William Lloyd, fifty-eight, working in local government although now semi-retired. He'd spent all of Sunday at the lake, caught a few small bream, then left at about 6pm, an hour or so after Walters.

'It was getting cold, and forecast for frost. I didn't think it was worth staying any longer, as the fish had been really quiet all day. Only likely to get less active, as it got colder.'

'Did you see Jason Reynolds?'

'No, I must have left before he arrived.'

Over the other side of the lake, it was a similar story. Reilly had opted to interview the three men together, as they were friends and had all been sitting together on Sunday. It seemed unlikely that there would be any significant difference in their stories.

They were younger than the average age of the other members, late twenties or early thirties. They had erected tents and camp beds, with a small gas stove and a selection of cans of beer. They clearly intended to make a night of it.

'We all work at the same place, and we'd booked a day off tomorrow anyway. Thought we might as well start the weekend early', said Danny, a stocky lad with a shock of spiky black hair, who seemed to have appointed himself spokesman for the group.

'So where were you last Sunday?'

'We were sitting around here. We like this spot. We always tend to come here, if it's free.'

'When did you arrive?'

'Friday night.'

'So you'd been camped out here all weekend?'

'Yeah, we like that. We bring plenty of food, tinnies, have a laugh. We wouldn't normally camp out in weather this cold, but with the record Crucian about, we thought it might be worth a go.'

'You seem very dedicated.'

'It's addictive, it is, carp fishing', chimed in one of the others, Andrew Murphy, who the other two referred to as 'Spud.' 'Once you get into it, you can't stop. But it's better than just getting pissed out your skull all the time.'

'Sometimes we do that, too' said the third, Eddie, and the others laughed. Spud coughed with mock seriousness. 'Except for Danny, of course, officer. He was the designated driver. He stayed sober.'

Reilly laughed with them. 'It's all right lads, I'm not interested in any of that. Nor any other stimulants you might have been taking to help you concentrate. Did you catch anything?'

'A few decent commons and mirrors. Biggest about 15 pounds. But no sign of the Lady, the Crucian.'

As darkness deepened, they lit their head lamps, but angled them down so as not to dazzle Reilly.

'So did you see Jason Reynolds at all?'

'Yeah, he arrived just before we packed up. We thought it was odd, him arriving just as it was getting freezing cold. That's when the feeding activity tends to fall.'

'What time was this?'

'Oh, just before 8, I guess.' The others nodded agreement.

'Did you speak to him?'

'I did', said Spud. 'He weren't interested though. Just said he'd come out for some peace.'

The others grunted in scorn.

'You didn't believe him?' Reilly asked.

'Well, he was a strange guy', said Danny. 'We reckoned he was up to something, but we didn't know what.'

'How so?'

'Well, he never seemed that into fishing, really. Seemed to spend a lot of time making calls. And all his gear was brand new, top of the range – like he'd walked into a tackle shop and said, 'Give me a matching set of everything."

'Why's that strange?'

'Well, we've all got bits and pieces we've picked up over the years, whenever we could afford. He just seemed to have picked it all up in one go.'

'He didn't use his Dad's stuff?'

Spud laughed. 'Old Greg's stuff was out of the Ark. I think only he knew how to use it.'

'He still caught loads, to be fair', said Danny.

'Any of you ever hear about Jason opening a tackle shop?'

All three shook their heads. 'I don't think that would be up his street', said Danny. 'He knew the basics, like, but he didn't strike me as much of an expert. You've got to know more than your customers to make a go of something like that.'

Back at the lean-to, Hopkins was speaking to the second fisherman, Kenny Stagg. He was forty-ish, blond-haired, mid-height, with a wide, open-looking face that seemed always ready to break into a grin, but with a restless air. He seemed constantly to be seeking something, looking around, occasionally losing the thread of the conversation, so Hopkins had to steer him back. Multiple chunky gold chains competed around his neck.

'What do you do for a living, Mr Stagg?'

'Oh, bit of this, bit of that. Used to have a stall on the market, then worked as a security guard and a bouncer, but I'm working on a building site at the moment.'

'Did you know Jason Reynolds at all?'

'Oh yeah. We used to chat a lot. Not close mates, like, but we got on.'

'Really? The others said he didn't talk much.'

'Well, we got similar interests, see? He was thinking of starting a business, I've started a couple of businesses myself, buying and selling stuff, like. I said I could help him, he was thinking about us going in as partners.'

'And this was his fishing tackle business?'

'Yeah. He'd got a place sorted out, low rent until he did it up and opened for business. He had a few ideas, but he was stuck for finance to do the work, get it started.'

'Had it got any further before he died?'

'Nah, not so far as I could tell.'

'Did you see him on Sunday night?'

'Just for a couple of minutes. He was arriving about 7.30, 8 ish, as I was leaving. I wanted a word with him, about the business, but he said he'd catch up with me next week.'

'And that was the last time you saw him?'

'Yeah.'

'And where were you for the rest of Sunday?'

'Went home. I was with my missis – we're not married, but we've been together ages.'

'All night?'

'Yep – she'll vouch for that.'

'Well, I think that's all for now, Mr Stagg. You can go now, if you want. Thanks for your time.'

'No problem.'

Kenny swaggered off to his car.

Hopkins walked over to Richards' car. Richards was talking to someone on his mobile. Hopkins moved into his line of sight and waved politely. Richards ended the call, then opened the car door, pocketing his phone as he stood up. Hopkins noticed that he did so awkwardly, as though his right hand were stiff, but Richards kept the hand in his pocket afterwards, preventing further observation.

'Finished with the interviews, Inspector?'

'I think so, sir. DS Reilly's just finishing up with the three on the other side.' He remembered. 'Oh yes, we've got to speak to Mr Locke, too.'

'Ah yes, our fearless pike hunter.'

'Could I ask you a few more questions, sir?'

'Of course, Inspector.'

'You weren't here at all on Sunday, were you?'

'No, I was fishing on Saturday, but I had some work to catch up on, on Sunday, so I stayed at home.'

'Can anyone vouch for that?'

'My wife. My eldest daughter and her fiancé dropped by in the evening, too.'

'And what time was that?'

'Oh, about 8 until 10, something like that.'

'And after that, it was just you and your wife?'

'Yes, that's right.'

'I was wondering if you knew anything about any works around the lake in the past year or so. You know, any drainage, septic tanks, anything like that.'

'Nothing I'm aware of Inspector. But that's all Craig's responsibility.'

'You haven't seen any invoices or receipts for big jobs? Been asked to authorise any temporary closures?'

'No, nothing like that.'

'Do you know if the farmer, Mr Lewis, has been on the land to do anything?'

'Well, he comes on now and again to clear the channels into his field drains, take some brushwood for his fire, that sort of thing. Nothing major I'm aware of though.'

It was now almost dark. As Hopkins opened his mouth to ask another question, there was a sudden loud *thwack*, like a canoeist's paddle slapping the water flat on, that made Hopkins jump. He looked to where ripples were spreading out from a massive disturbance, about twenty feet out from the banking.

'What was that?'

'Looks like Rob has caught something. That must have been the fish's tail slapping the surface.'

Hopkins could see headlamps bobbing along the opposite bank, where the three fishermen, with Reilly, were jogging towards where Robert Locke sat. Richards and Hopkins set off too.

When they reached Locke, he was standing, braced, holding his rod almost vertical with both hands. The rod arched viciously, and it seemed impossible to Hopkins that it did not break. The fish was obviously nearer the bank, now, as the unbelievably taut line stretched into the water a few feet out, and was zig-zagging slowly from side to side, as though something massive just below the surface were shaking its head.

Locke lowered the rod swiftly then reeled in the slack created, thus gaining another few feet of line. He then started lifting the rod slowly again to the vertical, grunting with the effort. He was only half way there, however, when the reel screamed and line started to run out again.

'Still got plenty of fight in him', said one of the fishermen.

Locke began the laborious task of drawing the fish to the banking again. There were several more sudden, violent runs, but at last, he reached down with his left hand and lifted a net, which seemed big enough to Hopkins to envelop a grown man, on a long

123

pole. He slid it into the water, beneath the surface, and then drew the rod back once more, pulling the fish over the net.

As he lifted the net out of the water, Hopkins could see something huge thrashing in the folds of the net; a dark green curve of smooth, slick muscle, flecked with yellow.

Locke carried the net over to a large padded mat and laid the fish on it, then knelt astride it. He reached one gloved hand into the back of the gill flap, opening the mouth so that he could reach inside from the front, using long-nosed artery forceps to remove the hooks. That done, he slid the fish into a long sling under a tripod, made a couple of adjustments, then said, 'Twenty-five pounds twelve ounces.'

'Our biggest pike yet!' said Richards. 'Come on, let's have a look.'

Locke was now kneeling again, holding the great fish beneath its jaw and the base of the tail, while the other three fishermen took pictures on their phone cameras. Hopkins walked closer and then suppressed a shudder as he looked at the first pike he had ever seen in real life.

The fish to him didn't look like a fish at all. Its wide, flat head was more reptilian, like a crocodile's. When the mouth gaped open briefly, he saw a huge pink maw, into which he could have easily fitted both hands, lined with needle-sharp, backwards-curving teeth. In the light of the headlamps, the pike's soulless, yellow-rimmed black eyes seemed to gaze at him. He knew it was ridiculous – the pike's eyes would be adapted to seeing under water and so he and the others must be just blurs to it. But nonetheless, he felt as if the fish was directing a flat, evil stare at him.

Locke stood up, gently cradling the huge length of the fish, and slowly lowered it back into the water. He held on to the end of its body, just in front of the tail, for a few seconds, slowly swishing the great fish's tail back and forth, to revive it.

Then, with a sudden, violent contraction of muscle, the pike beat its powerful tail and was gone.

Chapter 14

Covered faults

Time shall uncover what plighted cunning hides.
Who cover faults, at last shame them derides.
Shakespeare, *King Lear*

As Hopkins stood staring at the swirls left in the water, Locke rose to his feet and Hopkins found himself looking directly into his eyes. Locke looked to be a similar age to Hopkins, but slightly taller with short, grey hair and a neat, pointed beard. In spite of Locke's capture of the huge pike, Hopkins realised he had not seen him smile once. He was not smiling now, either.

'I gather you want to talk to me.'

The tone was neutral, neither helpful nor combative. Locke sat down in his canvas seat, staring up at the two policemen. He didn't offer to move to the seating area, and something in his manner suggested he would be unwilling to do so. The other fishermen went back to their rods and Richards to the lean-to.

'If you wouldn't mind, Mr Locke.'

'Rob.'

'OK, Rob. As you know, we're trying to eliminate people from our enquiries. Were you at the lake at all on Sunday?'

'No, I wasn't.'

'Are you sure? Not even for a short while?'

'No, I just told you.'

'We found some fish heads in the water a bit higher up the bank.' Hopkins indicated. 'I understand you sometimes come to the lake the night before fishing, to pre-bait the area you want to fish. Are you sure that wasn't you?'

'No, must have been someone else.'

'Who else fishes for pike?'

'A couple of regulars, then a few others dabble from time to time.'

'Can you give me their names?'

Locke gave two names, which Reilly wrote down, then added, 'But I don't know about the others. Could have been anyone.'

'And where were you Sunday night?'

'At home until about 9. Then I went to the village pub for about an hour. Then home.'

'Anyone see you at the pub?'

'The landlord, couple of regulars.'

'Can anyone vouch for the time you were at home?'

'No, I live alone. Got divorced a few years ago.'

His tone was flat, unforthcoming, unhelpful. It didn't seem as if they were going to get anything out of him. Hopkins looked at Reilly, who shook his head.

'Very well, Mr Locke, thanks for your time.'

Locke nodded curtly then returned to re-baiting his rod, which he then cast out into the darkness. After a few seconds, they heard a faint splash. He re-set the bite alarm, which gave a feeble electronic cheep and flashed a green light a couple of times.

Hopkins and Reilly walked back along the now completely darkened path, towards the light emanating from the lean-to. Richards was sitting inside, looking at his phone.

He looked up. 'Hello, all finished? At least we managed to lay on a bit of excitement for you.'

'Yes, thank you sir. I was wondering, have you got time for a quick couple of questions, just to clarify a few points?'

'Of course.'

'Kenny Stagg told us he was talking about going into business with Jason Reynolds – an online fishing tackle shop, or something. Did you hear anything about that? I mean, presumably they would be promoting the idea around members, get them interested before the start-up, and so on?'

Richards chuckled.

'I'm afraid the idea of going into business together may have been entirely in Kenny's own imagination. He's a bit of a Del Boy character – always got some get rich quick scheme on the go, always comes to nothing. He's a perfectly nice chap, if a bit pushy, but the members have learned now never to buy anything off him. I'm not saying Jason wasn't planning anything – I certainly hadn't heard about it – but Kenny was probably badgering him for a share in return for his 'expertise', and Jason hadn't had the heart to say no to him. I doubt this partnership went any further than Kenny's head.'

'Thank you, sir. And Robert Locke – he says he wasn't here pre-baiting on Sunday. Is there anyone you know who's that keen? Like these two, for instance?'

Richards looked at the names. 'Possible, but unlikely, especially on such a cold night. Rob's the one who's really into the pike. The others just dabble a bit.'

Reilly, inadvertently speaking his thoughts aloud, said to Hopkins, 'But we haven't got his car on CCTV.' He instantly regretted it but, as Hopkins turned to him, Richards said,

'Oh, you wouldn't. Rob only lives in the village over there. He comes on his bike on the track across the fields when he's just dropping bait in. I've seen him propping it up against the side of the lean-to here.'

He thumped the corrugated metal wall for effect.

...

The two detectives were sitting in Hopkins' car, sipping coffee. They had driven their separate cars from the lake to a McDonald's in an industrial estate off the M4.

'I'm really sorry, sir', said Reilly. 'I was just thinking, and it slipped out.'

'Well, I'd rather Richards didn't know who we have and haven't got on CCTV. But I think any harm done was outweighed by that little snippet about the bike. That was useful to know, and we wouldn't have found it out otherwise.'

'Why do you think Locke was so resistant, sir? Like he really had a grudge against us. You don't expect that attitude from someone his age and background.'

'Yes, see what you and the team can find out about his background. Also about Kenny Stagg. And can you see if we can line up somebody from the Drugs Team to talk us through what they know about the current scene, any links to our case, etc. Tomorrow morning would be good.'

'OK sir.'

Something suddenly occurred to Hopkins. 'You know, Richards was so keen to get the lake opened, but he never once asked what we found in the roped-off area. Which means he's either not curious at all about it, which doesn't sit with the description of him we got from the Hanger, or – '

'He knows about it already, and didn't want to raise it.'

'Exactly, John.'

They sipped in silence for a few moments. Then Reilly said, 'Well, I'd better get off, sir. See you in the morning.' He paused, half-in, half-out of the door, and turned as if to ask Hopkins something.

But Hopkins, politely but firmly, said 'Yes, John. See you tomorrow.'

Reilly walked over to his car, got in, then took the turning onto the motorway for Cardiff. Hopkins watched him go, then sat staring out at the dark, watching the lorries roaring past on the motorway above him.

Chapter 15

Pits and perfidy

A half truth is a whole lie.
Jewish proverb

The unusually fine spell of weather had come to an end on Friday morning, and a thin, mean rain was slanting miserably across the HQ carpark as Hopkins locked his car and hurried inside.

When he got to his desk, there was already a mug of fresh coffee there, with a saucer over the top to keep it warm, and a small plastic box of Welsh cakes.

'What's all this? It's not St David's day until tomorrow.'

'Catrin made them for you, sir' said Reilly, embarrassed. 'She'd like the box back, if that's OK.'

'Well, tell her thank you very much. That's very kind of her. But there's really no need, I'm fine.'

Reilly cleared his throat, to cover his embarrassment, then said, 'Right, well, Nick Goodall from the Drugs Team is free any time this morning, if you want to catch up.'

'No time like the present. Can you get him to come over?'

Fifteen minutes later, the two detectives and Goodall were sitting in the Murder Room, Goodall flipping open his laptop. 'So what do you want to know?'

Reilly began.

'We're interested in the current local drugs scene. In particular, whether you've noticed anything new in the last year or so, as that seems to tie in with the period our victim may have been trading.'

'Well,' said Goodall, 'There are a couple of established gangs in the area. But as regards new developments, there has been an increase in supply over the past year. Cocaine, ketamine, pills. A couple of our informants pointed us to Shadows nightclub, but they were too scared to give us any names. We put undercover officers in there for a few nights, witnessed some minor dealing, which was enough to get a search warrant. But when we busted the place, it was clean.'

'And I guess the owners denied all knowledge.'

'Exactly. Showed us the certificates to say all their bouncers have been on drug awareness courses and said they operated a zero tolerance policy on drugs.'

'And who are the owners?'

'Well, this guy, Andy McMahon is on the lease.' Goodall turned his laptop around to show a picture of a tall, heavily-built blond man in his forties with a short beard and a neck tattoo. 'Hard man from Glasgow. Done some time up there for gang-related stuff.'

'The Bar-L', said Reilly.

Hopkins looked at him.

'Barlinnie jail, in Glasgow' said Reilly, embarrassed. It was something he'd picked up from reading Inspector Rebus novels.

'How on earth did he get on the licence, if he's got a criminal record? The magistrates normally don't like that', asked Hopkins.

'He's not the licensee. Just one of the tenants. This lady holds the licence.'

Goodall turned the laptop back to himself, tapped a few keys, then turned it again towards Hopkins and Reilly.

'Alexandra Watkins, known as Sandra or Sandie, originally from Walthamstow, East London. McMahon's partner, in both senses of the word, so far as we can tell. No previous convictions. Our info from the Met is that she ran an elite escort agency in London, got out of there because she crossed some local gang boss, but no proof of that.'

The picture showed a striking looking woman in her fifties, with a mane of wavy blonde hair. The picture had been taken from a distance, and she was striding along a street in a leather jacket and close-fitting jeans.

'Could this be our Sandra / Alex?' wondered Hopkins.

'She looks a bit old for Jason, though, doesn't she?' said Reilly. 'I mean, she's good-looking and that, but I can't see him cheating on Lisa with someone twenty years older.'

'Stranger things have happened, John.' Hopkins turned to Goodall. 'Would you mind if we talked to her? Would that cross any lines for you?'

Goodall thought for a minute. 'No, that should be OK, but stick to the murder enquiry line, if you can? We wouldn't want her knowing she's part of an ongoing drugs investigation. As far as she's aware, the raid was due to some duff information, and it's all over now.'

'I don't suppose you've got contact details for her, have you? She must have filed them with the magistrates when she applied for the licence.'

'Sure, I'll e-mail them across to you.'

'From our side, obviously you know all about the septic tank and that it was being used for storage. But we thought it likely they'd need somewhere else nearer town, to stockpile smaller batches of drugs and break them down for street sale.'

'That makes sense. Less risk of losing a whole consignment, that way. But the only premises we've had on our radar was the club. Not a sniff of anything else so far.'

'OK. Anything else we should know?'

Goodall hesitated. 'Well, we're really into the realms of rumour and speculation now, but our contact in Police Service Scotland said McMahon was known on the street as 'Mr 9 millimetre', or just '9', allegedly because he knew how to get hold of handguns for people. I've got to stress, though, that's just a rumour that was passed on.'

'OK, thanks a lot, Nick.'

They stood and filed out.

A few minutes later, Reilly called over from his desk, 'Got the details on Sandra. Her phone number doesn't match the one in Jason's phone.'

'I wouldn't expect it to, if she's a professional. The number in Jason's phone is probably unregistered.'

'Shall I get her in?'

'Yes, see if she's free this afternoon. This morning, I was thinking of tackling Jimmy Lewis. Let's see him there, near the scene of the crime. And we won't phone ahead – let's just surprise him.'

...

Hopkins drove into the yard of Lewis' farm about 10.30. Both men got out and crossed to the farmhouse, an old whitewashed stone building. Reilly knocked. Immediately, what sounded like a pack of ferocious wolves set up a furious barking and howling. Reilly, looking nervous, stood back.

A strong-looking woman with brown, weather-beaten skin and wrinkles round her eyes, opened the door. Her greying dark hair was tied up in a loose bun from which a few loose strands escaped, and she wore dungarees over a checked flannel shirt.

The wolf pack turned out to be two black and white collies, who were immediately silent once the door opened. Both trotted out, tails wagging, to sniff the detectives' trouser legs. Hopkins tentatively reached out to stroke one dog's head, and it leaned appreciatively against him.

'Mrs Lewis?' Reilly showed his ID and introduced them. 'I wonder, could we have a quick word with your husband?'

'He's not here. He should be down by the old barns, over there.' She pointed to two large stone buildings, about a hundred yards down a rough track leading from the farmyard. 'Can I help?'

'No thanks, Mrs Lewis' said Hopkins. 'We just want to ask him a couple of things about the fishing club.'

'Oh yes, we heard. That poor man. Well, you should find him down there.'

Hopkins and Reilly picked their way through the yard, skirting around patches of mud and dried cow pats now moistened again by the rain, to a steel gate at one corner. Reilly opened it and ushered Hopkins through with a courtly flourish. He closed the gate again and both walked along the rutted lane.

They now had a clear view of the barns, but Lewis was nowhere to be seen. As they drew nearer, he came out from behind one of the buildings, shoving a phone back into the pocket of his overalls.

'Think she phoned ahead, to warn him?' said Reilly, quietly.

'Probably. She's bound to know about it.'

Hopkins raised his voice.

'Hello, Mr Lewis, is it? Just wondered if we could ask you a few questions.'

'No problem. We can sit by here.' He pointed inside the nearest barn. They went inside, and Lewis clicked a switch attached to a thick yellow cable. Temporary lights came on, their bulbs shielded by mesh cages, illuminating a fresh concrete floor and newly rendered walls.

'Looks like you've been busy', said Hopkins.

'Yes, trying to convert the barns into cottages for holiday lets, or maybe selling on. Started about two years ago, but with working the farm and money being tight, we just do bits when we can. We sold the milk cattle on a few years ago, no money in it, so we just have beef and sheep now. But even so, we struggle, so this is the retirement plan.'

He gestured around. 'Nearly finished this one. Just need to do windows and doors and a bit of internal work. The other one needs more work.

136

Hopefully pouring the concrete floor soon, when it's a bit less cold. Have a seat', he gestured to some plastic chairs scattered around a packing box.

'Thanks, Mr Lewis' said Hopkins. 'Well, as I'm sure you've heard, a man's body was found in the fishing lake on Monday morning. We're treating it as suspicious.'

Lewis nodded. 'Yes, I heard.'

'Did you know him?'

'No, I only heard his name later.'

'Never had any contact with him?'

'No, I always dealt with Craig, Craig Walters, the bailiff.'

'You own the land the lake is on, is that right?'

'Yes, my Dad leased it to them first, in the 1990s, then I carried on the arrangement when he passed away. Doesn't pay much, but they take on all the hassle of keeping the site safe, maintaining it and all that.'

'But you occasionally do bits of work there?'

'Yeah, I've got a key in case I need to go in and clear the drainage channels that run under the fence, that sort of thing.'

'We understand you put a septic tank in for the club, about two years ago.'

'The one by the metal container, yes.'

'Was there another one?'

'No, not so far as I know.' But he looked nervous.

'Mr Lewis, did you install a second septic tank at the lake, about a year ago? On the left hand side, about a hundred yards or so past the shipping container?'

'No, definitely not.'

137

Hopkins paused and looked at him regretfully.

Reilly stepped in, his voice hard.

'You've just lied to us, Mr Lewis.'

'What? No – that's ridiculous. I don't know anything about another tank.'

'You've lied to us, and we can prove it', said Reilly, standing up and walking closer, until he stood over where Lewis was sitting.

He reached into his pocket and produced a folded sheet of paper, which he passed over. 'Copy of the sales invoice from the supplier to you. Make and serial number match the one we found – no doubt you've seen the blue tape around where we found it. Now, if we were to get a team in and dig at the location you've given the supplier, which is your barn renovation, would we find it?'

Lewis stayed silent.

Hopkins spoke again, in a quiet, reasonable tone.

'Come on, Mr Lewis. This is a murder investigation and that's our main interest right now. I don't know why you bought and installed the second septic tank, maybe someone threatened you, maybe you didn't know what it was for. But I do need to know everything about it, all the background. And if I find out you're hiding anything – you'll be charged with obstruction, perverting the course of justice, maybe even accessory to murder.'

'Plus we'd get a team in here and dig up all these nice new floors' said Reilly, with a wolfish grin. 'No telling what else you might have buried down there. Useful stuff, concrete.'

'All right, all right! I had to do it. They threatened me.'

'Who did, Jason?' Hopkins asked.

'He was there. But it was another guy who did all the talking. Said he'd make it worth my while, I'd be quids in, but I still didn't want to do it. Then he threatened my wife. Said it must get lonely for her in the house all day, while I'm out working on the farm. I knew what he meant, so I caved in.'

'Who was this man?'

'I can't say.'

'Can't or won't?' intervened Reilly, harshly.

'He'll kill me! He'll kill my wife!' Lewis was near to tears now.

'So tell me how and when you installed it', said Hopkins, the quiet voice of reason again.

'It was just over a year ago. Maybe early February. Jason said the bailiff was going to be away – winter sun holiday. The other guy said he could make sure no-one came to the lake that night. I hired the mini-digger again, plus an arc light, and dug the hole. I tipped the spoil over my side of the fence – if anyone saw it, they'd think I'd been clearing out drains. I moved it the next day and spread it out. Jason and I lifted the tank in – it wasn't big, and then we backfilled around it with spades. He'd brought one of those manhole covers you use for patios, you know? Sort of like a tray, so you can put matching paving stones in it. But we put a square of the turf we'd cut in it. Then we looked around and found some old piles of brushwood. We took a bit from each pile and made a new one over the top, to hide it. It was quite a way off the path, anyway, and in amongst some bushes. Jason said he'd keep the brush topped up, until the grass grew back around the edges.'

'So that wasn't Walters covering it up?'

'Not at first. Then, because there was a pile there, I think he started adding to it. There was new stuff there a few times when I went in there. He probably thought he'd put it there in the first place, and carried on.'

'How much did they pay you?'

'Ten grand, cash. I spent it on building supplies.'

Reilly came in again. 'What about these characters riding around your land on quad bikes or off-roaders. Who are they?'

'I don't know, kids after rabbits or messing about?'

'Have you ever reported them to the police, or put up stronger fences, barriers, that sort of thing? Wouldn't have thought it was good for your livestock, having them roaming around.'

'No.'

'They told you to ignore it, didn't they?'

Lewis looked down, then nodded. 'They seemed to be there the nights Jason was there.'

'How do you know that?'

'Well, a few times after the tank was installed, he called in. Probably to check on me, make sure I was keeping quiet. It was those nights I first noticed the lights in the fields.'

'And what did you think they were doing?' asked Hopkins.

'I can't be sure. I didn't want to know. I didn't want to be implicated in any of it.'

'But you are, Mr Lewis', said Reilly menacingly. 'And you won't tell us who threatened you. That's obstruction.'

'They'll kill us! You don't know what it's like –
living out here on our own. It'd be easy for someone
to just come and get us one night.'

'We can offer protection', said Hopkins.

'They say they've got people in the police – they
say they'd still be able to find us. Can you guarantee
we'd be safe?'

No matter how much they pressed, Lewis would
not be budged. He also claimed to have been in the
farmhouse all Sunday night, and that his wife would
vouch for that.

'Very well, we'll leave it for now. But we are likely
to have more questions for you, Mr Lewis' said
Hopkins. 'And, whatever you do, don't talk to anyone
about what we've discussed. That could put you in
danger.'

'And you think I'm not already?' asked Lewis,
bitterly, as they walked back down the lane. He
opened the gate for them, then watched them get into
Hopkins' car and drive away.

...

'Why can't I be the good cop, sometimes, sir?'
asked Reilly.

'Because you have such a natural talent for playing
the bad cop, John.' Hopkins thought for a moment. 'I
don't like using that tactic on non-criminals though.
It feels wrong.'

'The non-crims are the only people it works on.
The hardened crims are used to it.'

'But still. I felt sorry for Lewis.'

'He lied to us. In a murder investigation.'

'But nonetheless, he didn't have a choice, did he?'

'He could have come to us at the start.'

141

'Would you, John, if you thought your family was at risk?'

Reilly was silent for a few moments. 'So, what we need to do is find out who this guy is that Lewis was so frightened of.'

'I think Sandra may be able to help us there.'

'You think it's Andy McMahon then?'

'Could be. If he was a gang enforcer up in Glasgow, it sounds like his sort of thing. Of course, there are several local characters who would fit the bill, too.'

'But none of them are linked to a new supply of drugs, according to the Drugs Team. Remember, all this started about a year ago, which is about the same time the new septic tank was put in.'

'How did you get on fixing a meeting with Sandra?'

'She won't come into the station, and won't meet us at her home or the club. She wants to meet us in a coffee shop in town, about 3.30. I didn't want to frighten her off, so I agreed.'

'Sounds like she's worried about being seen with us by McMahon – or somebody.'

Reilly nodded.

'One more thing, John, the timing of the installation of the second tank. Get Davy or Sue to call Walters and check on the exact dates he was away last year. Then could you call Richards and tell him we want access to the e-mails from the club to members during that period, plus two weeks either side. I want to see if anyone sent an e-mail telling members the lake was closed for the night the tank was installed. Otherwise, how could Jason be so sure that the coast was clear?'

Reilly had his phone out. 'E-mailing Davy and Sue now.'

'And tell Richards forwarding copy e-mails isn't enough. We want actual access to the server or whatever. Actual log-in details so we have the same access as an administrator. If he does know about the second tank, I don't want him sending us an edited set of e-mails. Threaten him with a warrant if he won't comply.'

...

It was 12.30 when they got back to HQ. Reilly went straight to his desk, where he had sandwiches. Hopkins decided to walk to the canteen. The rain had stopped, although he took care to avoid the puddles that lay on the tarmac between the building where MCIT were based, and the main admin building. His phone buzzed and he pulled it out. A number he didn't recognise. He accepted the call.

'Inspector? It's Amrita Madhvani here.' He could hear road noise in the background. For some reason, he was glad he was out of earshot of his colleagues.

'Hello. You sound like you're driving.'

'Very astute of you, Inspector. I can see you'll have the case cracked in no time.'

'You'd better be on hands-free, Doctor, or I'll give your registration to the traffic police.'

'OK, truce!' she laughed.

'What's this about?' Hopkins asked.

'I was just calling to invite you for lunch. I'm on my way back from Swansea. I'll be passing Bridgend in about fifteen minutes.'

Hopkins was about to make an excuse, then thought, 'Why not?' And perhaps he could kill two birds with one stone.

'There's a place I've heard of that I've been meaning to try. Shadows, off Wyndham Street. Your satnav should be able to find it.'

Chapter 16

Past wounds

Wandering among them in that great wood, was Phoenician Dido with her wound still fresh.
Virgil, *The Aeneid*

As Hopkins walked into Shadows, he began to worry that coming here was a mistake.

The cocktail bar area was tastefully, and expensively, furnished in the style of a Prohibition-era speakeasy. Three-sided, intimate booths were ranged along the walls on either side. If they were not real leather, they were an incredibly good imitation. Large wood and cane fans turned slowly from the ceiling. Mirrors, surrounded by an edging of shiny black mosaic tiles, covered most of the walls, interspersed with framed reproduction posters for boxing matches and theatre shows from the thirties. There was a three sided cocktail bar, with a vast array of various coloured bottles, and beyond it, roped off and unlit, Hopkins could see what was presumably the dancefloor area.

The whole effect was a bit too much for what he had intended – would Madhvani think he was trying to impress her? His intention had been that, if she did have some ulterior motive for prying into the case, going to the place that seemed to crop up again and again, might throw her off balance. However, he saw her waving at him from a corner booth, grinning wickedly. Whatever his plans, she was not going to be the one off balance.

'Well, Inspector,' she began. 'You do have hidden depths, don't you? I would never have suspected you would be a frequenter of places like this.'

'OK, cards on the table,' he sighed. 'I heard about this place in connection with a case, and I thought I'd give it the once-over. But I didn't know it would be as high-end as this. We can go somewhere else if you like.'

'So you're combining lunch with me with work?' She laughed at his discomfiture. 'No, it's fine. I sort of like it. It's so kitsch, it's actually quite good.'

One of the waiters, dressed in a white shirt and dicky bow, came over to take their order. Hopkins ordered a pastrami salad bagel. Madhvani went for a New York club sandwich.

'Drinks?'

'Oh, just sparkling water for me.' Hopkins waved to Madhvani.

'Coke Zero, please', she said. 'Although if I wasn't driving, I think I'd have a cocktail.'

The drinks arrived.

Hopkins cleared his throat awkwardly. 'Look, I'm very flattered you asked me out for lunch, – '

'But you're wondering what's behind it?'

'Not to put too fine a point on it, yes.'

'OK, time for me to put my cards on the table too. You don't need to worry – I'm not trying to seduce you.'

Hopkins spluttered into his drink. 'I never thought – '

'I know you didn't. That's why I thought I could trust you. Most of the cops I meet in my line of work are either scared of me, like your sergeant, or they're alpha males who just want to get me into bed. The truth is, I need a friend, however pathetic that sounds. I was doing well in West Midlands, next in line for promotion, when a senior officer, who I won't name, made a pass at me. He didn't like it when I said no, and started harassing me. Dripping poison in the ears of my colleagues and my boss at the Home Office. He was very well-connected. So in the end, I saw my career going down the tubes and decided to move on. That's when I applied for this job.'

Hopkins thought it was best just to listen, and let her tell her story. He nodded, silently.

She carried on. 'But this senior officer, he's a vindictive bastard and I think he's probably trying to mess things up for me here, too. It wouldn't surprise me if he's been in contact with senior officers here.'

'So you want me as an ally? Sort of a knight in shining armour?'

'More prosaic than that. I wanted to go the extra mile, show I'm interested and involved in the case, helping to move it forward and so on, then you'd hopefully tell the higher-ups how good I am at my job and they won't listen to all the rubbish coming from West Midlands. Plus, I like you. You seem like someone I could have an intelligent conversation with.'

Hopkins waved a self-deprecating hand. 'Very kind of you. But why didn't you bring a harassment claim against him?'

'Well, he was very subtle about it. Nothing in writing or that anyone would swear to. Also, I hate playing the victim.'

'Well, I think you're right about the contact from West Midlands. My boss pulled me in to ask me, amongst other things, what I thought of you.'

'I hope you were suitably glowing.'

'I said you seemed very efficient.'

'And now?'

'I'd upgrade that to excellent. And you did find a key piece of evidence on Reynolds.'

At that moment, a gruff voice with a Glaswegian accent came from over Hopkins' shoulder. 'Pastrami and a club sandwich?'

Hopkins turned, and saw Andy McMahon, whom he recognised from the photo Goodall had showed him. He wondered whether McMahon had overheard any of what he had just said. Nothing showed on his face.

Madhvani, not noticing anything amiss, said

'Yes. Mine's the club sandwich.'

McMahon put the food down, displaying broad, tattooed forearms protruding from his rolled-up white sleeves, and walked away.

Madhvani, catching Hopkins' look, asked, 'What's wrong?'

'I think I just made a mistake.'

She looked at him. 'This place is connected with the Reynolds case, isn't it?'

'I don't want to say any more here. Let's eat.'

After a few mouthfuls, Hopkins asked, 'Do you mind if I tell my boss about all this? In strictest confidence of course. He hates all that kind of stuff

148

that you've described. He may not spout on about diversity, equity and so on like some, but he believes in giving everyone a fair crack of the whip. And he's a strict Presbyterian with two daughters. He should be able to deflect any misinformation coming over Offa's Dyke.'

'Offa's what?'

'The ancient border between England and Wales. Built by a Saxon king because he was so scared of the Welsh.'

She thought for a few moments. 'OK, I'll trust your judgement. But make sure he knows it's in strict confidence.'

'Absolutely.'

'And can I help with the case? There might be something I could contribute to, from the medical side.'

'Well, I can't bring you into the core team. That would be unprecedented, and raise eyebrows in a way which wouldn't be helpful. But I will share anything with you that might have a medical bearing.'

'That would be great.' She held out her hand, mock-seriously. 'Friends?'

He took it. 'Friends.'

...

Hopkins decided to wait in Bridgend town centre, rather than drive to HQ and have to turn almost straight round and come back for the meeting with Sandra. He called Reilly and told him he'd meet him at the café, ten minutes before they were due to meet Sandra.

He then walked along the side of the river Ogwr, down to the old stone bridge, just wide enough for one

149

cart in the old days, and now pedestrianised. He looked at the benches by the bridge, but decided against it, as they still looked damp from the morning's rain. He walked on, through the little streets of the old market town part of the centre.

He cursed himself for his slip in front of McMahon. What had the man heard? Potentially the name of the case, and that they had a new piece of evidence. What would that do? Warn him off, or trigger him to act? Hopkins wondered if he needed to report himself to the Hanger, but then decided against it,

Even as he was thinking that, his phone rang. The name on the screen said 'Supt. Jeffries.'

Hopkins accepted the call. 'Hello, sir?'

'What have you been doing to wind up Bryn Richards?' asked the Hanger, without preliminaries.

'What?'

'He says you want access to all e-mails to and from club members for a certain period, and you want admin privileges, not just copies. He's arguing it's not relevant and also insulting to him personally, as you seem to think he would delete e-mails.'

'I can explain, sir.'

'I think you better had.'

Hopkins spoke quickly and concisely. 'We found a second septic tank, hidden by the lake. We know it was used for storing drugs – quite large quantities. It was purchased and installed by a local farmer, Jimmy Lewis, we think acting under duress from Reynolds and another man, as yet unknown. We know the period the tank was installed and that the bailiff was away for that period. But Reynolds couldn't have guaranteed that no members would turn up the night the tank was installed. Unless there was some sort of message to members, telling them the lake was closed and to stay away. That could lead us to Reynolds' killer.'

There was a pause. 'OK, I see your reasoning. And I agree, which is good, because I've already gone out on a limb with friend Richards, and sent him away with a flea in his ear. A very polite flea, but a flea nonetheless. I told him I'd review the evidence with you, but that you're one of our best, and I didn't think you'd make a request needlessly. I also told him that, if I agreed that disclosure of these e-mails was necessary, I'd back you in applying for a warrant.'

Hopkins felt weak. He had expected to be cut off at the knees, but was being offered praise and support instead.

'Thank you, sir', was all he could come up with.

'Just make sure it's relevant and justifiable.'

'It is, sir.'

'Hmm. Good.' The Hanger rang off.

Hopkins looked at his watch, and realised it was nearly time to meet Reilly. He went back into the old centre of town, crossed a couple of streets, then arrived at a small teashop called 'Y Tegell Gopr', the Copper Kettle. Indeed, there were a multitude of such vessels displayed in the window and hanging from pegs on the walls. While Hopkins was hovering outside the door, Reilly appeared.

'Doesn't really look like our sort of place, sir. Bit chintzy. Shall we go in?'

Hopkins pushed at the door and a little bell tinkled. Immediately, he saw that Sandra had beaten them to it.

Clearly, she had wanted to prepare the ground, so the interview would be on her terms, as much as possible. She had chosen a table right at the back, partially hidden by the serving counter, and she sat with her back to the wall, so that she could see everyone coming in or out, but a casual passerby looking through the window would not see her. She had a small tablet open on the table in front of her, with her smart phone lying next to it, for all the world the successful businesswoman, working through her coffee break.

Hopkins made introductions, and they ordered drinks from the waitress. Hopkins, determined not to repeat his earlier mistake, made small talk until the waitress arrived with their drinks.

Once the drinks had been served, Sandra said, 'Right, so what's all this about? I'm busy. I haven't got all day to sit around talking about the weather and how my club's doing.'

She looked challengingly at Hopkins. She was undeniably attractive, but like Reilly, he couldn't quite see Jason and this woman being an item, and not just because of the age difference. He could not imagine her doing anything that was not to her advantage.

'We're looking into the death of Jason Reynolds. He was found in a lake on Monday and we're treating it as suspicious.'

'Yeah, I heard. But what's it got to do with me?' Her voice still held a trace of Cockney, but was mostly well-spoken, middle class Southern English.

'We think he may have had some connection with you.'

'Well he didn't. I'd never heard of him before I heard his name on the news.'

'You never spoke to him, on the phone, say?'

'Never. You're welcome to check.' She slid her phone across the table.

Hopkins switched his cup from his right to his left hand, and blew on his tea. The prearranged signal. He prayed that his gamble would pay off. Surreptitiously, beneath the table, Reilly pressed the 'call' button on his phone.

Sandra started to say something else, then froze as a buzzing sound came from her handbag.

'I think someone wants to speak to you, Ms Watkins. You can pick it up if you want, we'll wait.'

She glared at Hopkins. 'You bastard. I could just leave now.'

Hopkins knew she wouldn't. She would want to find out how much they knew.

'We found that number on an unregistered phone in Mr Reynolds' possession. I take it your other phone is also an unregistered phone?'

'It's not illegal.'

'No, but it does tend to show that you may have something to hide. The number was listed as 'Alex.' Is that you?'

'Yes. Alex is what I used to be called. Now I go by Sandra or Sandie.'

'Why is that?'

153

'Don't want some people from my past finding me.'

'So what was your relationship with Mr Reynolds? Was it business, or personal?'

Though she disguised it well, Hopkins could sense her mind whirring, desperately trying to work out how much they knew. After a pause, she said,

'Personal.' Then, more quietly, 'We were having an affair.'

'And how long did this affair last?'

Again, Hopkins could sense her trying to think fast, working out how many months the phone records might go back.

'I dunno, it was sort of off/on, over several months.'

'I see, and are you in a long-term relationship with someone else?'

'Yes.'

'Were you at the time?'

'Yes.'

'And is your long-term partner Andy McMahon, the other owner of the nightclub?'

'You can't ask him about this', said Sandra.

'Ms Watkins, if he's being abusive or threatening, we can help you.'

She laughed contemptuously.

'Since when have you lot ever helped me? You'd threaten me with arrest to force me to snitch, then when you'd got what you wanted, you dropped me and left me to the wolves.'

'We're not the Met vice squad, Ms Watkins. You can trust us.'

'Yeah, right.'

'Why don't you want us to speak to Andy?'

'Why do you think? He'd go mad. You know his background, you know what he's like.'

Reilly stepped in.

'Was there any chance Andy knew about you and Jason?'

'No, I'm sure of that.'

'Because that would give him a pretty strong motive for killing Jason.'

'He didn't, I'm sure of it. When do you think it happened?'

'Last Sunday night, between about 11pm and early hours of the morning.'

'We were stock taking all Sunday night. It's the only night we don't open. One of the assistant barmen was helping us – I can give you his name. Then we went to bed. He didn't go out at all that night. Plus he hasn't got a key for the lake.'

Hopkins said, 'So you know the lake needs a key to get in?'

He could see Sandra mentally kicking herself, then she said, 'Yeah. Jason must have mentioned it.'

'Talk about fishing much, did you?'

'Leave it out. Do I look like I'd be interested in fishing?'

'So, he never talked about a business he was thinking of setting up – a tackle shop? I gather he had rented some premises.'

'No, he never said anything about that. But we didn't talk about ourselves much, if you know what I mean', she said.

She took advantage of the two men's momentary embarrassment to rise and put her tablet and phone

155

away. 'And now, unless you two gentlemen have anything else to ask, I've got a business to run.'

Neither man spoke, so she gathered up her coat and bag, and marched out of the café, leaving only the merry tinkle of the bell behind her.

...

Back at HQ, Hopkins gathered the team at 5.30 for a catch-up meeting in the Murder Room. He stood in front of the whiteboard with its photos of persons of interest and interconnecting lines. He noticed that more lines were starting to converge on Shadows nightclub.

'Right, well we've made progress on eliminating people. Craig Walters, while initially our prime suspect due to his background, has an alibi for the night of the murder, and also it appears Jason took steps to get him out of the way when the second tank was installed. As far as we know, he knew nothing about it. So I think he's out.'

Nods of agreement.

'Jimmy Lewis. Clearly involved in installing the tank, and the only one with a key, who could have approached the lake without being seen on CCTV. But I can't see him as our killer. It seems he was forced to do what he did, and we'd have trouble proving he knew it was for drugs. Also, he has an alibi, although also provided by his wife, who we suspect knows all about the tank too. It's just about a possibility that they're lying to cover each other, and one of them sneaked into the lake and killed Jason, maybe to take away the threat to them. But it seems unlikely, particularly as they were more scared of this other man, than Jason. So I think we keep him in for now, but as a low priority. Agreed?'

Reilly spoke up. 'Sir, Lewis isn't the only one who could have got past the CCTV camera. Rob Locke lives in the village, remember, which is only five minutes' walk across the fields, maybe less on a bike. And Richards said he'd seen him arriving on a bike before.'

'Quite right, John. Dave, Sue, either of you get any background on Locke?'

Sue Wilshaw spoke up. 'One interesting thing, sir. Locke had a daughter, his only child. She died of a drugs overdose. She wasn't a habitual user, just one E from a batch that was cut with something dodgy. Went into cardiac arrest in a club in Cardiff and the medics couldn't save her. She was only 19. It seems he and his wife divorced a couple of years after that.'

'Yes, I remember that case. About five years ago, wasn't it?' Sue nodded.

'So, a possible motive for Locke. Revenge for his daughter, or maybe wanting to stop it from happening to anyone else. It also explains his resentment towards us, maybe he thinks we should have stopped the supply of drugs that killed his daughter. He denies he was there, but he hasn't got an alibi for the whole night, and there would have been time for him to get to the lake after he was seen in the pub, within the time frame for Jason's death. Do we know anything about Kenny Stagg?'

Dave Lane spoke this time. 'No convictions, but when I started looking further, I came across a locked file marked confidential. Officer responsible is DS Goodall, Drugs Team. I went to see him, and he told me Kenny's a small-time wheeler-dealer, probably receiving stolen goods and flogging them on. But he's never been charged, because he's a source.'

'A snitch?' asked Reilly.

'Yeah. Apparently he's given them some good stuff in the past, so they overlook his dodgy deals. Although Goodall said he was off-target recently. He wouldn't say any more, but I guess from that, that he must have been the one who pointed the finger at Shadows, but it drew a blank.'

'Interesting' said Hopkins. 'I don't want to spoil your wonderful creation, John, would you mind adding another connection to Shadows?'

Reilly got up and inked in a dotted line, indicating a possible, rather than a definite connection, between Stagg's picture and the club.

'Moving on to the five we interviewed, I think we can discount all of them, except Stagg of course. No connection to Jason, and they weren't there at the relevant time. We've got all their cars leaving on CCTV, including Stagg's, well before the time of the murder.'

Hopkins paused.

'Which brings us to Richards. Not even there on Sunday, what looks like a solid alibi, although the second part's only backed by his wife. Can't see any motive or connection, but he does seem keen to point the finger at other people. First Walters, then Locke. He never asked us about what we'd found in the search area, which doesn't fit with his character. And he's been trying to pull strings with the Chief to withhold evidence. Didn't get him anywhere, I'm pleased to say. Maybe it's just because he likes to feel important, make us dance to his tune, but I'm not sure. So let's keep him in for now, too.'

'And lastly, our Bonnie and Clyde. Sandra Watkins and Andy McMahon. Co-owners of the club, although only she is listed as the licensee, probably because McMahon's record would stand against him with the licensing magistrates. Both have an alibi, although for the latter part of the night, it's self-supporting. And neither has a key. What did you think about our little chat with Sandra, John?'

'I thought she was lying', Reilly said bluntly. 'Pretty much any woman you've ever met, should be able to give you precise dates for the beginning and end of a relationship. Right Sue?'

'Misogynistically put, but basically correct, Sarge', replied Wilshaw.

'OK, sorry. But she was incredibly vague about it. I think she made up the story of an affair to cover for the fact it was a business relationship. Also, she knew you need a key to get into the lake – why would she know that? It seems unlikely to have been pillow-talk between them. She does seem to be genuinely scared of McMahon, though, and doesn't trust coppers.'

'I can't see either of them being directly in the frame for the murder, though', said Hopkins. 'There's no connection to the scene at the relevant time and no real motive, if we assume that the affair story was made up.'

'Well, plenty to think about over the weekend.' Hopkins was about to wrap the meeting up, when Reilly waved to get his attention.

'What about the issue over Jason's parentage, sir? Do you think that's worth pursuing? Only, I ran down

Copeland, through the Solicitors' Regulatory Authority records. He's still alive, retired last year, so he's still on the Roll as a solicitor, but not practicing. I rang their office and, after a bit of pushing, they gave me his home address. He lives in Henley, near Reading.'

'Good work, John. I'm still not sure how relevant it is. Finding out about his parentage seems to have triggered Jason's spiral into crime, and he spoke to Lisa about meeting an 'uncle', who she didn't think was at the funeral of the person we now know to be his adoptive father. But I don't see where it gets us.'

'Should I see if he'll speak to us, sir? I've got a hunch about this one.'

'Very well, John. See if you can set it up.'

Hopkins gathered up his papers. 'Well, if there's nothing else, have a good weekend, everyone. I certainly intend to.'

Chapter 17

Peace and parentage

...yet was his mother fair, there was good sport at his making, and the whoreson must be acknowledged. Shakespeare, *King Lear*

Unusually for Hopkins, the weekend proved uneventful, at least from a work point of view. Normally, there were at least a few calls and on Sundays, he usually went into the office for a few hours to catch up on paperwork, but Mair absolutely forbade it.

'You're going to start looking after yourself, Tomos Hopkins' she said fiercely, when he mentioned the possibility. 'Starting from now.'

On the Saturday, St David's Day, the first day of spring, the weather was fine and sunny, so they went for a walk over Craig yr Allt, a long, ridge-backed hill between Cardiff and Caerphilly, with fine views Southwards, across the waters of the Hafren, and on the other side inland, to Caerphilly Castle and the valley of the Taf.

The walk had happy memories for Hopkins, as his parents had lived in the small former mining village just below, Tongwynlais. Plus, there were two excellent pubs on the route.

On Sunday, the fine weather was replaced by the more usual rain and wind, but Mair had scheduled two trial visits to local gyms, and drove a protesting Hopkins out of the house. To his surprise, he enjoyed the tours and light workouts, particularly sitting in the sauna of the second gym afterwards. Under the guise of seeming to relax, he found it was an excellent place to think about the case.

He felt now that there was something eluding him, something right under his nose, annoyingly out of reach. Normally, when he started to get that feeling with a case, it meant he was near to getting the crucial breakthrough, but here, he had no idea what it might be. There were still so many leads open, and several of the most promising ones seemed to be dead ends.

He reviewed the persons of interest and possible links and motivations again and again, shuffling them like a pack of cards, until, checking his cheap plastic watch (expensive watches and police work didn't tend to mix), he saw it was ten minutes past the time he said he would meet Mair in the reception area.

When he rushed out, full of apologies, Mair said, 'No, I'm glad you were relaxing for a change.' He decided not to enlighten her.

They picked up the brochures and membership documents to complete later, and were just walking out into the car park, when Hopkins' phone rang. It was Reilly. Seeing Mair's accusing glance, he held up an apologetic hand, whispered, 'I'll only be a minute', and accepted the call.

'Sorry to bother you on the weekend, sir.'

'That's OK, John. It's very nearly not the weekend now, anyway. What is it?'

'I got a call back from Copeland. Jason's possible biological father. He's willing to talk to us, but he wants to do it there, in Henley. And it has to be tomorrow, as he and his wife are flying off to join a cruise on Tuesday. So I thought if we left early, 7.30 say, we could be there by 9.30 to ten-ish, talk to him and get back by early afternoon.'

'Sounds a good idea, John. I'll pick you up on the way through, if you could get Catrin to drop you off at Cardiff West Services on junction 33. That's not too far from you, is it?'

'No, that'll be great, see you then.'

Hopkins left the house at 6.45 the next day. The traffic on the motorway was starting to get busy when he reached Cardiff, but was still moving fairly freely. He hoped there wouldn't be any hold-ups at the Bryn Glas tunnels near Newport, a notorious black spot.

As he turned into the services, he saw Reilly waiting like a hitchhiker on the grass verge by an HGV layby, holding two cups of coffee. Hopkins swung into the layby and Reilly jumped in, slotting the coffees into the cupholders in the central console.

'Surprised you didn't get offered a lift by a lorry driver, standing there.'

'A couple did slow down. I think they were just surprised to see a hitcher wearing a suit.'

Hopkins pulled back onto the motorway. As they went around Newport, and traffic got heavier, Reilly moaned about the 50mph zones on the M4. When they got to the Severn Bridge, Hopkins complained about the decision to re-name it the Prince of Wales Bridge, without consulting the Welsh people. They both complained about the seemingly interminable distance between Bristol and the turn off on junction 12 at Theale, for Henley.

Nothing of consequence was discussed. A couple of times, Reilly looked over at Hopkins and opened his mouth to speak, but Hopkins gazed straight ahead, or reverted to discussing the case.

By about 9.45, they were pulling up outside a large, 1930s detached house in Henley, set a couple of streets back from the river Thames. Reilly whistled as he looked at the size of the house and the sweeping lawn. 'Wonder what a place like this is worth?'

'Beyond our wildest dreams, John.'

'But we do it because we love the job, don't we? Otherwise, we could be millionaires.'

They reached the large front door, divided into Georgian panes of stained glass, and Reilly pressed the bell. A melodic chime sounded, followed by a single, deep bark. After a brief pause, the door was opened by a man who looked to be in his mid-sixties, tanned and fit-looking, wearing an open-necked country shirt and a sports jacket. A large, slightly overweight yellow Labrador stood next to him, wagging its tail enthusiastically.

'Mr Copeland?' The man nodded. 'Detective Sergeant Reilly, we spoke on the phone, and this is Detective Inspector Hopkins. May we come in?'

'Certainly. Sorry for the long drive, gentlemen. But with us leaving on holiday tomorrow, I didn't think I could manage the journey to Wales.'

Copeland had a trace, the barest trace, of a South Wales accent, but otherwise sounded upper middle-class English.

They went through into a sunlit conservatory, Copeland limping slightly and leaning on a walking stick.

'There's fresh coffee in the pot on the sideboard there. Do help yourselves. I had my hip done a few weeks ago. Struggle with getting up and down.'

He sank into a raised armchair with an electronic control pad and tilted it to a comfortable angle.

'My wife's out with our daughter. Given the subject matter, I thought it best. She knows the story, or most of it, but I didn't want to distress her. Where do you want to start?'

'Well,' said Hopkins, 'I suppose let's start with your relationship with Gwen, Gwen Reynolds to be.'

'I'd just qualified as a solicitor, and I was working for a small firm in Swansea. My family were from Maesteg, and I met her at a social function in the Workmen's Institute. Very traditional. We only went out for about four months before we got engaged, but I had my doubts. I thought I was happy, but I gradually realised working in the same area I grew up, in a small firm, wasn't what I wanted.'

'You were ambitious?'

'Maybe I was. Driven, to be more honest. All my life, I'd had to play second fiddle to my older brother. He was the apple of my father's eye. Did everything for him. I was very much the afterthought. 'Why can't you be as good as your brother?', that sort of thing.

'Then, my Dad put the house up as a guarantee, when my brother got his offer of partnership in the accountancy firm. In those days, you had to buy yourself in, with a loan, and my Dad put the house up as collateral. That was it, for me. I knew he would never have done the same for me. I cut all ties with him and my brother, started applying for jobs in London. I got a good offer, firms were expanding rapidly at that time to cope with the boom in the City. However, during that time, while I was looking to move to London, making my plans, and working out my six-month notice period, I met Gwen.'

'And she didn't want to move with you?'

'She would have hated it. Very much a home girl. So, although we were very much in love, I thought the kindest thing was to break it off. I moved to London, heard she'd got married about a year later.'

'But then, you returned, and started an affair with her?'

'That's the story we agreed on. She called me out of the blue, in a panic, asked for help, so I felt duty bound to come back. She explained she was pregnant.'

His face darkened. 'Another thing my dear brother had to spoil for me. Of course, he wouldn't have been interested in acknowledging the child, or helping Gwen, not that she told him. Gwen was distraught – she said she knew the child was his, given the timings. I didn't enquire as to the details, but I believed her. She was always honest, at least with me.'

'We decided that it would be easier on Greg, more understandable, if we said that the child was mine, she'd made a terrible mistake, rekindling an old affair, that sort of thing, rather than having an affair with my brother, who even then, was not universally popular in the area, though he'd moved to London a few years before. So that's what she did, and I didn't correct her.'

'Did you have any contact with Gwen after that?'

'No. I thought it better to let everyone believe I was the villain of the piece, as I never intended going back to Maesteg again. Then I heard a few years ago, quite by chance, that she'd died of motor neurone disease. She could only have been about sixty one, sixty two.'

'And Greg died last year. He was older than her, of course. Some industrial disease, we gather.'

'Very sad. But, I'm ashamed to say, I was so remote from it all, it didn't really affect me that much. It was so long ago, and I thought I'd done my bit.' He pondered for a moment. 'I didn't even go back for my own father's funeral.'

'And what happened to your brother?'

'Oh, he returned from London, the conquering hero, and started building his empire in South Wales.'

'So, did you ever meet Jason?'

'Yes, about ten, eleven years ago. He would have been in his twenties. He rang me out of the blue, asked to meet. Given the history, I agreed. But it wasn't a pleasant meeting.'

'Why was that, sir?'

'It was clear he was only interested in money. Said he'd got himself into trouble with loan sharks, wanted me to give him money to help him get out of it.'

'And did you?'

'Well initially, I was cautious. I mean, he could have been anyone. But he knew enough of the backstory, things that no-one else would know, to convince me that's who he was. But while I was hesitating, trying to figure out what best to do, he blackmailed me.'

'Blackmailed you?'

'Yes, threatened to reveal the story of my affair with his mother to Elspeth, my wife. I had told her the story, of course, because she wondered why I never had any contact with my family. But I didn't want her distressed, and we had just adopted our daughter. We couldn't have our own children. She was nine years old, when she came to us, and had had a bad time of it before. She was just settling in, and it would have been a very bad time to cause a disturbance.'

'So I paid him. Twenty thousand. I have no idea if his story about loan sharks was true, or just an attempt to pull on the heartstrings. I told him not to come back, or I'd report him to the police for blackmail and take the consequences.'

'And you haven't seen him since?'

'No.'

'Did you tell him you weren't his real father?'

'No, but I think I might have shouted in anger that if he wanted more money, he should go and see his uncle Bryn.'

Hopkins' mind spun and nearly fell off its axis. Bryn – business empire – came back from London.

As calmly as he could, he asked, 'Sir, what is your brother's name?'

'Bryn – Bryn Richards.'

'But you're not Richards.'

'No, I changed my name by deed poll when I split with my father and brother. Copeland was my mother's name – she was always kind to me. Also I loved the music of Aaron Copland, the American composer. One letter different, but pronounced the same. I was particularly fond of his 'Fanfare for the Common Man.' I saw myself as a common man, struggling in the world, and it seemed fitting that my first initial was already A. A Copeland. That's what I was calling myself when I met Gwen.'

168

'Mr Copeland, would you mind showing us your hands?'

Copeland extended both hands. The little finger and ring finger on the right hand were curled inwards, almost touching the palm. He smiled. 'Ah yes, the Vikings' curse. I take it Jason was developing it? He wasn't when I saw him.'

'He was. Does your brother have it too?'

'Yes. He's quite vain about it – he'd just had an operation to straighten the fingers when I went back for our mother's funeral, the last time I saw him. His right hand was bandaged. But my doctor told me it nearly always comes back, so I never bothered. It's not the biggest problem to have. A mutual contact told me he nearly always hides it in gloves or a pocket these days.'

Hopkins remembered Richards awkwardly holding his phone, then quickly stuffing his hand in his pocket in the car park at dusk, the previous Thursday. His mind was still trying to process what this meant, when Reilly's phone rang. He picked it up, listened for a moment, then walked out into the hall. Hopkins could hear him talking, quietly and urgently.

Then he came back into the conservatory and said, 'Sir, we've got to go. Now. It's urgent.'

They quickly said their goodbyes to Copeland and hurried back to the car.

'What is it, John?'

'Kenny Stagg's gone missing, sir.'

They reached the car.

'I think I'd better drive, sir' said Reilly, climbing into the driver's seat as soon as Hopkins clicked the unlock button. He leaned over as Hopkins got in on the passenger side and opened the glove compartment. 'No blue light?'

'No, do we need one?'

'I guess we'll just have to square it with the traffic boys if we get flashed.'

Reilly gunned the engine and set off back for the A-road to Theale. He resumed his story.

'Set off for his job at the building site, at 7am, never arrived. The site foreman rang his missus to see where he was. She tried calling his mobile, friends, family, nothing. So then she called us in a panic.'

'Why is she in such a state? He could just be off on one of his dodgy deals.'

'She said he was always chasing some get rich quick scheme. But this time, he said it was the big one, it was finally going to make them rich. But last week, after Jason died, he started acting funny.'

'In what way?'

'Said it was going to be a bit tricky for a while, told her to watch out for anyone maybe following her, watching the house. Then he said, 'But I've got an insurance policy. If anything happens to me, get in touch with Rob Locke asap.''

'Has she called Locke?'

'Not yet, she says. She says she doesn't trust Kenny's plans.'

'Sensible woman. OK, I'll call Davy now. I want uniforms at Locke's house immediately, prevent him from going anywhere or hiding or destroying any evidence. In particular, don't let him open his computer. If he argues, they need to arrest him for obstruction, whatever, we just need to keep him there.'

Reilly heard him speaking on the phone to Wilshaw, rattling off instructions. 'And get a team over to Shadows. Search it again, thoroughly. Particularly look for any false floors, behind boxes and barrels, anywhere that could hide a man.'

He ended the call.

'Right, we're going to Lewis' farm first. We'll only be five minutes there. Then Locke's house.'

'What about Richards?'

'I need to think about that, but while it's a stunning piece of info, I can't see how it ties him to the crime. You've always got to be careful, John, when something big and shiny falls into your lap, something distracting. It's tempting to run after it and ignore the basics in front of your face. Richards is a nasty sod, granted, but he's not connected to the drugs, he wasn't at the scene at the time, and we've got no motive. Yes, we'll follow it up in due course, but right now, the priority's finding Kenny.'

'You think he's been abducted, sir?'

'I'm nearly sure of it. And I think he's in real danger.'

They hit the M4 Westbound and Reilly merged aggressively, weaving between vehicles to get into the fast lane, ignoring the chorus of horns behind him. He floored the accelerator and the speed climbed above eighty, then kept climbing.

Chapter 18

Truths compelled and withheld

And ye shall know the truth, and the truth shall make you free.
John, 8:32-32

It was 12.25 when Reilly pulled into the Lewis' farmyard, scattering indignant hens in all directions. Hopkins was out of the passenger door almost before the car had stopped moving.

Hearing the sound of machinery from the barns, he marched straight down the short lane, Reilly catching him up as he reached the buildings. The sound came from the other barn, the one Lewis had said he was going to lay a concrete floor in. As they went in, they saw Lewis with his back to them, operating a mini concrete mixer and wearing ear-defenders.

Hopkins grabbed him by the arm and turned him round, while Reilly pressed the 'Stop' button on the mixer.

'What the hell – ', began Lewis, dragging the defenders off his head, but Hopkins cut him off.

'Who was the man who threatened you? I need his name, now!'

'I can't, I told you!'

'One man is dead, and another has disappeared and is in danger. We have to move quickly to be in with a chance of saving him. So tell me, now!'

'I can't!'

Reilly stepped forward, and Lewis flinched, remembering his aggression during their previous encounter. But Reilly said, in a calming voice,

'I think there may be an easier way.' He held up his phone and showed Lewis a picture. 'Is this him? All you need to do is say yes or no, and we'll be gone.'

Visibly shaking, Lewis muttered,

'Yes.'

The two policemen didn't bother saying goodbye, just ran (or in Hopkins' case, jogged) back to the car. As they got in and Reilly pressed the ignition, he said,

'I've just realised – I just got to be the good cop for once.'

...

To get to Locke's house, they had to drive round effectively three sides of a square – back down the lane and past the lake, to skirt the edge of the industrial estate, then make another right turn onto the lane leading to Rhyd yr Afon. Although it took only five minutes to drive, Hopkins was reminded that cutting directly across the fields from the village on foot or a bike would only take about the same time.

As they pulled up outside Locke's house, they saw a marked police van parked outside. They hurried up the garden path to a pretty, well-kept farm worker's cottage, where a uniformed officer let them inside.

...

Kenny Stagg woke slowly from unconsciousness and groaned. He became immediately aware of the pain flooding from all over his body. His arms were bound tightly behind him with duct tape and he was sitting in a hard wooden chair. His legs were taped to each of its two front legs.

'Ah, back with us then?' said a voice.

Kenny's fuddled mind remembered setting out that morning, taking his usual short-cut down a single-track country lane with high hedgerows, then a white van coming towards him, refusing to stop, forcing him to pull into the nearest passing place. It then stopped opposite him, blocking him in.

Three men in balaclavas had jumped out and, before he could lock the doors, had dragged him out and bundled him into the back of the van, where two of them tied him up with duct tape while the third drove off. A black cloth sack had been forced over his head.

They drove for some time, Kenny guessed about half an hour. All the while he was cursing himself. He'd let his guard down, taken the same route too often, all because they'd said they agreed his terms, they were going to pay. Then the van stopped, and he was forced out into a building, empty he guessed by the echoing sound their feet made, and up two flights of stairs.

Then the ordeal began.

'Well then', the voice said pleasantly, as if they were sitting side by side having a drink. 'You told me during our last little chat that you have an insurance policy. Very wise, very – ' he paused, seeking the word. 'Prudent.'

The man leaned closer, his lips almost touching Kenny's ear. 'But you know, the thing about insurance policies. They're only any good, as long as you have the documentation. So I'm asking you, where's the documentation?'

Kenny shook his head and said nothing. Once they had his insurance, they'd kill him. His only chance was to hold out and hope Rob Locke came through. Come on, Rob, hurry, he pleaded in his mind.

...

In Locke's house, the two detectives sat on a sofa facing Locke. He was glaring at them, making no secret of his resentment at being held in his own house.

'What's all this about?', he began to bluster.

'Kenny Stagg's disappeared, we think abducted', said Hopkins. 'We think he's in danger.'

'And what's that got to do with me?'

'Kenny's wife came to us soon after he disappeared this morning. She said Kenny was worried he was in some sort of danger. She also said you were holding something for him – an 'Insurance policy'.'

'It's just another of Kenny's mad schemes – all completely in his own head.'

'Mr Locke, Kenny's probably being tortured right now, to divulge the location of whatever he's got. If he gives them the information, they'll kill him. Then they'll come after you.'

'Shame you lot didn't do your jobs properly a few years ago', Locke said bitterly. 'Then my daughter would still be alive and we wouldn't be here.'

'Mr Locke, what happened to your daughter was terrible. But by holding out, you're helping people like the ones who supplied the drugs to her. Whatever scheme you had with Kenny, it can't work now. We're his best chance. His only chance.'

Locke cursed under his breath, then got up and said,

'I need to go into the kitchen.'

'OK. But we're coming with you.'

Locke went through into the small galley-style kitchen, and opened the fridge door. He removed the salad drawer and turned it round. Taped to the back was a small flash drive, which he tore off and held out.

'What is it?' asked Hopkins.

'Pictures of Reynolds opening the trapdoor to the fake septic tank, taking drugs out, and passing them through the fence to one of the guys on off-roaders. Plus Kenny's written statement of what he saw.'

'How did he get the pictures?'

'He asked to borrow my night-vision camera. We used to go for a pint together every now and then, in the village pub here, and I'd mentioned I sometimes took it with me when I went fishing, to take pictures of owls, foxes, stuff like that.'

'Did he say what for?'

'Not at the time. But a few days after, he came to my house, all excited. He said he thought Jason was acting a bit suspiciously one night when Kenny was there fishing. Takes one to know one, I suppose. Jason was fishing near where you found the tank. Kenny was the only other one there. He was on the other side, with the island in the way, so he was out of sight. But Jason came round, looked like he was checking up on Kenny, seeing what he could see, whether he was asleep, maybe. Never tried to talk to him. So Kenny kept quiet, pretended to be asleep, then after a bit, he sneaked round after Jason, making sure he kept in the shadows off the path.'

'What did he see?'

'At first, Jason just sat, doing nothing. Then he got his phone out, looked like he was reading messages, then made a couple of calls. Kenny couldn't hear what he was saying, he was speaking so quietly. Then, after about half an hour, Kenny hears an engine and sees a headlight coming across the fields. The rider stopped and killed the light a couple of hundred yards away and Kenny couldn't see where he went in the dark. But he saw Jason get up and go to the fence. At first he thought he was just going for a pee. Then he saw him lean forward and heard voices, as if he was talking to someone on the other side. Then he saw Jason come back, turn on his headlamp, open the trapdoor and lift stuff out. Then he passed it through the fence to the other guy.'

'Jason was surely taking a bit of a risk, when he knew Kenny was there?', thought Reilly, out loud.

'Not really', said Locke. 'It's so dark there at night, with the trees and everything, that you could be thirty, even twenty yards away from someone, and unless they lit a torch or made a noise, you'd never know they were there. Jason would have been quite safe, so long as he knew who was fishing and where.'

'So anyway', Locke continued, 'he asked to borrow my camera, but he didn't tell me what he wanted it for at the time. I guessed it was one of his schemes, but we were mates and I reckoned I could count on him to bring it back. After that, after he'd borrowed my camera, he left his car at my place. There's a back lane, a private road, where his car'd be out of sight. I didn't want the neighbours wondering what was going on. Then he sneaked over the fields. He'd get there before Jason and hide behind the container. It took Kenny a couple of attempts. He got no luck the first night – Jason didn't show. But then the second night, Jason came and Kenny took the pictures. That was when he came to me and gave me the full story.'

'I asked him why he was telling me all this and why he'd taken the pictures. Then he said it's because of what happened to my daughter. The police were useless, he said, no point going to them. Let's hit the dealers where it hurts, in the pockets, and make ourselves a bit of money at the same time.'

'He wanted to blackmail Jason?'

'He didn't call it that, but yes. I know I shouldn't have believed that one of Kenny's crazy schemes could work, but I was interested in getting revenge. If it had worked, I'd have given the money to a drug rehab charity.'

'So you were his insurance?'

'Yes. He gave me a copy of the photos, because he knew there were people higher up than Jason who might come looking for him. So that was his tactic, to warn them off by saying there were copies somewhere else, but they'd stay hidden as long as he stayed safe. If he disappeared, I was meant to contact them through Jason, and say if he wasn't released, I'd take the photos to the police. Kenny said it was like 'The Firm', that was how Tom Cruise stayed safe from the Mafia.'

'But of course, with Jason dead, that threat has much less weight. All they'll be interested in now is

178

whether he's got anything on the higher-up gang members. I assume you don't know who they are?'

'No. Kenny hinted he might. But he never said.'

'And have you ever seen this man?' Reilly showed his phone again.

Locke shook his head.

'Why did you lie to us about not being at the lake on Sunday night?' asked Hopkins matter-of-factly, as if asking about the weather outside.

'I wasn't – '

'Please don't carry on lying, Mr Locke. You're in enough trouble as it is. Your alibi only covers you to 10pm. You could get across the footpath from the village to the lake in five minutes, maybe less on a bike. We know that you've sometimes gone on your bike at nights to pre-bait for pike. I assume that's how the fish heads got there?'

Locke's shoulders slumped.

'I thought you'd suspect me, because of my daughter. You'd think I killed him for revenge. But I didn't. Kenny wanted me to go there that night, the night of the murder, to put pressure on Jason, because Jason had been dragging his heels about agreeing to pay, and he was avoiding Kenny. I wasn't keen, because if I was meant to be the insurance, then Jason and his bosses would know who I was. So I went along, but I bottled it. I said hello to Jason, threw in the bait, and left by about half ten, quarter to eleven, something like that.'

'Can anyone prove that?'

'No. But there was someone there after me.'

'How do you know?'

'Well, I thought I saw someone on the path in front of me, on the way back, but then when I got to where I thought I'd seen them, there was no-one there, so I thought I must have imagined it. But then, I was nearly at the village, and I heard the gate being opened. You know, the big screech it makes. The sound travels a long way at night.'

'I wish you'd told us that earlier, Mr Locke. It might have saved your friend Kenny from being kidnapped, for one thing. Have you any idea where Kenny might be being held?'

Locke shook his head.

'Right', said Hopkins. 'You haven't been formally arrested, but if Kenny is being interrogated, which I strongly suspect, the gang are likely to find out your name sooner or later. So I'm going to ask the officers to stay here for now, and I would strongly advise you not to leave the house or contact anyone.'

'How long will that be for?'

'I don't know, Mr Locke. But things seem to be moving fast. We'll let you know.'

Chapter 19

Shadow of a gunman

*And I looked, and behold a pale horse: and his
name that sat on him was Death...*
Revelation 6:8

'We've got to work out where they're holding him,
and fast', said Reilly, as he drove Hopkins' car back to
HQ. 'We can't do anything until we know that.'

'I know, John, but it could be anywhere. If we
assume that McMahon's got him, which seems a
reasonable prospect, as it was him who threatened
Lewis and is connected with Jason and the drugs,
then it's got to be somewhere connected with him.'

'And he could be #9, from Jason's burner phone –
Mr 9 millimetre.'

'Yes, that would make sense. Any word back from
the search on the club?'

'Seen a text from them just as we were leaving
Locke's. They looked all over. But they found nothing.
Sandra gave them a hard time, saying she was trying
to get ready to open up for lunchtime.'

'Yes, a repeat of the drugs bust outcome. So, is the
answer to the two failed searches at Shadows the
same – that there's a separate staging post
somewhere to split the drugs, and that's where they're
holding Kenny?'

'That seems the best we've got to go on, right now, sir. Although, could it be something else connected with fishing, I dunno, does the club own any other premises, lock ups, that kind of thing?'

Hopkins smacked his forehead.

'Oh my God. It's been staring us in the face all this time.'

'What, sir?'

'Jason's business. His fishing tackle company, which the other fishermen thought he wasn't expert enough to run. The place he leased at a low rent until he did it up, which he never did. The derelict building he showed to Lisa, presumably to impress her that he was starting his own business, and throw her off the scent as to what he was really up to.'

'And Lisa should remember where it was!'

Hopkins was already dialling her mobile.

'Lisa? Sorry to bother you, Inspector Hopkins here. I just wondered if I could ask you a quick question, just to clear up a point for me. Where was Jason's business, you know, the online shop he was going to start?'

He listened carefully, then said, 'Thank you very much, that's very helpful', and ended the call.

'It's the old mill building off Ewenny Road. She said it's not the mill itself, but a small stone building, behind it, like a granary or something. Two floors.'

'I know the mill building, sir. Never seen if there's anything behind it. Want to go straight there?'

'No, we need back-up. A couple of uniforms who're trained to use the Enforcer and have one in their van.'

'The big red key? Definitely. I think we need an armed response team too, sir. Mr 9 millimetre – may be just a rumour, but I think we should play it safe. But how long's that going to take to put together?'

'I'll ring Jeffries now, get him to pull rank and see if he can speed things up.'

Hopkins started dialling again. Reilly heard him explain the position, say there was a strong likelihood of a hostage situation, with the hostage-taker possibly armed.

'Yes sir, immediate danger to life and limb. No need for a search warrant. Thank you, sir.'

He ended the call. 'He's going to get back to me.'

'He'd better be quick. We're only ten minutes away from HQ now.'

'But we're only about the same from Ewenny Road. Let's go there now, park up somewhere we can't be seen, and see if we can work out where he's being held.'

Reilly took the turning off the roundabout before the one that led to HQ, and followed a wide road with garages and commercial properties, before taking a left turn signposted for Ogmore and Ewenny. The properties lining the road changed to residential, then they were out in the country, with fields on either side and the river Ogwr on their left.

'I think it's the next left, sir'

'Carry on, just slow down so I can have a quick look. I don't want to drive into the yard and alert them.'

Reilly slowed to twenty, causing the car behind to honk indignantly and then overtake on the wrong side. As they went past the wide entrance to the yard,

Hopkins saw the old mill building, and also a smaller, stone building behind and off to the right.

'I think I can see where it is, John. Carry on and park as soon as you can.'

Hopkins' phone rang. 'Hello sir? Is that the best they can do? Well, I suppose we'll just have to make the best of it. Thank you.' He ended the call.

'Bad news?'

'They'll be half an hour. Best we can expect, I suppose, but I'd hoped they'd be quicker.'

Reilly parked in a layby next to the bridge where the road crossed over the Ogwr.

'Want to try another drive-by, sir?'

'No, I think we'd be too conspicuous if we did it again. Hopefully, anyone who saw us would have just thought we were lost. And although we're only a hundred yards or so down the road, two guys in suits walking along the pavement and peering in through the gate is going to look odd, too.'

'There's the old Heronston lane, sir. I've run along there, coming back up the river from the coast. It used to get used as a rat-run, so they closed it to through traffic. It's pretty quiet now, and there might be a back way into the mill.'

'OK, let's have a drive along there and see.'

Reilly pulled out, then turned left before crossing the bridge, and started driving slowly up the narrow lane, obeying the 20mph sign. They could see the taller mill building, and the roof of the outbuilding, over the hedges, but there did not appear to be any way in. A high stone wall, backed by a straggly hedge, ran all the way along the back of the property. What might have been an entrance for the mill workers, a narrow doorway in the stonework, had been bricked up.

As they reached a small hamlet, Hopkins' phone rang. 'Really? How far? That's great!. Look, turn your sirens off on the approach. We want as much surprise as possible.'

He turned to Reilly. 'Turn round and get back to the mill entrance. There's only one ART on duty, but their car was closer than the despatcher thought. They're coming straight here now and the uniforms with the ram are coming from HQ. They'll both be here in 10 minutes. Turn around and drive slowly back to the entrance. We'll wait by the side of the road until we see them coming, then swing in after them.'

Reilly turned round in the drive of a neat bungalow, ignoring the 'No turning!' sign and headed back to the main road. They pulled up slightly back from the mill entrance and waited. Within a few minutes, they saw blue lights up ahead, coming from the Bridgend direction.

As the vehicles got closer, they saw a marked BMW X5 in the lead, carrying the armed response team, with a police van following close behind. Reilly flashed his lights at them, and both vehicles swung into the mill yard. Reilly gunned the engine and turned in behind them.

The two officers from the van were already out, clad in body armour, and pulling on riot helmets. They went round the back of the van and lifted out the heavy, red battering ram. The two firearms officers, also in body armour, pulled on baseball caps and removed their weapons from the locked safe in the boot. One strapped a Heckler and Koch carbine across his chest, the other put a 9mm Glock pistol into his holster.

'That building, there!' Reilly shouted and pointed to the outbuilding. The officers ran to the door and quickly assembled, the two with the ram in front, the firearms team behind them, and then Hopkins and Reilly. One of the officers who carried the ram quickly ran his fingers round the door. 'Not solid steel – just a metal plate over wood. Yale and mortice locks in the middle. Should be easy to break.'

Hopkins nodded, the armed officers switched on torches, one under the barrel of his carbine, the other on the front of his body armour, then the two uniforms swung the ram against the locks.

With a huge crash, the door burst inwards, the two armed officers rushing in first, yelling 'Armed Police!' The uniforms followed with heavy-duty torches and drawn batons. Hopkins and Reilly made up the rear.

The torches swept the small area of the ground floor. It was empty. No crates, boxes, nothing. Nowhere a man could be hidden.

'First floor!' said Reilly, pointing to some stone steps in the corner. The armed officers went first, shouting their challenge, and pivoting to cover each other from the dark spaces at the open top and sides of the stairs.

'Clear!' came the shout from above, and Hopkins and Reilly ran up. Again, there was nothing. The small room was quite empty.

The six men stood, staring at each other. 'So what do we do now?' asked Reilly.

Hopkins stood, defeated. For once, he had no suggestion, no plan to make. He had been so sure it was McMahon, so sure it was this place. But he had led them all on a wild goose chase and worse, time was still ticking away for Kenny. It might even have run out, while they followed false trails.

His shoulders slumped. 'I don't know, John. I really don't.'

Perhaps it was time to give up. Perhaps the disease had affected his mental powers, skewed his reasoning. He could be putting people's lives at risk by pretending, by carrying on.

At that moment, there came a muffled cry from above them. Hopkins spun and saw, partly hidden behind him in the shadows, a steep, open staircase, more like a ladder. Without thinking, he turned and started to run up it.

'No, wait!' yelled Reilly desperately, but Hopkins was already near the top, pushing open a trapdoor, and climbing through. The officer with the Glock shoved past Reilly and flung himself up the stairs after Hopkins. Reilly ran after him.

There was a single shot, reverberating shockingly loud in the empty building, a loud crash, then silence.

Chapter 20

Folly and friendship

I was angry with my friend;
I told my wrath, my wrath did end.
William Blake, *The Poison Tree*

Hopkins knew he was being an idiot, he should let the armed officers go first, but something he couldn't explain impelled him to charge up the stairs.

He pushed open the trapdoor, which fell to one side with a crash. There was a small attic room, unlit except for a bare bulb dangling in the middle, where the figure of a man sat tied to a chair. He was gagged, but seemed to have managed to work it to one side.

Hopkins climbed fully into the attic. 'Kenny? You're safe now.'

'I wouldnae bet on that', growled a Glaswegian voice, and McMahon stepped out of the shadows, levelling a black automatic pistol at Hopkins' head.

Time seemed to slow down, milliseconds becoming seconds. Hopkins was sure he saw McMahon's knuckles whiten as he increased pressure on the trigger, and he tried to fling himself sideways, knowing it would be far too late.

The first firearms officer's head and shoulders appeared through the trap door. He was out of breath and off balance and Hopkins was partly in his line of fire, though moving sideways. He saw he had no time to save Hopkins by going by the book and waiting for a clear shot at McMahon's torso. Praying, he snapped off a shot on pure instinct.

The heavy 9mm slug, instead of being a killing shot to McMahon's chest, slammed into his right shoulder, spinning him round. The gun dropped to the floor and slid into the shadows. McMahon fell with a heavy crash.

The first firearms officer ran over to McMahon, kicked the gun further out of reach, and trained his gun on McMahon's head. Reilly appeared next, closely followed by the second armed officer, already radioing for an ambulance. The two firearms officers quickly searched McMahon, then began to administer first aid.

Reilly leaned against a beam, chest heaving, then turned furiously to Hopkins, who was just picking himself up from the floor.

'You – bloody – idiot! Don't you ever do anything like that again! What the hell is the matter with you? Got a death wish or something?'

'I'm sorry, John', said Hopkins, mildly.

'Sorry? There's been something going on for weeks, and you won't tell me! You're my best mate, we're partners, I've got a right to know!'

As the adrenaline in Reilly's system subsided, he calmed somewhat. 'Right, after we've finished up here, we're going to the nearest pub. We're going to have a drink, and you're going to tell me what's going on.'

'Very well, John', said Hopkins meekly. 'But in future, when you give an order to a superior officer, would you mind calling me 'sir'?'

...

Reilly paid the barman, nodded his thanks, and stuffed his wallet back in his pocket. Then he carried two pints of bitter over to the corner table where Hopkins sat. The pub was quiet, lunch trade having departed, and it being too early for the evening customers.

'Thanks John.'

'Cheers.'

Both sat in silence and drank deeply, observing the unwritten rule that nothing serious could be discussed until drink had been taken.

'I don't really know where to begin, John.'

'The beginning's usually a good place, so I find, sir.'

'Look, when we're not in work, I think you can drop all the 'sir' stuff. We've known each other too many years. Call me Tom.'

'OK sir – Tom.' It felt awkward on Reilly's tongue.

'Well, here goes.' And Hopkins began the story of how he had started to feel fatigued and weary, taking longer to complete tasks than before. 'I thought it was just age, slowing down, maybe a touch of anaemia at worst. Mair talked me into seeing the GP, he referred me for tests, then I saw a specialist on Wednesday last week.'

Reilly was listening attentively and nodding, as he might do with a witness.

Hopkins took a deep breath and told him. 'It's a blood disorder called myelofibrosis. Not too serious at the moment, but it can turn into cancer. They think they can control it for ten years, maybe longer, with drugs. After that, could be tricky. I might have to have a bone marrow transplant. I don't know how that works, but it doesn't sound nice.'

Reilly thought. Hopkins was grateful he hadn't shown sympathy, or made exclamations of shock or sadness.

After a while, he said, 'I thought it must be something like that.'

'I've been falling down on the job, you mean?'

'Not at all. But you've seemed, I dunno, like angry with yourself, or something. Frustrated. Like you felt you weren't up to your usual standards. Well, let me tell you, that's bullshit.'

'Thanks for the loyalty, John.'

'No, I mean it. If you can't do the paperwork, who cares? You're still just as brilliant at the important stuff. You've just showed that. And you saved a man's life by it.'

Hopkins was silent.

'Looks like you were right about the staging post, too.' Before they had left the scene, Reilly had called the Drugs Team, who were now engaged in searching through the boxes and packaging Reilly and Hopkins had seen in the attic room.

Reilly went on, 'This drug, can it stop the disease?'

'They say so. Maybe even reverse it a bit.'

'So you'll still be able to do what you're doing now. Maybe a bit better. You can delegate the grunt stuff to the junior guys and gals. And ten years – who can say where any of us will be in ten years? Think about today, bugger tomorrow, as my grandad used to say.'

'The doctor said I should start doing some exercise.'

191

'Well, I agree with him on that.' Reilly pulled a card out of his wallet and showed Hopkins. 'Did I ever tell you I'm a qualified running coach? We could start having a couple of sessions a week, at lunchtimes, if you want.'

'I'm not going up any mountains with you, John.'

'No, of course not, that's the second lesson. Only joking', he added hastily. 'We'll just take it easy, walking then a bit of gentle jogging, gradually increase the time you spend running and decrease the time walking. But the important thing is, you slow down or stop as soon as you need. You don't push yourself.'

'That sounds surprisingly less masochistic than I was imagining. Yes, let's give it a try.'

They both drank in silence for a few minutes.

'That was a good collar for us, though, wasn't it?'

'Yes, John. One major dealer off the streets, and caught literally red-handed. Shouldn't be a problem getting a conviction, and he should go down for quite a few years. But I still don't think he's our killer.'

'Why not, sir?'

'All the stuff we've discussed before. Can't place him at the scene, motive, weapon, all of that. And he's a hardened pro. He'll just deny whatever we haven't got strong evidence for.'

'At least we got him alive, though. Hopefully he can fill in the background about Jason and the blackmail, maybe it'll lead us to whoever did it.'

'Yes, maybe. But – I wonder?'

'What, sir?' Reilly grimaced. 'Tom'.

'It's OK, I think we're back in work now. What if we pulled in Sandra? She may not have been directly involved, but I bet she knows what's going on. Tell Dave and Sue to go and arrest her, would you?'

'What for?'

'Oh, conspiracy to kidnap, for starters. But the main thing is, I want her frightened, looking at a possible jail sentence, looking for a way out.'

Chapter 21

Sandra's story

When lovely woman stoops to folly;
And finds too late that men betray
T S Eliot, *The Waste Land* (quoting Oliver
Goldsmith)

It was after five when they arrived back at HQ.

'Can you stay on for a bit, John?' asked Hopkins.
'I think we should interview Sandra as soon as
possible. Is she in yet?'

Reilly went over to check with Sue Wilshaw, then
returned. 'Yep, they booked her in about half an hour
ago. She's in a cell now.'

'Does she want a solicitor present?'

'Apparently not. They asked her, but she said no.
She used her phone call to call the club, tell the staff
what they needed to be doing, to open up tonight.'

'OK, we'll give her another half an hour to think
about things, then do the interview.'

Reilly went off to call Catrin and explain he would
be late. Hopkins called Mair. As he suspected, she was
not pleased.

'Twm, you said you were going to start looking
after yourself. It's not even a week since the diagnosis.
And you've been down to Henley and back today. You
must be shattered.'

He decided not to tell her he had nearly been shot, as well. 'We're getting very close to cracking the case. I can feel it. We just need to give it one more push.'

'That's what you always say. And then there's always another urgent case.'

'This time it's different, *cariad*. I really will change my ways. John and I have had a good talk about sharing out my workload. He's even offered to give me coaching sessions.'

'You, running?' She laughed.

'He says we won't do anything too strenuous at first. I'm actually looking forward to it.'

'Well, I suppose you must be serious about changing. Make sure you have something proper to eat, tonight – not just crisps and chocolate. I'll see you when you get in.'

'Thanks, *cariad*. Love you.'

'What's got into you? Love you too. Now go and do whatever it is you have to do.'

...

Reilly spoke into the recorder. 'Interview commencing 18:00, Alexandra Watkins, DI Hopkins and DS Reilly present.'

Sandra sat across the table from them, looking coldly furious. Being arrested and spending an hour in the cells did not seem to have made her more co-operative. But then, reflected Hopkins, even though she had never been convicted, she had probably seen the inside of police cells a few times.

'Ms Watkins', Hopkins began, 'I understand you don't want a solicitor present?'

'Don't need one. I've done nothing wrong.' The London accent was sounding more pronounced.

'Today we arrested your partner, Andrew McMahon, for abduction, false imprisonment, grievous bodily harm, wounding with intent and attempted murder.'

'Where is he?'

'In hospital. He received a gunshot wound while resisting arrest. He's stable.'

Reilly took over. 'We found a large quantity of drugs at the place where he was apprehended. We suspect you've been running the club as a front for drug-dealing and using it to launder the profits.'

'That's not true!'

'The Drugs Team are getting a search warrant right now to seize all your accounts and records. Are you certain they're all going to hold up to examination by a team of forensic accountants?'

Sandra was silent.

Hopkins took over. 'Look, Sandra, this is serious. You did the books. It's your name on the licence. If this all comes back to you, you're looking at some serious jail time.'

'I didn't do anything, OK?'

Hopkins continued, as if she hadn't spoken. 'And that's not to mention conspiring to kidnap and torture Kenny Stagg.'

'I don't know anything about that!'

'So Andy never discussed any of that with you? He was acting entirely on his own?'

'Yeah!' she said defiantly.

'I think a jury may find that hard to believe. Particularly if the accounts show you've been fiddling the books to hide a drugs operation.'

'You can't pin any of that on me.'

Reilly intervened. He passed across stills of Jason's Kia, taken by traffic cameras along the M4.

'You claimed when we spoke last, that you were having an affair with Jason. Here are pictures, with dates, of his car driving eastbound on the M4, then returning, late at night. Now, here's a list of all the calls he made to you. Guess what? They all correspond. Hard to see how you could be having a romantic evening together, when he was driving up and down the M4 most of the night.'

Hopkins went on.

'What this looks like, is Jason went to meet his county lines contact, somewhere near Magor, to collect shipments of drugs. He then called you, presumably to confirm how much and what type, and make arrangements for collection from the lake.'

'Bastards. You never give me a bloody break, do you? All my life. For Christ's sake.'

There were tears in her eyes now.

Hopkins leaned forward.

'Ms Watkins, I know you were frightened of Andy. That was clear the first time we met. If you did all this under duress, then the Crown Prosecution Service may see it as not in the public interest to prosecute, or to proceed with lighter charges. But you have to co-operate with us, tell us everything, so we can understand what went on.'

'Yeah, I know the score. I've been down this road before, remember?'

'What's different, Ms Watkins, is that this time, you've got a chance to get out for good. Andy's going down for a good stretch for what we caught him doing, maybe ten years, but with good behaviour, he could be out in five.'

He saw the fear in her eyes.

'But if we could get everything on the drugs business, the full works, and you co-operate with the forensic accountants, he could be gone much longer. Giving you time to make a life somewhere else. We'd offer you protection, of course.'

'Doesn't look like I have much choice, does it?'

The two detectives waited.

'Jesus! If it wasn't for that bloody little snitch Kenny, we wouldn't be in this mess.'

'Andy knew Kenny was an informer?'

'Course he did. Kenny wasn't the brightest, not great at covering his tracks. But Andy thought he could play him. Get him to feed false information back to the cops, throw them off the scent. Of course, it had to be convincing, so he'd get chicken feed to pass back – a few small amounts of drugs, some genuine info on rival gangs, that sort of thing. But everything about Andy's operation – that was false. Andy enjoyed it – said he felt like a sort of Cold War spymaster. He passed all the info through Jason to Kenny. He never met him directly himself.'

'So why did things go sour?'

'Kenny got greedy. Took some photos of Jason moving the drugs. He said he wanted a slice of the action, a big pay day. And he wanted to be shot of it all, stop being used to feed info back. He was starting to worry the cops were on to him, after some of his info didn't pan out. Jason passed the message back to Andy.'

'How did Andy react?'

'How do you think? He went ballistic. If I hadn't calmed him down, he'd have gone out that night and topped Kenny.'

'So what happened?'

'Andy spoke to Jason, told him he wasn't going to pay. It was Jason's problem – he was the one who'd got himself photographed. He said Jason would have to take it out of his own cut, if Kenny had to be paid. Jason said he couldn't afford that, and if he tried to take it out of the cash he was funnelling back to the suppliers in London, they'd give him something a bit worse than a P.45. So Andy said to stall Kenny, say his bosses were thinking about it. That went on for a couple of weeks. Then we heard Jason was dead.'

Reilly broke in.

'Andy didn't kill him?'

'No, I know he didn't. He was stocktaking, like I said, and then he was with me for the rest of the night. We figured it must have been another gang who did it. Anyway, Andy had no reason to kill Jason. It was Kenny who was trying to blackmail him.'

'But once Jason was dead, then presumably, Andy realised Kenny didn't have so much of a hold any more. Seeing as Kenny never met Andy face to face.'

'That's right. Andy was going to take him out straight away, but then he thought he needed to know how much Kenny knew about the operation, what he might have passed on to the cops, all that. But what triggered him to make his move, was he overheard some cop in the club one lunchtime, saying there was new evidence on Jason's murder.'

Hopkins reddened, but Reilly didn't notice. He pressed on.

'So what did Andy do?'

'I didn't help him do any of this, OK? I just heard him talking on the phone. They'd worked out his route to work, so Andy and a couple of other guys were going to stop his car, shove him in the back of a van, and take him somewhere for a chat. That's all I know.'

'Did you know about the building at Ewenny Road? The old granary behind the mill? Jason rented it and used it as a staging post for breaking the drugs up for street sale.'

She shook her head. 'No, never heard of it.'

'Were you frightened of Andy? Was he abusive?'

'No, he never hit me or anything. He always treated me well. We were real partners, business and personal. But I realised after a bit that he wasn't normal – there was something missing. It was like he had no empathy, no thought about other people. Everything was like a transaction to him – I do this, you do that. And he had no restraint as far as violence goes. I had no doubt that, if I crossed him, he'd have killed me. He might have regretted it, but he'd have done it anyway.'

'Do you think he'd killed before?'

'Yes. I mean, no specifics, but from stuff he said about when he was in Glasgow – I believed he had.'

Reilly said, 'And I take it you weren't having an affair with Jason?'

'No, he wasn't really my type. On the nights when he picked up a shipment from London, he'd drop it off at the lake, then go round to my flat. I gave him a spare key. I was always out at the club. He'd have a shower and change his clothes, leave his worn clothes there for me to wash. He always took a set of clean clothes with him, that looked the same as the ones he had on. He didn't want any residue on him or his clothes when he got home, in case his place was ever searched.'

'I see', said Hopkins. 'Well, I think that's all we need for now.'

'Wait a minute, what happens to me?'

'Well, you are still under arrest, although we'll be recommending to the CPS not to proceed with the charge of conspiracy to kidnap, seeing as you say you weren't involved. The rest is up to them. We'll suggest it's not in the public interest to prosecute you, if you co-operate. I think you'd better stay here tonight, for your own safety. We'll make you as comfortable as we can. After that, we'll see about getting you into a safe house. But I'd stress that's conditional on you co-operating with the forensic accountants.'

'And what about my club?'

'I would think the magistrates will suspend your licence pretty quickly, when they hear about this. And we're bound to tell them, I'm afraid.'

'Shame. I worked hard on that place. One of the few things in my life I've been proud of.'

...

The MCIT room was dark, save for a pool of light in one corner, where someone worked on. Reilly went over to have a brief chat, then came back to Hopkins, who was making coffee in the kitchen.

'Well, what do you make of that, sir?'

'Not here, John. Murder Room.'

They carried their mugs through to the Murder Room.

'So it looks like Kenny spun Rob Locke a complete pack of lies, to get him involved. Kenny was in it all along, first as a snitch, then as a kind of double agent.'

'I suppose, given the history with Locke's daughter, he would never have helped Kenny if he'd believed Kenny was a part of it. And then he would never have agreed to be Kenny's insurance policy.'

'And what about this mystery cop supposedly blabbing in Shadows? That's got to be a cock and bull story.'

Hopkins sighed heavily. 'It wasn't, John. It was me.'

Reilly's face was incredulous. 'You? In Shadows?'

'It was really stupid, I know. But I wanted to take a look at it, as several leads seemed to point there, then Dr Madhvani rang me, wanted to talk about the case over lunch. I thought I could kill two birds with one stone.'

'You took Dr Madhvani to Shadows?' Reilly whistled. 'I bet she thought you were taking her on a date.'

'Look it's not funny, John, OK? But yes, it was a little embarrassing, for a while.'

'So what happened?'

'Well, we were discussing the case, and just as I mentioned the phone, McMahon came up behind me to serve the food. I didn't mention the phone specifically – just said there was a key piece of evidence. I didn't know whether he'd heard me at the time. But – my God, if that's what triggered him to grab Kenny, then it's all my fault.'

'That's rubbish, sir. You know it was only a matter of time until McMahon moved against Kenny, once

Jason was dead. It would still have happened, with or without your slip.'

Hopkins looked miserable.

'Look, sir, what Sandra said about what McMahon says he heard, is hearsay. That means it's not admissible and can't go into her official statement, or it would just get struck out. So it's not going to come out that way. And if you and me both keep schtum, who's ever going to know?'

'What if McMahon raises it? Points me out in court? He's bound to have recognised me at the mill.'

'What good would it do him? It just shows he was already planning to grab Kenny, and speeded up his plans to avoid discovery. That's an aggravating factor on sentencing. And if he does raise it, all you've got to say is that you were there, as part of the investigation, but you don't remember using those precise words. The jury'll think he's just trying to throw mud at us.'

'You're suggesting I lie, John? That's something I swore I would never do.'

'Well, it's not going to affect the outcome, is it? It's a minor detail. There's enough evidence to prove all the charges, especially with Sandra's statement. Nothing you said has any bearing on that. And given the weight of evidence, he might just plead guilty anyway, in which case it never comes to light.'

'I hope you're right John, I hope you're right.'

'Look, sir, go home and get some sleep. It'll all look better in the morning.'

Hopkins sighed. 'Yes, you're right. Did we get anywhere with those log-in details for the fishing club e-mails?'

'Came in while we were out. Got the tech guys looking at the relevant dates. They'll batch the e-mails from the relevant period and send them to us tomorrow.'

Hopkins said goodnight, then went out to his car. He sat in the driving seat for a while, staring out at the cold, friendless night, then started the engine and drove home.

Chapter 22

Lost souls and absolution

These dwell among the blackest souls, loaded down deep by sins of differing types. If you sink far enough, you'll see them all.
Dante Alighieri, *Inferno*

Contrary to Reilly's advice of the evening before, things didn't look better in the morning for Hopkins.

After, a brief, wonderful moment between sleeping and waking when he had thought it had all been a bad dream, reality came flooding back. Though he now accepted he hadn't caused what had happened to Kenny – McMahon would have kidnapped him anyway – there was now the decision of what to do.

If he kept quiet and told half-truths or outright lies to cover it up, he would be going against his whole reason for joining the police in the first place. While he recognised his youthful naïveté, he had never compromised on his principles, had never twisted or withheld evidence to improve the chances of a conviction. Was he going to break those principles now, just to save his own neck?

His dilemma wasn't improved when he reached the office. Reilly was waiting for him with a message.

'McMahon wants to speak to you, in hospital. He says just you – no-one else.'

Hopkins thought a moment.

'Then I suppose I'd better go.'

'Are you sure, sir? He's bound to try and twist what you say to suit him. I doubt he wants to see you to confess.'

'Then I'll have to try to use words that can't be twisted. I think I need to see him. Then I'll know where I stand. Maybe we can see Kenny at the same time – get his statement.'

'The doctors say he's not ready to be interviewed yet. He's in the Burns Unit and he's suffered huge mental trauma, as well as other injuries.'

'The Burns Unit?'

Reilly nodded, looking sick.

'First of all, McMahon beat him up, pretty badly. Three broken ribs, broken nose, suspected liver damage. Then he cut him with a knife. Arms, chest and legs. Then, just before we arrived, he covered his arms in petrol, and set them alight. Let them burn for a few seconds, then put them out with a fire extinguisher.'

Hopkins remembered Sandra's words. Something missing...no empathy, no restraint. He shook his head. He couldn't think of words adequate to respond.

He pulled his jacket on, which he had only just removed. 'Well, I'd better get going.'

'Want me to come along sir? For support?'

'No. I think I've got to do this myself.'

...

Hopkins walked along a ward corridor and saw a uniformed officer standing outside the door to a private room. He looked bored, but straightened up when he saw Hopkins.

'Morning, sir', he said smartly.

'Morning. How is he?'

The uniformed cop grinned. 'He'll live. But I doubt he'll ever compete in the javelin.'

Hopkins hid a grimace at the black humour. But cops didn't like it when someone tried to harm one of their own, so maybe it was justified.

'I'm going in to see him, at his request. I won't be long.'

'Righto sir.'

Hopkins pushed open the door. McMahon lay in bed, one shoulder swathed in bandages, his good arm handcuffed to the bed rail.

He grunted. 'You sweating, yet, pig?'

'If we're not going to have a civil conversation, I'm going.'

'I heard what you said the other day, when you were with your ladyfriend in the club. Could be very embarrassing for you, if that came out in court.'

Hopkins said nothing, just waited.

'These charges against me. Attempted murder of a copper, that's a biggie.'

'Maybe we can arrange for you to be transferred back to the – Bar-L, do you call it? I'm sure there's plenty of your old friends there, who would love to see you back.'

'That doesnae scare me. But see here, I wasnae gonna kill you. I wanted a hostage, so I could walk out of there.'

'That's very reassuring.'

'And if you could maybe say that you didn't think I was going to kill you, I might forget about what I heard in the club.'

Hopkins remembered McMahon's finger tightening on the trigger, the absolute certainty he was facing death. He also remembered again Sandra's words – something missing, no empathy, no restraint.

'That's an interesting offer, Mr McMahon. But I don't do deals with vermin.'

He turned on his heel and left.

...

On his return to the office, he marched straight through the MCIT room. Reilly stood up to intercept him, waving a sheaf of papers, but Hopkins carried on.

'Later, John. I'm going to see Jeffries.'

'Sir, you're not going to – '

'I'm going to do what I should have done in the first place, John.'

He walked to Jeffries' door and knocked.

'Come in!'

'Sir, I wondered if I could have a minute? There's something I need to tell you. Well, two things actually.'

'This sounds ominous. Sit down.'

Hopkins did so, took a deep breath, and launched into the story of his ill-fated lunch at Shadows, ending with the recent conversation with McMahon. Jeffries listened in silence, his face betraying nothing.

When Hopkins had finished, he thought for a few minutes, then leaned back in his chair.

'Well, I don't know what shocks me more, the fact that an officer of your experience would discuss details of a case while in a location connected with that case, or the thought of you consorting with a lady pathologist in a night club.'

'I wasn't – ', but the Hanger waved to cut him off.

'Fortunately, I can't see what bearing it has on the case against McMahon. He's not being charged in connection with Reynolds, so whatever you said about Reynolds is irrelevant. And it also shows him in a worse light – it shows premeditation and calculation. Not likely to improve his chances on sentencing. If I was his barrister, I'd advise him not to mention it. He might still do so, out of spite, of course.'

'Yes, sir.'

'But I can't pretend it isn't a potential embarrassment. We're going to have to make sure prosecuting counsel is fully briefed. There's nothing they hate more than some unexpected question cropping up about the conduct of the investigating team. However. I can't see it as affecting the likely outcome in any way.'

'Thank you, sir.'

'There's still the question of how I deal with this from a disciplinary point of view.'

Hopkins' heart sank. He knew it wasn't serious enough to lose his job over, but what if he were suspended, or given an official warning? With a sense of shame, he realised that the thing he was most worried about would be his colleagues knowing, sniggering behind his back. Vanity, all is vanity.

'I honestly don't know what you were thinking of. But you've never been in any kind of trouble before. And I can't see you ever doing anything like this again. The embarrassment to the service, if it happens, will be minor. So I think a first verbal warning, not to go on your record, would be appropriate.'

'Thank you, sir.'

'This is the verbal warning.' The Hanger's lips twitched, in an almost-smile. 'If you should have the irresistible urge to take a pathologist to lunch in the future, do not, under any circumstances, do so in a place of interest to the case, and do not, under any circumstances, discuss confidential details of said case in such a place. Clear?'

'Yes, sir.'

'And I'm not going to say anything to West Midlands about Dr Madhvani's role in this. I trust you more than I trust that lecherous old Saxon over there. Now, what was the other thing?'

'Well, I went to see a consultant last Wednesday, sir, and it appears I have a serious, well, possibly serious, blood condition.' Hopkins gave him the details of the diagnosis and treatment.

'I'm impressed, Tom.'

'Sir?'

'A lesser man would have told me that first, to try and get my sympathy.'

'Would it have worked?'

'Of course not. I'm widely known to have a heart of flint.' He paused, then went on. 'Is there anything we can do to support you now? Do you need some time off?'

'No, sir. The doctor says I can carry on, more or less as normal, for the time being. This drug may disrupt things a bit and I may need a day or two off, maybe for a transfusion, but once it settles down, I should be OK. I think I'd rather carry on and see how things develop.'

'Very well. But I want you to be less hard on yourself. Delegate more to the younger ones. I know you wouldn't ask them to do anything you wouldn't do yourself, and you've always led by example, but the time has come to take it a bit easier. One of the privileges of rank – and age.'

'I'll try, sir.'

'Good. Anything else?'

'No, sir.'

As Hopkins walked back to his desk, Reilly mouthed 'What happened?', but Hopkins waved to him, then showed five fingers. He needed some time to process what had just happened. The enormous feeling of relief, and of having a plan to deal with any fallout, overwhelmed him.

Later, as they had a coffee in the Murder Room, Hopkins told Reilly what had gone on in Jeffries' office. Reilly punched the air in glee.

'You got off!'

'Yes, I suppose I did. Strange, though.'

'What?'

'For a strict Chapel man, I think he found the whole thing quite amusing. So, back to normality. Where are we on those e-mails?'

Reilly looked glum.

'Nothing of any interest between the relevant dates, when Walters was away. Just general chit-chat, some stuff about a competition to raise money for charity, couple of complaints or suggestions, that sort of thing. Nothing about closing the lake.'

'Would we be able to tell if something had been deleted?'

'The tech guys say not. It's a standard Outlook account, no backup or anything. So if a message was deleted from the Inbox and then manually deleted from the Trash, it wouldn't show.'

'Could it be on a server or something?'

'The provider does keep a backup for their own purposes, usually so they can restore everything in the event of a system failure, but the time period varies. After six months, at most a year, it seems unlikely they'd still have it. And we'd need to get a court order to force them to disclose any copies, which would take time.'

'But there must have been something. If it went out to all members, surely someone would have kept a copy?'

'Well, it might not have gone to all members. Or Walters would have seen it, for a start, and he says he didn't. And we'd have to search the e-mails of seventy members, and hope one of them hadn't deleted it. As it's over a year old, the chances are, they have.'

'Unless they had a reason for keeping it.'

They both came to the same conclusion at the same time.

'Kenny.'

Chapter 23

You've got mail

I beseech you, sir, pardon me. It is a letter from my brother, that I have not all o'er-read; and for so much as I have perused, I find it not fit for your o'er-looking.
Shakespeare, *King Lear*

Unfortunately, the opinion of the doctors was that Kenny wouldn't be in a condition to be interviewed for another forty-eight hours, maybe longer. Sue Wilshaw had been to Kenny's house and persuaded his wife to hand over his laptop. The tech team were trying to unlock it, but apparently, Kenny was better at devising passwords than Jason Reynolds had been.

Therefore, the investigation was deadlocked for the present.

'Could we bring Bryn Richards in?', suggested Reilly. 'Tackle him about being Jason's dad?'

'I don't want to do that, until we know what possible connection there might be to the murder', said Hopkins. 'I can't see one at the moment. And either Richards already knows, in which case it's old news, or he doesn't, in which case we'd be causing him unnecessary distress. We'll have to tell him at some point, but I'd rather do it once the investigation's complete, and not in the context of interviewing him as a suspect.'

'Is there any CCTV in the village?' wondered Dave Lane. 'Or any of the approach roads? See if we can pick up any vehicle that might be associated with the guy who was at the lake after Rob Locke?'

Reilly shook his head. 'Nothing till you get back to the A-road, and then there'd be so much traffic, it would be meaningless. We got Jason on the M4 because we knew what we were looking for. You'd have no chance unless one of the cars on the list happened to go by, out of the hundreds, maybe thousands of others. Even then, you wouldn't be able to tell if a car was turning off for the village or going straight on. And there's more than one way in – three lanes meet just outside the village, so there's several potential routes.'

'We could see if there's a Community Liaison Officer for the village. Maybe the Neighbourhood Watch reported illegal or nuisance parking, something like that', suggested Sue Wilshaw.

'Good idea', said Hopkins. 'Long shot, but worth trying. Can you follow it up?'

'Will do, sir.'

'Right, well, unless there's anything else, let's wrap it up', said Hopkins. 'I've got an afternoon off.'

'Doing anything good, sir?', asked Reilly, after the other two had left.

'I wish. Bone marrow test, to confirm that it is myelofibrosis.'

'Doesn't sound nice.'

'From what I understand, they bore into your hip at the back, where the skin's thinnest, and take a sample from the core. I'll be having a local anaesthetic, though, so hopefully it won't be too bad.'

'Well, good luck with it, sir.'

...

Two days passed, and nothing of any value to the Reynolds investigation came in. Sue Wilshaw and Dave Lane were left, not quite twiddling their thumbs, but resorting to checking statements, CCTV records and other evidence to try to find inconsistencies or points they might have missed. By the end of Friday, the Hanger was making noises about assigning them to other duties.

'It's not like we haven't got other urgent cases piling up. And yours seems to have come to a standstill for the moment.'

'But sir – '

'We'll review it on Monday. You can have them back if something new comes in.'

Hopkins felt it, though, and so did Reilly. The investigation was losing momentum. They needed a breakthrough.

...

On the Sunday afternoon, despite Mair's protestations, Hopkins went to visit Kenny Stagg in the hospital. He had rung ahead and the doctors were, reluctantly, of the opinion that he could now be interviewed. Hopkins didn't intend to ask him in detail about what had gone on in the attic. Much of that was self-evident and a full statement could be taken later. What Hopkins was desperate for, was some new information to re-energise the investigation, and to persuade the Hanger not to divert resources to other cases.

The corridors were surprisingly busy, for a Sunday, then Hopkins remembered that it was the start of visiting time. Scores of relatives bearing food, books, magazines and other gifts were processing to the main lifts. When he got to the lift lobby, it was crammed with people waiting, and he saw that only two out of the six lifts were in operation. Hopkins opted to take the stairs, and consoled himself that it would count towards his new exercise target.

Arriving two floors up, only slightly out of breath, he walked along the long corridor to the ward number he had been given. As with McMahon, there was a guard outside the door. Stagg wasn't under arrest, at least not yet, but McMahon's associates, including the ones who had helped kidnap Kenny, were still at large. Hopkins acknowledged the officer with a wave, not waiting for any black humour, and walked straight in.

'How are you doing, Kenny?' As soon as he said it, he realised it wasn't the most diplomatic question. Most of Kenny's face was swathed in bandages, and what parts could be seen were bruised and swollen. His forearms too were heavily bandaged. But still, he raised a smile.

'Champion, as you can see, Inspector.' He half raised his arms.

Hopkins sat down opposite him.

'What on earth made you think your insurance policy could work, Kenny? Who was Rob Locke supposed to threaten, with Jason gone? You just ended up putting Rob at risk, too.'

'I suppose I didn't think it through properly.'

'Hmm. Seems to be a feature of your schemes.'

'Rob's OK, though, isn't he?'

'He's OK, but he wouldn't be if McMahon had got hold of his name. What works in the movies doesn't always work in real life.'

Kenny was silent for a few moments.

'It was you who was first up the stairs – back at the mill, I mean?'

'Yes. Not my brightest move.'

'Well, it was bloody brave. You saved my life. I reckon I owe you one.'

'Funny you should mention that. There was something I wanted to ask you.'

Kenny's eyes wrinkled in suspicion. He hadn't meant the promise to be taken literally. More a sort of pub promise you make, when someone buys you a pint.

'Your laptop, Kenny. Your good lady gave it to us voluntarily. We need to look at the e-mails to and from the fishing club. I need your password to open the laptop, and any confidential files relating to the fishing club.'

'That's all?'

'I promise that's all I'll look for, and I won't pass it on to anyone else. Apart from anything else, all your dealings with my colleagues in, a different department, we might say, are subject to strict confidentiality arrangements. Once we've found what we're looking for, it goes straight back to your missus.'

'I was hoping to trade that.'

'Kenny, you're in enough trouble already. Blackmail, concealing a crime, probably a few other things. You know we can't make deals. But what you've been through, plus the fact that you're co-operating, will be taken into account. I shouldn't think CPS will think it's worth prosecuting you.'

'What are you looking for, specifically?'

'I'd rather you didn't know. It might put you in danger again. I just need to know where you've stored e-mails to and from the club, and if you've saved any specifically, I need to know how to get into them.'

Understanding dawned on what Hopkins could see of Kenny's face.

'I think I might know what you're after, Inspector.'

'Yes, well don't speculate or discuss it with anyone else. You don't want to end up in another attic. I might not be there, next time. Just tell me the passwords.'

'OK. This one's the general one, to get into the laptop.'

Hopkins took out his notebook, wrote down what Kenny dictated, then showed what he had written to Kenny. Kenny nodded.

'I'm already logged into Gmail, so it shouldn't ask you for the password. But just in case, here it is.' He paused while Hopkins wrote it down and showed it to him again.

'But what I think you're looking for, is in a separate folder, and this is the password.' A third time, they went through the process.

'Is that it?' asked Hopkins. 'Is that everything I need?'

'Should be. You'll be surprised. He always seems so respectable, doesn't he? Hey, don't rush off, I don't get many visitors.'

'If this works out, Kenny, I'll come back with a great big bunch of flowers and a basket of fruit.'

'I'll hold you to that, Inspector.'

As Hopkins reached the door, Kenny called out, 'Hey Inspector? Just had a thought. I bet I could sell my story to the tabloids, after this is all over!'

Kenny, the undefeated, the ever-optimistic, still believing that one day, his big break would come.

'Goodbye, Kenny' said Hopkins, and firmly shut the door.

...

Risking Mair's wrath, Hopkins drove straight from the hospital into the office. The MCIT room was deserted and in darkness. He went and retrieved Kenny's laptop from the evidence storage room, signing it out in the book, and took it back to his desk.

Technology was not Hopkins' strong point, and it took him several attempts to input the random jumble of letters, numerals and symbols that Kenny had given him to gain access to the laptop. He assumed Kenny must have used a random password generator to get such a complex password.

Once in, he navigated fairly quickly to Kenny's Gmail account, which didn't ask him to sign in, as Kenny had left it signed in. He then found the sub-folder entitled 'Fishy Stuff'.

The password here was much simpler. It was 'Cruc14nC4rp.' There was one e-mail saved in the folder.

Hopkins opened and read it in disbelief. Then checked and re-checked what he was reading. At last, he shook his head, picked up his phone and dialled Reilly's number.

'Hello sir – er, Tom?'

Hopkins could hear wild shrieks in the background.

'Hope I'm not disturbing you, John.'

'No, just Mad Half Hour, before bed. Trying to wear them out playing games, so they'll get to sleep.'

'Listen, John. I've found the e-mail on Kenny's laptop, the one closing the lake for the night. It says for essential drains maintenance. The date's within the relevant period. It was clever, it had a time period on it to self-delete after thirty days, but Kenny must have smelled a rat, maybe he suspected Jason even then, because he e-mailed a copy to himself and saved it. I didn't believe who sent it at first, but I've checked and re-checked.'

'And?'

Hopkins could hear the tension in Reilly's voice.

'John – it's Craig Walters.'

Chapter 24

Friendly and unfriendly fire

Thrice is he arm'd that hath his quarrel just,
And he but naked, though lock'd up in steel,
Whose conscience with injustice is corrupted.
Shakespeare, *Henry VI Part 2*

The four team members were in the Murder Room on Monday morning. The Hanger had, as he put it, 'suspended execution' while they saw how the lead played out. All had a copy of the e-mail in front of them, and Hopkins had just finished explaining how he had got hold of it.

'But how did he do it? He was sunning himself in Lanzarote at the time', said Reilly.

Dave Lane spoke up. 'He could've taken his laptop with him.'

'Or,' said Sue Wilshaw, 'he could have used a computer at his hotel, or an internet café, if he wanted to hide his IP address.'

'Funny he used his own e-mail address, though', said Hopkins. 'You'd think he would have taken steps to disguise himself.'

'But then it wouldn't have worked, would it sir?', said Reilly. 'Walters is the only one who can authorise stuff like that, we've heard it from multiple sources. And he did put a timed self-delete on it, which he could do, as an admin. He must have thought no-one would keep a copy.'

'And', said Lane, 'he took care to distance himself from the actual works. He wasn't the one who threatened Lewis, and he made sure he was away when it was done.'

'Yes,' said Reilly, 'he must have worked out Lewis was the weak link in the chain, so he kept himself out of any face to face contact with him, and got Jason to convince Lewis that Walters knew nothing about it.'

Hopkins sighed. 'I think you're all making strong arguments, and I think you're probably right. I just didn't see this coming, that's all. I still can't quite believe it.'

'Shall we get him in, then sir?'

'Yes. See if you can get two of the big lads, from the ones who work the town centre on Friday and Saturday nights, to come with us. Despite his age, I bet Walters can do some damage if he cuts up rough. And check if he's got a firearms licence. I don't fancy having a gun stuck in my face again. We'll go when that's done.'

...

It was nearly eleven when they arrived at Walters' house, a small detached house in a new estate on the edge of Bridgend. The front garden was rigorously well-kept, if austere. They arrived in Hopkins' car, with the two back-up officers in a marked police vehicle.

Reilly knocked at the door. 'What do we do if he's out? Go and try the lake?'

But before Hopkins could answer, the door was opened by Walters himself. He didn't look particularly surprised to see them, just stood there impassively. His eyes flicked to the two well-built uniformed officers standing behind Hopkins and Reilly.

When Reilly informed him he was being arrested for drug trafficking offences and on suspicion of the murder of Jason Reynolds, Walters simply nodded to indicate that he had understood the caution, then held out his wrists for the handcuffs. However, before they started to walk down the short garden path to the waiting cars, he turned his head and called,

'Jess? You know who to call.'

Then he marched down the path with them, head held high, as if he led them and not the other way round. Hopkins and Reilly watched him being seated in the rear of the marked car, one officer's hand on his head, to keep him from striking it on the rim of the door. Then both detectives looked at each other with a strange sense of anti-climax, and walked to Hopkins' car.

...

Several hours' delay ensued. Walters insisted on his right to have a solicitor present. His chosen solicitor, whom presumably he had asked his wife Jess to contact, was based in Plymouth. As that was where the Marines were headquartered, Hopkins guessed that the solicitor specialised in defending them. The solicitor had arrived shortly after 2pm and the two of them were now closeted together.

'Let's give them another half an hour, then get Walters in the interview room', said Hopkins.

'Righto, sir' said Reilly, but before he could convey the message to the custody sergeant, his phone rang.

'That was Custody, sir. He's ready for us now.'
'Right then. Let's go and do battle.'
...

As Reilly read the details into the recorder and asked Walters and his solicitor to confirm, Hopkins studied Walters and his solicitor. Walters did not appear at all concerned to be there. His solicitor, introduced as Charles Bristow, was a slim man in his forties with close-cropped blond hair. He looked combatively back at Hopkins through steel-rimmed spectacles.

Hopkins began.

'When we first spoke to you, Mr Walters, you seemed annoyed that Mr Richards told us about the off-road bikes that were occasionally near the lake at nights. Why was that?'

'I didn't think it was anything to do with us. Not on our land. I didn't want the club getting a bad reputation.'

'Now you may remember, Mr Walters, that at our last interview, which was voluntary, you confirmed that you were solely responsible for carrying out works at the lake.'

'That's correct.'

'And that you had previously engaged Mr James Lewis, the farmer on whose land the lake is situated, to install a septic tank by the shipping container on site, about two years ago?'

'Correct.'

'We have discovered a second septic tank, installed about a hundred yards further along the left bank of the lake, in amongst some bushes, up against the fence. Do you know where I'm talking about?'

'Yes, I know the location.'

He did not sound particularly surprised, but Hopkins surmised that it could be down to his interrogation training.

'Did you also know what was found in the second septic tank?'

'No.'

'Then let me enlighten you. A large quantity of cocaine, ketamine and pills, including MDMA and Ecstasy.'

'I don't know anything about that.'

'Really? You accept you're the only person authorised to carry out or commission works at the lake?'

'Yes. But I didn't authorise that.'

'You're sure?'

'Positive.'

Having got him to repeat the denial, Hopkins nodded to Reilly, who sprang the trap.

'That's strange, Mr Walters, because we have here an e-mail from you, to all members, informing them that the lake would be closed for fishing from 18:00 on the night of Sunday 11th February 2024 until 08:00 the following day, to allow the farmer, Mr Lewis to carry out drainage maintenance work using machinery.' Reilly passed over a copy. 'Is that your e-mail address?'

Walters looked at it, then passed it to his solicitor.

After a few moments, he responded.

'It is my e-mail address. But I didn't send it.'

'You seem very sure about that.'

'I was on holiday in Lanzarote, with my wife. I didn't take my laptop with me.'

'You could have used another computer, in your hotel or an internet café, say. All you'd need would be your login details.'

'I could. But I didn't.'

'How did this e-mail go out from your e-mail address?'

'I don't know. Someone must have hacked my e-mail.'

'That sounds very convenient. Did you notice any other unusual activity, other e-mails being sent in your name, for instance?'

'No.'

'And you didn't notice that this e-mail had gone out in your absence?'

'No, but I wouldn't. It wasn't addressed to me, was it?'

'You didn't see it in your Sent Items box?'

'No, but I don't often look in there, and if someone hacked my e-mails, they could have deleted the copy from my account.'

'We think you sent this, then put an automatic thirty-day self-delete on it to cover your tracks.'

Bristow, the solicitor, intervened.

'My client has already confirmed several times that he didn't send the e-mail. He doesn't need to keep answering variations of the same question.'

Walters grunted, 'I can answer them all day, Chas. The answer'll still be no.'

Bristow asked, 'Have you investigated whether my client's e-mail has been hacked?'

The two detectives looked for a second nonplussed, then Hopkins said,

'No, because until now, that possibility was never raised.'

'Well, my client will be happy to turn over all his devices to your IT team.' He looked across to Walters to confirm, who nodded. 'And until they report their findings, I do not think this line of questioning can usefully be continued.'

'Was your e-mail account with the club password-protected?' asked Hopkins.

'No, but it's a members-only fishing club, not a gambling syndicate. Most of the guys are over sixty and barely know how to turn on a computer, never mind hack one.'

'Well, let's go to the night in question, Sunday 16th February. You say you were at home all night, with your wife.'

'I was.'

'We have information that someone entered through the gate to the lake, at about 10.30pm that night.'

'It wasn't me.'

'But it would be easy for you to drive through the back roads, park your car in the village, then walk through the fields to the gate, thus avoiding the CCTV?'

'I could, but I didn't.'

'And no one else, other than your wife, can confirm your alibi?'

'No.'

Hopkins pulled out a photograph of Reynolds' upper body, lying on a mortuary slab. Walters looked at it without flinching.

'You will notice,' said Hopkins, 'That the fatal wound is precisely between the fourth and fifth rib on the left hand side, penetrating straight to the heart.'

'Yes.'

'And you confirmed to me at our last interview that, while in the Marines, you had training on how to kill using a knife?'

'I did. But we wouldn't have done it that way.'

'Could you explain?'

'You can't see where a man's ribs are when he's wearing clothing. If you try to stab him in the chest, there's a chance the blow will get blocked or turned by a rib. Instead, you aim for below the ribs, angling the blade upwards. Or if you're behind him, you go for the neck.'

Walters pointed to the photo. 'Whoever did that,' he said, 'wasn't an expert. He got lucky.'

'I would comment at this point,' said Bristow, 'that my client will not be answering any questions about the historic allegations against him by the MOD, which he totally denies. Those matters have no relevance to this case, and are subject to ongoing investigations. It was improper of you to raise them in his first interview. If he is asked about them, he will answer 'No comment' to any such questions.'

...

The interview terminated shortly after that. As Walters was being led back to the cells, Bristow caught up with Hopkins and Reilly.

'It's clear that you haven't got even a *prima facie* case against my client. If he's not released today, then I will file claims for wrongful arrest and false imprisonment first thing tomorrow, with an urgent application for immediate release. I'm personally sick of ex-members of the Forces, who've served our country, being arrested based on character profiling and type-casting. I will make sure it gets all the publicity I can. Good day, gentlemen.'

He pushed past them and walked quickly down the corridor towards the front desk and the exit.

'Well, that was a fiasco', said Hopkins to Reilly. Reilly nodded glumly. 'We'd better go and tell Jeffries. He needs to know about any threats of legal action.'

Later, in Jeffries' office, after he had listened to their account of what had gone on in the interview room, he leaned forward, his hands on his desk.

'I can't recommend extending custody in the circumstances. You've no new leads, no new evidence that might come in in the next few hours?'

They shook their heads.

'Then we're going to have to release him. And get a driver to take him home. We want to try and keep on his good side, in case he decides to make a complaint.'

He went on.

'I don't blame you. That e-mail did look like a smoking gun, and anyone less tough might have folded in the interview room. We still can't be sure he isn't your man – he looks like the best candidate to me. But we have to let him go, for now.'

'And what about the investigation, sir?' asked Hopkins.

'Well, unless you have any new lines of enquiry, I'm going to have to transfer Lane and Wilshaw onto other cases. I'm sorry, but we're running a huge backlog and I can't justify it. You two carry on with it, alongside the rest of your cases of course, but as of today, it's no longer our main priority.'

...

'Fancy a drink, sir?' asked Reilly, as they left the office, heading for the car park. 'Just the one?'

'No, thanks, John. I'm not in the mood. I'm all in. See you tomorrow.'

'See you tomorrow, sir. Onwards and upwards, eh?'

Hopkins nodded and climbed into his car. He watched Reilly's long-snouted dark blue Capri slide, like some predatory animal, under the raising barrier and turn left out of the gate. Then, with a sigh, he switched on his own engine and drove home in the gathering darkness.

Chapter 25

Becalmed

Sailors on a becalmed sea, we sense the stirring of a breeze.
Carl Sagan, *Pale Blue Dot: A Vision of the Human Future in Space*

The following day, Tuesday, Hopkins had his follow-up appointment with the consultant, Dr Bradley. This time, instead of the smart private hospital, the appointment was in the consultant's regular NHS haematology clinic at the hospital.

Hopkins first needed to have blood samples taken, so he took a numbered, arrowhead-shaped ticket from the sort of dispenser he remembered being in use at the deli counter at the local supermarket, when he was a child. Then he joined all the others waiting to have bloods taken, sitting outside the phlebotomy room.

Bloods taken, Hopkins went to get a coffee, then returned to the clinic waiting area. It seemed quite crowded and he worried about how long it would take. Then, after a while, he worked out that there were three doctors working in the clinic, and patients were called to one or other of them. The patients seemed to be a wide cross-section of ages – he had imagined they would be mostly his age or older.

The time for his appointment came and went, without him being called. He had been warned by Dr Bradley's receptionist that delays were not unusual, but still he grew more and more restless, the more time passed. He repeatedly checked his e-mails, but nothing of any interest appeared, just more admin and minor details on other cases.

Eventually, he heard his name being called and stood up awkwardly, balancing coat, laptop bag, phone and empty coffee-cup. He saw a pedal bin to one side and levered the lid up to toss his cup in. The lid fell with a loud clang behind him, as he hastened to where he had heard the voice call his name, which appeared to be around a corner off the main waiting room.

He rounded the corner and saw an open door, which he assumed was where he was meant to go. He entered and found Bradley, seated at a much smaller and very utilitarian desk, peering at a computer screen.

'Hello, how are you? Come in and close the door.' Bradley indicated a couple of plastic chairs. 'Sit down.'

Bradley brought up Hopkins' bone marrow and blood results.

'Well, as I thought, it's definitely myelofibrosis. The bone marrow sample was classically fibrotic.'

Hopkins remembered, after the surprisingly painful procedure, Bradley showing him the sample he had taken. It had looked like a dried-up, greyish white twig, sitting at the bottom of the vial, with a couple of small tendrils of blood curling up into the sterile solution.

'However, your bloods are holding up and seem to be stable. At least, based on the evidence of the last few weeks. So it doesn't seem to be progressing much, at this stage. I'll give you a note for the receptionist to book you in for regular six-weekly monitoring.'

Hopkins nodded.

'And what about the medication you mentioned?' He struggled to remember the name.

'Ruxolitinib? Yes, now that myelofibrosis is confirmed, that's the next step. As I said, I'll put you on a high dose to begin with, twenty milligrammes twice a day. Then we'll review it at our next meeting. It is normal for your haemoglobin levels to fall in the first few weeks, so if you feel more than usually fatigued, I want you to phone and come in straight away. You may need a transfusion to tide you over. Any questions?'

'Will this affect my ability to work?'

'Not usually. But, as I say, if you feel any unusual levels of tiredness, dizziness, etc., ring the clinic and book an appointment as soon as possible. Anything else?'

Hopkins had had several more questions, but his mind had gone blank and he couldn't remember them.

'Right then. See you in six weeks if all goes well.'

...

Hopkins went into the kitchen when he arrived at HQ. Nobody seemed to be watching so, with some misgivings, he took out the box of pills from his briefcase and quickly swilled one down.

Then, he made himself a coffee and went to his desk. He opened his e-mails and saw a long list of unopened mail. He started working through it. There seemed to be an increase in street crime, particularly violent robbery, with the assailants riding scooters or e-bikes – an unwelcome import from London.

In the latest robbery, the victim, an elderly woman, had bravely tried to hold onto her handbag, been knocked to the floor and sustained serious, potentially life-threatening injuries. The level of violence, together with the apparent degree of organisation, meant this was a matter for MCIT, rather than CID. The Hanger would want results on this quickly – it had been reported widely in the local papers and people were worried.

Hopkins started trying to read into the file, but try as he might, his mind kept slipping back to the Reynolds case. He realised now that he had been carried along too easily by the appearance of a big break. He had had his doubts, hadn't he? But he had allowed his colleagues' optimism to over-ride them. Self-doubt assailed him once more. Perhaps it was time to pack it in. He would be eligible for early retirement, particularly if he cited medical grounds.

He forced himself to look back at his e-mails. One was from Goodall, in the Drugs Team. His covering e-mail was short,

'Thought you might like to see this. Not sure if it takes you any further, but could be relevant.'

Attached was an extract from the forensic accountants' preliminary report into the accounts of Shadows. It appeared that Sandra was keeping her word, and had taken them through how the cash receipts from the drugs transactions had been disguised in the bar takings. They were impressed at her ingenuity. Apparently, they could have worked it out eventually, but Sandra's explanation had cut the time it would have taken significantly.

However, that was not the point that Goodall wanted to highlight. A few paragraphs on, underlined in black ink, was the fact that Shadows' owners, as tenants, were paying more than twice the going market rent for a property of that size and nature. This was due to a 'ratchet clause' in the lease, by which the rent initially started low, but once the club was operational, the rent increased to a full market rent, plus a proportionate share of the profits made. As the accountants drily concluded,

'Such clauses were once common in London commercial properties but are rarely, if ever, found elsewhere and are now less common even in London, due to their onerous nature. We recommend further investigation into this, as a possible money-laundering mechanism.'

Hopkins picked up his phone and dialled Sandra, on her main number. She picked up, although she sounded less than pleased to hear from him.

'Inspector? What can I do for you?', she asked warily.

'It's about your rental payment on the club. The accountants have picked up how it started low, and then increased in line with profits, to the point where it was more than twice the going rate.'

'So? We thought the club was going to be a winner, and it meant we didn't have to find the capital up front for the lease, so we could spend more on the renovations. I won't say that it wasn't starting to sting, though. We were hoping to renegotiate with the landlord.'

'Sandra – was the reason for this ratchet clause that your landlord knew about the drugs side of the business, and wanted his cut?'

There was a silence.

'I can't say.'

'Who is your landlord?'

'I'm not going to tell you that either.'

'I can find out from the Land Registry.'

'Do that, then.'

'Come on, Sandra. Remember you've got an agreement to co-operate with us.'

'That only covers the business in Shadows. I didn't sign up to be your grass forever.'

'Are you frightened of him?'

'Not so much him. More who he works for. And they're still on the outside.'

...

Hopkins re-read the extract from the forensic accountants' report. Unfortunately, the page he had been given did not reveal the name of the landlord, although he guessed it was probably a company. Nonetheless, companies had directors, who could be traced through Companies House. He e-mailed Goodall to request the name.

He walked over to Reilly's desk.

'Fancy going for a coffee? I want to get out of here for a bit.'

They walked across the car park to the vast, monolithic main building, which had once been an armaments factory. In the canteen, there was the usual cheery background noise of uniforms on a break. A few nodded to the two detectives as they entered. Reilly got the coffees while Hopkins found a corner table.

'I just wanted a quick word, John', Hopkins began.

'That sounds ominous. What have I done?'

Hopkins laughed. 'It's not you. First of all, I wanted to say sorry for keeping you in the dark. I think I was scared – didn't want to admit it to myself.'

'You don't need to apologise. It's OK, I get it.'

'Thanks. Well, I wanted to ask you a favour.'

'Anything.'

'Wait till you hear what it is first. Look, I've just started on this drug. It's quite a high dosage to begin with and it may cause anaemia, fatigue, that sort of thing. I want you to promise that, if you think I'm not getting it right, or my judgement's off, you'll tell me?'

'Sure, but that's not going to ...'

'It might, John. And I'd rather know, as I might not be able to admit it to myself.'

Hopkins took a sip of his coffee and grimaced.

'God, it doesn't get any better in here, does it?'

'You wanted to come here, sir. Should I be reporting that to you as a lapse of judgement?'

They both grinned, relaxing.

'Any joy on Walters' computer yet?' asked Hopkins. Walters had handed over his laptop upon being dropped back at his house, apparently keen for the hacking theory put forward by his lawyer to be investigated.

'Not yet, the tech guys say they'll be a couple of days on it. They've got a bit of a backlog, and the Hanger's bumped us down the priority list.'

'Well, we may have another lead.' Hopkins told Reilly about the high rent on Shadows.

Reilly thought for a minute.

'Sounds like it might help from the drugs side of things. But I can't see where it gets us.'

'Neither can I, at the moment. But I've got a feeling about it. Can't hurt to run it down.'

'No, I guess not. But he might just be a tough landlord. Just because he charges a high rent doesn't necessarily mean he knew.'

'Although if he didn't know, presumably Sandra would have been clever enough to hide the profits from the club's non-legitimate business, so he wouldn't have known how much she was making.'

'She might, but then again, she was using the club's profits to hide the drug profits, so she'd have to disclose them somewhere, otherwise it wouldn't look like clean money.'

Hopkins guessed that Reilly was toning down his reaction, given that the team's earlier conviction that they had cracked the case had led to the fiasco of Walters' interview.

'So those are the two lines of enquiry open to us now. The potential hacking angle and tracking down the landlord.'

'And don't forget the Community Liaison Officer. We're still waiting on any reports from residents of suspicious vehicles, nuisance parking, that kind of thing. I'll give them a nudge.'

'Thanks, John.'

As they walked back in the Spring sunshine, Reilly asked, 'Think we'll ever crack this one, sir? All the leads seem to peter out and we haven't really got any live suspects any more.'

'I don't know. On the face of it, it should be easy. A closed membership club, with the suspect pool limited to those who had keys. But whoever did it, has been very good at covering their tracks. And that makes me even more determined to get the bugger.'

Chapter 26

Blood and rebirth

To get back up to the shining world from there
My guide and I went into that hidden tunnel,
And following its path, we took no care
To rest, but climbed: he first, then I - so far,
through a round aperture I saw appear
Some of the beautiful things that Heaven bears,
Where we came forth, and once more saw the
stars.

Dante Alighieri, *Inferno*

The next day, Hopkins had just got into the office when Reilly came over to his desk. He was clearly excited about something.

'PCSO Jones, the Community Liaison Officer for Rhyd yr Afon, wants to see us. I think you'll be interested in what she has to say.'

'Do you know what it's about?'

'She gave me the gist, sir, but I think it's best you hear it from the horse's mouth.'

'OK, let's have a chat in the Murder Room.'

They had managed to retain the room, despite requests from other teams.

A few minutes later, Reilly showed PCSO Jones into the room. She was a fresh-faced, keen-looking young woman and her eyes swept the room eagerly, clearly excited to be in a real Murder Room.

Introductions were made and she took a seat. She was carrying a black, police-issue holdall.

'Where do you want me to begin?'

'Tell Inspector Hopkins what you told me on the phone. Say it in exactly the order it happened and don't leave out any details. And don't jump ahead.' He winked at Hopkins. Reilly was really enjoying this, which was a good sign. Hopkins' pulse quickened.

'Yes sir. Well, I got your request for information on any suspicious vehicles, and I asked about, but nothing of any particular interest. Then I remembered Charlie Thomas, he's a retired civil servant who's chair of the Neighbourhood Watch. He's been banging on for ages about people parking in his road. It's a private road, not adopted, and people park there because it's close to the path across the fields, dog walkers and so on. He's been going on about it for ages, keeps a list of registrations, but there's not much we or the council can do about it, as it's private land. I've told him that we could only act if they were parked dangerously, like blocking access to emergency vehicles and so on.'

'So I dropped round his place, but he was in hospital for a couple of days. He came out yesterday and I went to see him in the evening. He was still keeping his list, and he said he'd particularly noticed these two – I've highlighted them – because they were parked up late at night. He saw them when he went out to let his dog do its business.'

She handed over a list, handwritten in block capitals, with dates and times. She had highlighted the two vehicles that had been parked late at night, in yellow marker pen.

'That's great work, well done!' said Hopkins.

'There's even better to come, sir', said Reilly, a broad grin breaking out now.

'Well, I thought about something else Charlie's always banging on about. The litter bins around the village only get emptied by the council every few weeks, because the village is quite a way out and only accessible along narrow lanes. It's not really our business, but I always let him have his say, keep him on side, and then I passed his query on to the council. Anyway, I wondered, might something that was dropped in there a few weeks ago, still be in there? So I went back first thing this morning, to have a look. There's two bins nearby. One near the end of Charlie's road and another near the entrance to the path over the fields, for dog poo. I left that one till last.'

'Understandable' said Hopkins.

'So I started going through the first one. Put the blue gloves on and did it properly, laid it all out on a plastic sheet, like they taught us. Got some funny looks from people, I can tell you. Anyway, I got nearly to the bottom, and then I found this.'

She reached into the holdall and pulled out a clear plastic evidence bag. Inside was a fish-filleting knife, with a blue handle bearing a red end cap, in a blue plastic sheath.

Hopkins stared at it, open-mouthed.

'Think it's our murder weapon, sir?' asked Reilly.

'It seems likely', said Hopkins, finding his voice after a few seconds. 'Why else would someone throw away a knife matching the murder weapon so near to the scene?'

'So he is human after all, sir. He made a mistake. And thanks to Officer Jones, here, we found it.'

Hopkins turned to Jones, beaming. 'That's brilliant work, officer. If I could promote you right now to full constable, I would. And I'm very glad you didn't have to look in the second bin.'

'So am I, sir. And I am applying to become a full constable.'

'Well, we'll both certainly put in a good word, a very good word, for you. That's absolutely fantastic.'

Jones positively glowed.

Reilly showed her out and then came back.

'Just goes to show the value of local knowledge, and good old-fashioned police work, doesn't it sir?'

'It certainly does. Let's get this fingerprinted, first', Hopkins said. 'Maybe he made more than one mistake. Then, let's get it over to Dr Madhvani asap. See if she can find any blood or other residue on it.'

'Let's hope he was in a panic, and didn't wipe it, or didn't do a good enough job.'

'Absolutely. I think I'll give Dr Madhvani a call now, so she can set things up.'

'Oh! I'd better leave you two in private then, sir.'

'John!' Hopkins protested, but Reilly was already out of the door, still grinning like a Cheshire, or at least a Lancashire, cat.

Hopkins dialled her number.

'Hello, Inspector. To what do I owe the honour?' As always, she sounded slightly amused.

'Hello, Doctor. I think we may have found the murder weapon.'

'That does sound exciting. Do you want me to have a look at it?'

'Yes, I'm just getting it fingerprinted, then I'll get it driven over.'

'Any visible bloodstains?'

'No, but it was still in its sheath. We haven't taken it out yet.'

'Where was it found? In the water?'

'No, thank goodness. This type of knife is designed to float, so the killer would have known throwing it in the water wouldn't have worked. It was found in a bin, by a PCSO using her initiative and a pair of nitrile gloves.'

'Well done, her! One for the sisterhood. The fact it was in a bin is mainly good. It's protected from the elements and it's too early in the year for flies to have consumed any blood. But there's still a risk of contamination. Although that won't matter if we can get DNA from any residues.'

'That sounds great. Call me as soon as you know anything.'

'I will.'

She rang off.

Hopkins walked back to the MCIT room.

'The good doctor keeping well, sir?'

'I'm in a good mood, John, but don't presume it will last. I assume you are diligently working to identify the owners of those vehicles on the list?'

'Yes, sir.'

'Could you also get in touch with Companies House in Cardiff and ask for a full search on – ' he clicked on his e-mails and opened the latest one from Goodall. 'Shadows (Pty.) Limited. That's the name of the landlord on the lease of the club. Make sure they do the full search, the one that shows all linked companies, subsidiaries, parents, etc. Tell them it's urgent.'

'You still think that's relevant, sir? Now we've got the knife?'

'I think even more so. We've got to chase down all the angles, given the mistake I made in running with just one piece of evidence on Walters. I want to make sure we've got everything we possibly can.'

Hopkins thought a minute. 'Hang on a few minutes before you speak to Companies House, John.'

'What are you thinking, sir?'

'That the ratchet clause on Shadows sounded very similar to the arrangement Jason had for his shop. I'm just going to log into our account with the Land Registry. You can get details of who owns pretty much any bit of registered land.'

He concentrated for a few minutes, putting in address and postcode details.

'Here it is. Ewenny Mills (Pty.) Limited. Ask them to include that in the search as well.'

'Right, sir.'

'Any fingerprints on the knife?'

Reilly grimaced. 'No, out of luck on that score. They managed to lift one partial, smeary print from the end of the sheath, like someone accidentally touched it while wiping the rest. But they doubted it would be enough to give a complete match.'

'And how are the tech guys getting on with Walters' laptop?'

'I got onto them this morning after PCSO Jones phoned. Said we'd found the murder weapon and it was now priority. So they've bumped us up the list and said it should be early on tomorrow.'

'You managed to speak to Jeffries?'

'No sir. But I didn't tell them *whose* priority it was.'

'Don't you Catholics have something about sins of omission as well as commission?'

'Thank you for your concern for my immortal soul, sir. I'll remember to mention it to the priest when I see him next.'

...

After the initial excitement of the morning, they seemed to hit a hiatus. Hopkins tried to concentrate on some routine work, but the anticipation of where the various leads might go kept distracting him. Also, one theory was starting to gain ground in his mind. It seemed far-fetched at first, but the more he thought about it...

Reilly identified the owners of the cars parked late at night. On two occasions, it was Kenny Stagg's old Fiesta.

'That establishes Charlie's credibility', said Reilly. 'We knew Stagg was there round about that time, when he was trying to get Jason on camera, so the info checks out. But the one on the night of 16th February, the black BMW, is registered to a leasing company. I've put in a request to them for the name of whoever they leased it to.'

'Probably another company' said Hopkins. 'That sort of car's probably a company car, if it's being leased. But at least we should be able to get to the driver through them.'

About 3pm, Madhvani rang. Hopkins asked if he could put her on speakerphone, then hurried through to the Murder Room with Reilly.

'Can you hear us?' Hopkins checked.

'Perfectly, thank you. Good afternoon, sergeant.'

'Hello, doctor', Reilly answered stiffly.

'Well, I've completed my examination of the knife and the sheath. Steel and plastic are not very good at retaining blood, and it looks as if someone has wiped the knife.'

Hopkins looked at Reilly, disappointed. 'That's a shame. We thought we had a breakthrough.'

'I hadn't finished. I was talking about the knife. Inside the sheath, on the other hand, there was a substantial amount of blood.'

'So the killer put it back before he thought of wiping it?'

'It seems that way. There was evidence of wiping inside the sheath, as if someone had pushed a cloth or a tissue down inside. But they couldn't get all the way to the bottom. There was quite a lot of blood pooled there. Well, a lot in forensic terms – a couple of millilitres. Dried, of course.'

'Can you get anything from that?'

'Yes, indeed. DNA can be extracted from bloodstains for several months after the blood has dried. And up to fifteen years if it is stored correctly.'

'And?'

'The blood is definitely that of Jason Reynolds.'

'Yes!' shouted Reilly, punching the air.

'I thought that might make you gentlemen happy.'

'You have no idea,' said Hopkins. 'Anything else?'

'Microscopy indicated the presence of some fibres trapped in the crack where the blade joins the hilt, and also inside the sheath. I have managed to extract them and send them off to the lab for analysis. Now, it would be unlikely for the fibres to have come from the victim's jacket. It was waterproof, and fibres will not usually detach, due to the coating. However, if the knife was one owned and used by the killer, and not bought specially for the job, it may have collected fibres from his clothes, for instance if he wore it on a belt and moved his hand up and down his clothes when he took it out or put it back.'

'And how long will that take?'

'I asked them to make it as quick as possible. Hopefully tomorrow.'

'Well, that's more than we hoped for, Doctor. Many, many thanks. You've really done an excellent job.'

'As Mark Twain said, I can live for a month on a good compliment.'

Hopkins ended the call.

'Still not keen on our new pathologist?', he asked Reilly.

'You've got to admit, sir, she does think she's the cat's whiskers. But she is definitely starting to grow on me.'

...

Hopkins and Reilly agreed to get together the next day, once all the evidence they had requested was in. 'It might seem a bit theatrical, but I'd like us to examine everything together, at the same time. That way, we'll hopefully avoid pre-judging it and rushing to confirm a particular theory. We can also go and see Jeffries right after, when we've got a full story.'

'You think there'll be enough for an arrest warrant, sir?'

'I think so.'

'Any idea who?'

'Maybe. I'm not being cagey or holding out on you, John. I want you to come at it completely fresh and not spend the night building up a case to support some theory I've told you. I don't entirely trust myself on this, for health reasons and because of my slips last week, so I need you to be at your best and most critical. The best support you can give me, John, is to come at it from a completely neutral perspective, not to back me up.'

'Absolutely, sir. You've no need to worry about your judgement. But I'll act like the proverbial Devil's advocate.'

'Just independent will do, John. I think the Hanger will do the Devil's advocate bit, if I'm right.'

...

It was still only mid-afternoon. Hopkins decided not to go home and try to work through admin stuff remotely. Instead, he drove down to Ogmore again and parked at the bluffs overlooking the estuary.

The tide was on the way in, today, so he decided to walk up the river. The valley gradually narrowed and became greener, less sandy. The tide-meadow he crossed was dotted with shifting tide-pools, so there were several different paths to choose from, depending on the level of the tide. The river was beautifully clear, here, due to the filtering of the fine sand and the reeds higher up, and Hopkins saw several small flatfish skittering out of his shadow, kicking up puffs of sand as they went.

As he went higher up the valley, the trees on the opposite bank grew denser. He became aware of a great, grey heron, standing in the shallows under the trees, by the far bank. The Fisher King, he thought, recalling the Celtic legends of the heron being able to move between the earthly and spirit worlds, or embodying the spirit of a dead king, one day to return.

The bird saw him watching it and tensed, bending its legs and curling in its long neck, preparatory to leaping into flight. Then, deciding he was no threat, it slowly unbent its long appendages, and returned to the important business of fishing.

Fishing, ah yes, fishing. It all seemed to come back to that. Or at least to be linked by it.

Hopkins walked on. He was no longer consciously thinking of the case, just letting his mind wander where it would, unwinding, preparing. Like a soldier before battle, he thought. Or maybe a prisoner before execution. Which would it turn out to be?

He was now opposite the sand dunes at Merthyr Mawr, and could just see the top of the highest, the Big Dipper, where the Welsh rugby team sometimes trained. He remembered, when he and Mair were young, they had often walked over the dunes and picnicked on one of the tops, looking out over the valley and the sea.

He thought he would suggest coming here for their next weekend walk. She would call him a sentimental old fool and ask if the illness had got into his brains, and he smiled at the thought. He breathed deeply, luxuriating in the feeling of being alive, in this beautiful valley, with all his memories.

He turned and walked purposefully, no longer wandering, back along the river to the car park. He bought a coffee and then, on a whim, an ice cream, eating it looking out over the sea.

This afternoon it was clear, right across to the bluish hills of Somerset, no ships in sight. Over there, in those dreaming hills, had been King Arthur's ancient kingdom of Dumnonia. There also Aelfred, whom English called the Great, had hidden in the marshes, fugitive from the Danes, and rebuilt his nation from nearly nothing, following catastrophic defeat. So many stories, truths and half truths, unknowns and lies, weaving together like smoke curling from a storytelling fire of the ancients, or tendrils of blood rising in a laboratory vial of sterile fluid.

But he knew now that the tendrils could be unravelled.

He was prepared.

And what was more, he was alive again.

Chapter 27

ABC

Assume nothing; Believe nobody; Challenge everything! There is a need to be professionally curious.

College of Policing, *Practice guidance: Dealing with sudden unexpected death.*

Both Reilly and Hopkins got in early the next morning, Thursday 6th March. Hopkins was dropped off by Mair, as she had to take the Volvo in for its MOT. Hopkins hoped that the car had not been unduly distressed by Reilly's wild drive back from Henley, as it was totally unused to such treatment.

Both detectives were sitting in the Murder Room by 8am, steaming mugs in front of them. Each also had a stack of printed sheets.

'It's like waiting to open your presents on Christmas morning, isn't it?' said Reilly, barely containing his excitement.

'Let's keep it calm, John. We need to do this properly.'

'How shall we tackle it, then? Exchange each other's stuff?'

'No, I want to go through each piece together. I want the evidence to lead to the conclusion, not the other way round. Don't forget, we're going to have to lay all this out to the Hanger if we want him to approve a warrant.'

'Which bit first?'

'Let's start with the tech report into Walters' computer. Came into my e-mail overnight. Here's a copy. It's fairly short.'

He handed over a copy, and Reilly started to read. When he lifted his eyes, Hopkins continued.

'So what this shows, and my understanding of IT isn't the best, so feel free to correct me, is that Walters' laptop was not hacked, at least in the strict sense. There was no evidence of phishing, or malware, or anything like that. However, what can happen in a simple group system like this, if members haven't password-protected their accounts, is that the administrator can log in to any member's e-mail and send e-mails in their name. It would appear as if the member had sent it.'

'Now, according to the activity log, which Walters has helpfully not wiped, an administrator accessed his inbox shortly before the time and date the e-mail about closing the lake was sent, and sent an e-mail corresponding to the time and date of the copy of the one we have seen from Kenny. Of course, all copies of the e-mail have gone from Walters' computer.'

Reilly broke in, 'And the only other administrator was – '

'Bryn Richards.'

'But that doesn't prove it was him, though, does it sir?'

Hopkins nodded approvingly. 'You've seen the flaw.'

'If both he and Walters run a cut-throat defence, and each blames the other, we can't prove who did it.'

'Exactly, John. All we can prove is that *an* administrator logged into Walters' e-mail. It could have been Richards, or it could have been Walters covering his tracks, and logging in as an admin, rather than himself.'

'I.P. address sir? Does it show whose computer it came from?'

'Again, no luck. We know it couldn't have been Walters' laptop, because he left it at home. But it came via a VPN, to disguise the I.P. address – so either Walters could have done it from a computer in Lanzarote, or Richards used a VPN to disguise his home or business computer's I.P. address.'

'What shall we look at next, then sir?'

'I think the knife, or more precisely the sheath. This report came in early this morning, so Dr Madhvani did a good job of pushing the lab. The analysis of the fibres she found, show that they were wool, in three colours, not new but they can't pinpoint the age. From the dye and so on, they're saying it's probably a good quality tweed, maybe Harris.'

'And who do we know has a coat like that?'

'Exactly, John. But Walters may have one too. Without the garment to match it to, we can't say.'

'These presents are turning out to be pretty damp squibs so far, sir.'

'But they're important. We're building the foundations. You'll see in a short while, if the Companies House reports say what I hope.'

'Report, sir.'

'What?'

'This also came in overnight, sir. Just after I left, so someone worked late for us. But it's one report, not two. I haven't had time to read it.'

Reilly started flicking through the thick pile of papers.

'It looks like the reason is, sir, both the companies you asked for belong to the same group. So there's only one corporate structure.'

'OK, this is going to take some time to read through. Let's get another coffee.'

They stepped out of the room and walked through to the kitchen. 'You know', began Reilly, 'my money's on – '

'Wait, John. Let's not play Cluedo. Evidence before theories, OK?'

'OK. But I'm going to ask that new lad, Morgan, to run over to the canteen and get us bacon sandwiches. I'm starving. What do you say?'

Hopkins paused, thinking what Mair would say. But then with a small thrill of guilty pleasure, he said,

'Go on then. Here's the cash.'

As they walked back, Reilly asked, 'You don't have to tell me, sir, but you've got an idea, haven't you? I know you've been keeping something under your hat these last couple of days.'

'It's been growing on me, John. At first I didn't want to believe it. I didn't mean any disrespect to you, but given how our last rush to judgment ended with Walters, and our desperation for a breakthrough, I wanted to test the evidence with you first.'

They got back to the Murder Room and sat down with their coffees. Within a few minutes, Morgan arrived with the bacon sandwiches, having obviously

255

sprinted across the car park to impress his superiors. Hopkins and Reilly nodded their thanks, then dived into the sandwiches and the report, although one with greater fervour than the other.

Reilly took out a pen and started scribbling names and initials in boxes and linking them with arrows. Over the course of an hour, Hopkins noticed that the boxes were forming a pyramid, each tier shorter than the last. He himself was struggling with the corporate language and interlocking structures of nominees, different voting classes, companies with similar names but perhaps a different set of numbers or letters after the names, and so on. None of the directors' names appeared to have any connection with the case. After about an hour and a half, in desperation, he turned to the last page.

And there it was.

Reilly got there about the same time, looking across to Hopkins.

'Want me to summarise this one, sir?'

Hopkins nodded.

'Well, there's a separate company for every business lease. They seem to cover a large number of all the pubs and clubs in town and round about. I guess they've done it that way, so if one goes bust, the liability stops there and doesn't spread up the chain to the other companies. Then we have land holding companies, based on regions across Wales, which own or have options to purchase land for development. Above them, we have development companies, formed to deal with construction projects that are live or in planning. Again, to compartmentalise the risk. Each tier owns the ones below, through nominees, or owning a majority of the shares, or a 'golden share' – i.e. one that gives you power over all the other shares, sort of like the One Ring in Lord of the Rings.'

'For once, I get your reference, John', said Hopkins, 'but how do you know all this?'

'Corporate law was one of the options in my law and criminology course at Uni, sir. Bit rusty now, but I remember the basics.'

He continued, 'So, at last we get to the top co., Consolidated Land and Development (South Wales)(Holdings) Limited. That what you get too, sir?'

'Yes, but I'm afraid I cheated. I didn't understand any of it and just jumped straight to the end. You explained how it all links together much better. What is the purpose of all these tiers?'

'Like I said, sir, each one's limited liability. That means the buck stops with them if they go bust. Also they're often used for tax avoidance, legitimately, although I'm not an expert on how that works.'

'But if you were criminally-minded, it's also a good way to launder money, particularly where property's concerned. Money flows can go back and forth, expenses and purchases can be inflated a little bit, land could move from one to another but with some adjustments to prices to cover various costs, which then flows back again. And there's been quite a few cases of fraud and money laundering where mortgages are involved. It would take a whole squad of accountants weeks to work out where all the money's going and how much of it is legit. And you wouldn't be likely to start such a complicated and expensive investigation, unless you had pretty good evidence to base it on, to start with. So to the casual eye, it would all look clean and above-board.'

Hopkins spoke. 'And who is the person who is the Chairman and CEO of the top company?'

Reilly looked again, and his mouth fell open.

'The cunning sod. Hiding in plain sight like Gus Fring, all this time.'

'Gus who? Never mind, it's not important now.'

Hopkins turned over his final piece of paper.

'And that is also the person to whom the black BMW, parked at Rhyd yr Afon on the night of the murder, is leased.'

'Bloody hell.'

Chapter 28

A robe pulled aside

Through tattered clothes small vices do appear.
Robes and furred gowns hide all.
Shakespeare, *Measure for Measure*

Hopkins and Reilly walked into Jeffries' office, in response to his booming 'Come in!' at about 11.30am. He seemed surprised to see them. Then he said, 'Well, both of you gentlemen coming to see me at once can only mean one thing. Am I right?'

Hopkins said, without preamble, 'We want a warrant for the arrest of Bryn Richards, for the murder of Jason Reynolds. Search warrants too.'

He handed over the typed request forms.

'Certainly,' said the Hanger, deadpan. 'And how about one for the Lord Lieutenant of the County and the Moderator of the Free Church in Wales, while you're at it?'

'Sir, we're dead sure on this one', said Reilly.

'I seem to remember you were when I authorised the warrant to arrest Mr Walters, sergeant.'

He looked at the request forms.

'And you want all his computers and other devices, access to his car, plus – .' He paused. 'His tweed jacket and any other tweed garments he may have. Are you two gentlemen off to the County Show?'

259

Hopkins said, 'I know this all comes as a bit of a shock, sir. We didn't expect it either. But all the evidence leads us to him.'

Jeffries sighed, heavily.

'OK, take me through it. But this, as they say, had better be good.'

Hopkins began, meticulously laying out a summary of the evidence they had reviewed that morning. Almost immediately, Jeffries was asking questions, probing shrewdly, trying to poke holes. He shifted tack and came at it from a different perspective and asked left-field questions, posing alternative theories – 'What if – ?'

After an hour of grilling, Reilly was starting to sound truculent and defensive in his replies, but Hopkins stayed calm and reasonable, persuading, referring everything back to the evidence.

Finally, the Hanger said, 'You can place him at or near the murder scene, you may even be able to prove it's his knife, but you can't show if or why he struck the blow.'

'If the fibres from his jacket match those on the knife, we can prove it was his knife that struck the fatal blow, as the sheath had Jason's blood in it. We also have a strategy by which we think we can get him to admit to at least manslaughter, sir. But it needs a few final pieces of evidence which we can only get by arresting him and executing the search warrant.'

'And the money-laundering of drugs money. It seems he can just deny knowledge, unless you can demonstrate he knew from the start. Your computer evidence only gives you a 50:50 on that – Richards or

Walters. And he will have deleted the incriminating e-mail long ago.'

'Again sir, there's one piece, or possibly two pieces, of evidence we can only get via a search warrant, which we think will show he did know.'

'Hmm.' The Hanger sat back, pondering. Hopkins didn't envy him. If this call was wrong, the fallout for the department and Jeffries personally could be horrific. Finally, he spoke.

'I never liked him. I reckoned he'd sell his own mother to make a buck. But I never thought he'd be capable of this.'

'We think it would all have remained undiscovered, sir, if the blackmail by Stagg hadn't triggered off a series of events that he clearly wasn't prepared for. We think the murder might have been some sort of panic reaction to a situation he found himself in, a situation he couldn't control.'

Reilly took over. 'You see, sir, when Stagg blackmailed Reynolds, he put him in a bind. McMahon refused to help him, said it was his problem. Reynolds can't afford to pay Stagg himself, and if he tries to take it out of what he owes to the London suppliers for monthly supplies, they'll probably kill him. So we think he uses the family connection, like he did with Arthur Copeland, to try to blackmail Richards, because he worked out Richards was on the take from Shadows. When McMahon said to Lewis he could get the lake closed, Reynolds must have worked out there was some connection between them.'

Hopkins finished, 'But that put Richards in an untenable position. If he paid up, that would mean admitting his involvement in money laundering, so Reynolds would have a hold over him for ever.'

Jeffries took a deep breath.

'OK, I'm convinced. I'll get the forms authorised and sent off to the magistrates' office. But – .' He paused. 'There's one thing that still doesn't ring true. Why would a man as rich as Richards already was, when he came back from London, take such a risk as getting involved in drug dealing, even at such a remove?'

'Maybe he just enjoyed the thrill of the risk, sir? Some very rich people do', suggested Reilly.

'Possibly. But while we're waiting for the warrants, why don't you see if you can speak with one of his former partners in London? Find out what was going on before he left. Seems strange to leave such a prestigious firm when he was doing so well.'

'Very well, sir' said Hopkins, and he and Reilly took their leave.

...

Reilly and Hopkins looked at the website of Richards' former accountancy firm. It had grown significantly in recent years and now marketed itself as a multi-disciplinary consultancy service.

'There's over a hundred partners, sir', groaned Reilly.

'Let's have a look and see if there's a page that gives CVs or biopics of the partners. They usually like to advertise their years of experience and time with the firm.'

They started scrolling through the many biopics. After half an hour, Reilly looked at his notes.

'Well, we've got three who were there at the time Richards left. It was just a partnership then, not an LLP, and it was much smaller, so hopefully they'll remember something.'

He started dialling the contact numbers listed, which invariably were answered by a secretary. The first partner on the list said he barely knew Richards, and denied any knowledge of the reasons why Richards had left. The second, according to his secretary, was out at meetings all afternoon.

Reilly and Hopkins looked at the last name on the list, Reginald de Courcy.

'He went to Eton, of course, with a name like that', said Reilly.

'Interesting, how you often still find descendants of Normans in high places', observed Hopkins. 'Let's give him a try.'

Reilly dialled, gave his police details and stressed to the secretary it was an urgent matter. With some hesitation, she put him through.

'De Courcy. What can I do for you, sergeant? My secretary said it was urgent.'

The voice was exactly as expected – extremely well-spoken, but clipped and business-like, without any exaggerated drawl.

'I have my colleague, Detective Inspector Hopkins on the line, also', said Reilly. 'We'd like to ask you some questions. It won't take up too much of your time, sir.'

Hopkins took over. 'I know you're a busy man, so I'll be direct. We're currently investigating a number of serious charges, and the investigation is at a critical stage. We would like to know anything you can tell us about the circumstances surrounding the decision of your former partner, Bryn Richards, to leave your firm and return to Wales.'

'Good God, that's ancient history', said de Courcy.

'We believe it's very relevant, sir.'

'How so?'

'I'm afraid I can't say, sir.'

De Courcy sighed. 'Look, I'm really not happy talking about this. It could reflect badly on the firm. Could we agree to keep it confidential?'

'I can't rule out totally the possibility that you might have to give evidence, sir. But the more you can tell us, the more likely it is that we can make the charges stick, and avoid that outcome.'

De Courcy sighed again.

'Very well. But I'd appreciate it if you could do your level best to prevent this becoming public. It could be very damaging to our reputation.'

'I understand, sir. But it was a different firm then, differently set up, and had a different name. I assume you have good PR people who could help you distance yourself from it.'

'OK. Well, here goes. Basically, it came to light he'd been investing on the side. Nothing wrong with that, as long as the businesses he invested in had no conflict of interest. He told us he'd been quite successful at first, which gave him an appetite for risk. Well, at that time, there was lots of speculative building going on here in London, mainly new offices. Bryn had invested heavily in a development company that was building a major complex on a former industrial site near the docks. Unfortunately, the land turned out to be contaminated. There was no register for that, back then, so no way of searching. The major institutional investors pulled out and the company was left facing a huge clean-up bill. Of course, it collapsed.'

'But how would that affect Richards, sir?', asked Reilly. 'Presumably it was limited liability.'

'Yes, but you see, Bryn had put up nearly all the money for the land purchase – over a million. The banks thought it was too high-risk, and only decided to lend for the building work when he put his own money in for the land purchase. The company held the land, and once it had sold it at an undervalue to pay off creditors, there was nearly nothing left to repay the shareholders. The irony was, a few years later, the government brought in a registration system for dealing with contaminated land, plus grants and subsidised loans for clean-ups, another company bought up the site and made an absolute killing.'

'That's obviously where he learnt his later business model from', said Reilly to Hopkins.

'So how did this cause him to leave the firm?', asked Hopkins.

'Well, if an accountant goes bankrupt, he can no longer practice. Too much of a risk he might mess about with clients' money. Bryn was very nearly bankrupt, and came to see us, to ask if we would give him a loan. I was one of the partners on the management committee at the time.'

De Courcy sighed. 'I personally liked him. Very driven, unorthodox, bit of a rogue. But I got over-ruled. The others thought he was too high a risk. So they demanded his resignation as a partner, and bought his silence with a generous severance package. But it wouldn't have been enough to clear his losses, never mind start up again. I heard he'd been very successful after his return to Wales, and I often wondered how. I take it you think he was mixed up in something illegal?'

'I'm sorry sir, I really can't say. And I would be grateful if you could keep this all confidential.'

'Oh, don't worry. Not the sort of thing one wants to make public knowledge. Well, good afternoon, officers.'

Reilly put down the phone. 'I think we've just filled in another piece of the jigsaw, sir.'

Chapter 29

The hunt

I see you stand like greyhounds in the slips,
Straining upon the start. The game's afoot
Shakespeare, *Henry V*

At 3pm, the warrants arrived, duly authorised.

'Shall we go and get him, then, sir?' asked Reilly.

'Better ring him first. Check where he is. We don't want to go off on a wild goose chase and potentially alert him. Say we just have a few more questions.'

Reilly picked up his mobile and started dialling.

'No answer from his mobile, sir. I'll try his home, then his office.'

He dialled again. This time, someone picked up, and Hopkins heard Reilly saying

'No, there's no problem. We just had a few more things we wanted to check with him. Oh thanks, that's great.'

He ended the call and turned to Hopkins.

'That was his wife. He's at the lake. Gone fishing.'

Of course, thought Hopkins. That was where it was bound to end.

'We'd better hurry up. If, as we think, his wife gave him a false alibi, she's probably ringing him now to warn him. Have you still got the copy key to the gate?'

'Yes sir. I was just thinking – you had a lift in with Mair, this morning, didn't you sir? So – .'

Reilly left the sentence unfinished, looking hopeful.

'Yes, John', Hopkins sighed, resignedly. 'We can go in your car.'

...

Five minutes later, they were on the dual carriageway, the sleek snout of the Capri seeming to follow a scent, like a hunting shark. Reilly gunned the 2.8 litre engine and the needle swung up swiftly. Hopkins had to admit the old car's raw, vibrating power was thrilling, but it hadn't been built for comfort in 1987, and neither age nor Reilly's ministrations had mellowed it. He was sure he could feel every spring in his seat, and was grateful that the journey took only fifteen minutes, as opposed to the usual twenty.

They had to stop to unlock the gate first, Hopkins getting out to do the honours. Reilly was disappointed not to have been able to swing into the car park in an impressive swirl of gravel.

The car pulled up and Reilly got out, Hopkins walking to join him, having left the gate unlocked for their departure. They stood together, looking around. There were several fishermen there, a group of three to their right, two more across the lake, and one lone fisherman a short distance to their left.

'There he is, sir.'

Their arrival had already caused some interest, with the other fishermen standing up and peering to see what was going on.

They walked over to where Richards was sitting, in a luxurious padded canvas chair, wearing his tweed jacket. He stood up as they approached. They could see a knife, similar to the murder weapon, was strapped to his belt on the right side.

'Hello, officers. I wasn't expecting to see you again.' He looked across at Reilly's car. 'Looks like a remake of the Sweeney. I almost expected you to leap out yelling 'You're nicked!"

The smile on his face died, at the serious look on Hopkins' face.

'Bryn Richards, I am arresting you on suspicion of the murder of Jason Reynolds. You do not have to say anything, but it may harm your defence if you do not mention when questioned something which you later rely on in court. Anything you do say may be given in evidence.'

The look in Richards' eyes changed, and warning bells went off in Hopkins' head. Cornered rat, he thought. Then, no – the captured pike.

Richards' crabbed hand slipped slowly to his right hip.

Reilly stepped forward, blocking Hopkins with his body.

Reilly had a face which was all crags and angles, one which he himself laughingly admitted, 'Only a mother could love.' Most of the time, he looked like a genial ogre, but when necessary, he could summon a mask of such chilling brutality, that local hard men had been known to take a step back. Now, with his friend under threat, he did so, saying pleasantly at the same time,

'I wouldn't do that, sir.'

The effect was predictable. Richards quickly withdrew his hand. He returned to his usual, diffident manner.

'I didn't mean anything, officers. Well, I – er – suppose I'd better come quietly, as the saying goes.'

'Good decision, sir. Now if you wouldn't mind giving me your wrists. Thank you. I am now going to remove the knife from your belt.'

Reilly cuffed Richards and safely removed the knife. The pike de-fanged, Hopkins thought.

'Right, well', said Hopkins, breathing a sigh of relief. 'We'll just move over to the car and get you in, Mr Richards, before people start showing too much interest. You can make a call to your solicitor or whomever at headquarters.'

But they had no sooner turned to go, than the bite alarm on one of the rods behind Hopkins screamed.

Chapter 30

Leviathan

Canst thou draw out leviathan with an hook?
Job, 41:1

Hopkins stared at the rod, whose tip was bent over to the left, line running off the reel. One of the nearest group of fishermen shouted,

'Pick it up! We don't want a damaged fish.'

Hopkins looked at Reilly, who shrugged.

'You're nearest, sir.'

'Let me do it. Take these cuffs off', pleaded Richards, but Reilly said,

'Sorry, sir. I can't do that.'

As if in a dream, Hopkins picked up the rod. It pulsated gently as the fish ran, not yet feeling any significant resistance.

Panting slightly, the first fisherman of the three to their right joined him. It was Walters.

'Done this before?'

'Never.'

'Lift the rod up to 45 degrees, gently but firmly. Then throw that lever at the back of the reel.'

Immediately, the resistance increased and the line ran more slowly. The rod bent into an arc, like an archer's bow, and Hopkins felt the wild, juddering power of the fish as it took off on a run. He was amazed at how strong it felt.

'Let him run', advised Walters. 'It's only a light feeder rod, and I'm guessing only a light leader.' He looked at Richards, and said, 'That right? You said you were trying for the Crucian.'

Richards nodded.

He turned back to Hopkins.

'You've probably got a fish heavier than the line's breaking strain. That means you can't just reel it in, or the line will snap, and we'll end up with a fish with a hook stuck in its mouth. Ah, he's stopped running now.'

The wild charge had stopped, and the fish was now moving more slowly, but purposefully, off to the right.

'He's heading for the lily bed', said Walters. 'We don't want to let him in there, or he'll tangle the line round the stems and snap it.'

'What do I do?' asked Hopkins.

'Angle the rod to the left. Hold it lower, that's it. Now slowly pull back. Try and turn his head.'

Hopkins did so, and managed to manoeuvre the fish back into open water.

'Right, now he's a bit tired, let's try and get him closer. Raise the rod slowly up to vertical. Draw him gradually towards you. Then lower the rod and reel in as you do it. Keep the line tight or the hook might drop out – it's barbless.'

Hopkins did so. He then repeated the action several times, drawing the fish closer.

Then, as it got near to the bank, it sensed danger and took off on another wild run, pulling even more strongly than before. This time, Hopkins felt the rod tip being dragged inexorably down towards the water and felt sure something must break.

Walters reached over and fiddled with something at the front of the reel. Immediately, the tension eased in the rod.

'We can tighten the drag back up when he stops.'

'Why's the line got to be so light? We could just reel it in if it was higher breaking strain.'

'Because carp aren't stupid. They're not going to bite if you use a bloody anchor chain.'

Hopkins' wrists were aching. He snatched a glance at his watch. Amazingly, nearly fifteen minutes had passed and he hadn't noticed.

'OK', said Walters, 'Tighten down the drag. Turn that dial on the front of the reel two clicks to your left. Then start drawing him in. If he runs again, two clicks right and let him go.'

Hopkins started laboriously drawing the fish in once more. At last it was close to the shore, and for the first time, they saw a bronze swirl in the water.

Walters picked up the long-handled landing net and knelt on the bank, sliding the net out under the water.

'Now, try to pull him gently over the top of the net.'

Hopkins did so, pulling the fish up to the surface. A shout went up from the other fishermen, 'It's the Crucian!'

Walters swiftly raised the net, then lifted the handle, closing the net off like the neck of a sack. He carefully drew the net through the water, keeping the handle high, then lifted the fish out of the water and laid it on a thick, padded mat.

'Go and get your scales', he said to one of the others. 'We'll need two sets, and I want to get the fish back in the water asap.'

The man ran off.

Walters grunted. 'All that Lady of the Lake nonsense. I guessed it was probably a male.'

He deftly unhooked the fish with a pair of artery forceps, then sprayed disinfectant on the spot where the hook had been. Then he weighed it on Richards' scales.

'Five pounds, two ounces', he pronounced.

The other fisherman arrived back, breathless, and quickly set up his tripod, scales and sling. The fish was weighed again.

'Five pounds three ounces!'

A cheer went up. A few photos were quickly taken of the fish. Then Walters said,

'One with you.'

'What?' said Hopkins.

'We need one with the angler, for verification by the Records Committee. Don't worry, hold it gently under the rear of its head and its wrist – here, where the body joins the tail.'

Hopkins did so, smiling bemusedly. The fish was heavier than he expected, resting cold and slimy, but thankfully docile, in his hands.

Then the fish was taken from him, placed back into the net, and released.

Walters gave him a grim smile. 'You did alright for a first timer. Ever think of taking it up?' He looked at Richards. 'Looks like we'll have another vacancy.'

'Thanks, but no. We'd better get going.'

The three of them walked over to the Capri. Reilly guided Richards into the back seat. Hopkins climbed into the back on the other side, wincing. Even for a man of his small stature, the rear seats were cramped.

Reilly lowered the window and called to one of the fishermen, 'Would you mind locking the gate behind us?'

Then the Capri turned out onto the road, Reilly managing to resist a flamboyant exit, but still leaving a modest dust trail hanging in the air behind.

Chapter 31

Chess

And we shall play a game of chess
Pressing lidless eyes and waiting for a knock
upon the door.
T S Eliot, *The Waste Land*

They were back at HQ by 4.30pm. Hopkins and Reilly took Richards to be processed by Custody, where he was searched, possessions including belt and shoelaces removed, and fingerprints and cheek swabs taken. Last, Hopkins requested his tweed jacket, which he reluctantly handed over. Then, they left him to the Custody sergeant and went back to the MCIT room to wait.

Hopkins phoned Madhvani, to say he was sending over the cheek swabs and the jacket. He asked her to put pressure on the lab to speed up the results.

'Have we got Richards' laptop and devices yet?' he asked Reilly.

'Yes sir. The search warrant was executed at the same time as we were arresting Richards. His wife handed them over. SOC team are checking the house to see if he has any more. The tech guys are checking through what we have.'

'How long?'

'Even as a priority, several hours.'

'We need that tonight, if possible.'

'How do you want to play the interview, sir?'

'Well, first of all, we need to play for as much time as possible, to get the test results back on the swabs, jacket fibres and the computer. So, when his solicitor arrives, we give them as much time as they want. Then, in the first interview, I think we show him respect, listen to any suggestions or alternative scenarios he puts forward, make him think he's got a chance of talking his way out. Then, hopefully, he'll trip himself up and we pounce.'

Hopkins thought for a while.

'My guess is he'll hold out for a while, then probably, once he's had a chance to confer with his solicitor, come back with some kind of partial admission, maybe to manslaughter. What we need to do is play our cards right so that, when the test results and so on come back, we can prove he's lying, and then his argument falls apart. But I want to try to get him on record first, arguing something that we can then disprove.'

'Of course, sir, that depends on the results coming back showing what we hope they will.'

'Indeed it does, John. So for now, all we can do is wait.'

...

At just after 5pm, Richards' solicitor arrived. The two detectives went down to reception to see who Richards had chosen, and who their adversary might be. He was a thin, ferrety man called Jenkins, who Hopkins and Reilly knew well. He was from a small local firm, and Hopkins was surprised Richards had not engaged someone more prestigious. But then,

Jenkins had long experience in criminal law and knew the local courts well, so perhaps it was a wise choice.

'Well, you two gentlemen have excelled yourselves, this time.' Jenkins had a nasal, insinuating voice that he used to good effect to wind up police officers and prosecution witnesses. 'I should imagine you'll be lucky to be on traffic duty, after this.'

'We'll see, sir', said Hopkins, politely.

'I'll need at least an hour with him. This is all completely out of the blue.'

Hopkins pretended to consider this. He didn't want Jenkins guessing that they were playing for time. With feigned reluctance, he said,

'Very well, sir. Least we can do for such a pillar of the community. Shall we say 6.15?'

Jenkins nodded, and was led to a consultation room off the cells corridor.

...

'So, what do you think they have to do to confirm if you caught a record, sir?', Reilly asked as they waited in the Murder Room, nervously sipping coffee.

'I'd be grateful if you didn't tell anyone else about that little episode, John. I can do without all the jokes and distractions, at the moment. But from my reading, which was an excellent cure for sleeplessness, by the way, I gather they have to send both devices off to the British Record Fish Committee for calibration. Also the pictures they took, for verification that it's not a hybrid. Something to do with the number of scales, I gather. To be honest, I'd rather the whole thing hadn't happened.'

'I'll keep it quiet, sir. Shame the results on Walters' computer weren't more definite.'

The IT team, having had Walters' laptop for several days, had confirmed that there had been no attempt to delete or alter the activity log, and it was completely dormant for the period that Walters had been away on holiday. However, all that showed was that Walters had not tried to log in from that computer. He could still have done so from another computer, using a VPN to hide the IP address.

'Yes. It indicates Walters didn't send the e-mail closing the lake, but it doesn't completely remove the possibility. Richards is bound to blame him, as the only other admin.'

'Hopefully, the tech guys will find something on Richards' computers.'

Reilly checked his watch. 'Nearly 6.15. Shall we go down and see if they're ready?'

...

Reilly spoke into the recorder in the interview room. 'Interview with Bryn Richards commencing 18.25. Present: DI Hopkins and DS Reilly, and Mr Richards' solicitor, Gareth Jenkins.'

Hopkins began.

'In your first interview with us, you stated that you were at home all night on the night of 12th February 2025, when the murder of Jason Reynolds occurred. Do you still maintain that story?'

'I do.'

'We have information from a credible witness, that your car was parked in a private lane in the village of Rhyd yr Afon. This is very close to the entrance to a path across the fields belonging to Mr James Lewis, and which comes out on the lane near to the gate to the fishing lake.'

'He must have made a mistake', said Richards immediately. 'It would have been dark.'

'Who is this witness?' asked Jenkins.

'His name will be provided to you in due course on disclosure. However, for the moment, I would say that he is a resident of one of the houses on the private lane, who has been annoyed for some time about people parking there, and so he keeps a detailed list of times and registrations. In the other instances that we checked, his list was accurate and tallied with vehicles that we knew to be there. So we believe he is likely to be credible.'

Hopkins paused. 'So I'll ask again, do you have any explanation for your car being there?'

'I say the witness must have made a mistake.'

Jenkins jumped in. 'I'd say you might have a problem proving it was my client's car, if it was some old busybody with dodgy eyesight in the dark.'

'Very well, sir, we'll leave that there for now. I daresay we'll need to come back to it later.'

Reilly stepped in. He passed over a sheet showing pictures of the murder weapon.

'Do you recognise this knife, sir?'

'I've got one like it, but there are thousands out there. It's a very popular make.'

'It was found in a public bin, near to where your car was observed parked.'

'That wasn't my car.'

'So you say, sir. This knife has been forensically examined. There is no doubt it was the murder weapon – there was blood in the sheath, which was found to have Jason Reynolds' DNA.'

Jenkins laughed, derisively. 'In a bin, you say? Bound to be contaminated.'

'DNA can't be contaminated like that, Mr Jenkins. Our pathologist will swear to that on oath. There was also a partial fingerprint, which we're having checked against yours.'

'Partial?' said Jenkins, mockingly, but both Hopkins and Reilly noticed Richards was looking slightly uncomfortable now.

'It's not mine', he said. 'Although I do have one like it.'

'And what do you use it for, Mr Richards? You don't take the fish you catch home to eat.'

'Cutting up bait, like luncheon meat and so on. And deadbaits when I sometimes fish for pike.'

'So you maintain this isn't your knife?'

'Yes, I mean no, it's not.'

Hopkins and Reilly exchanged significant glances, which they made sure Richards could see.

'Yes, well I'm sure we'll come back to that, later, as well', said Hopkins. 'Now I'd like to change tack a little. Your companies, and ultimately the company of which you are Chairman and CEO, Consolidated Land and Development (South Wales)(Holdings) Limited, own both the Shadows night club and the derelict outbuilding at Ewenny Mill.'

Richards looked surprised at the change of direction, but said,

'Yes. But my companies own over a hundred properties. We buy and sell all the time.'

'It's a very complicated ownership structure, Mr Richards. Can you explain why?'

281

'It's on the advice of my tax consultants, to minimise tax liability. It's all legitimate.'

'I see. And not for any other purpose?'

'What sort of purpose?'

'Well, Shadows was recently shut down as one of the tenants, Mr Andrew McMahon, has been charged with offences related to drug dealing. At those premises and others. When DS Reilly and I searched the Ewenny Mill building, we found a large quantity of drugs there, plus the paraphernalia used for splitting them down for street sale. That would seem to be a bit of a coincidence, wouldn't it?'

Richards was visibly sweating now, as if he were wondering how much they knew, and how much he dared deny.

'Not at all. Like I said, my companies have over a hundred properties. I don't monitor what the tenants do with them.'

'Well, there is a further coincidence, sir. Each of those properties contained in their leases, a ratchet clause that increased rent in line with profits. Would that be a way of funnelling profits from drug dealing up into your chain of companies, where it could be disguised by inter-company transactions, mortgage charges and the like?'

'Absolutely not!' shouted Richards. 'It's a common business practice. I do it to encourage start-ups. They get a low rent at the start, so they can use all their finance to build up the business, then we get a return, if and when they're successful.'

'It seems you're accusing my client of being some kind of drug baron, with no actual evidence to connect him to any of it', sneered Jenkins. 'And it has no relevance to the charge of murder, which is what you arrested him for.'

'Forensic accountants are currently going through the accounts of Shadows, which they believe have been doctored to hide the profits from drug dealing', said Hopkins. 'If they find sufficient evidence, then my colleagues may be requesting a warrant for disclosure of all your companies' accounts and records. Do you think they will withstand detailed scrutiny, Mr Richards?'

'Of course!' said Richards, defiantly.

'Lots of coulds, shoulds and maybes, there, Inspector,' sniped Jenkins from the sidelines. 'Can't see a jury accepting that. And I still can't see why it's relevant.'

'I'll try to explain', said Hopkins. 'You see, we know that a member of your club, Kenny Stagg, had photographs of Jason Reynolds opening the trapdoor to the second septic tank that was discovered at the lake, taking out drugs, and handing them through the fence to couriers, who came across the fields on quad bikes or off-road bikes.'

Richards intervened. 'But I told you about those bikes, at our first meeting! Why would I have done that, if I was involved?'

'Possibly to divert suspicion away from you, sir. You also pushed us towards first Craig Walters, and then Rob Locke.'

'Speculation', said Jenkins, in a bored voice.

'Let me complete the story', said Hopkins, 'which is all supported by evidence. Stagg used this material to attempt to blackmail Reynolds into paying him substantial amounts of money. Reynolds couldn't afford this, and his associate McMahon refused to help him. If Reynolds had attempted to take the money out of payments to his London suppliers, then we can guess what would probably have happened to him.'

'All very interesting, Inspector, but where's the connection to my client?' asked Jenkins.

'I'm coming to that', said Hopkins. He noted Richards was sweating again, a sheen appearing on his brow in the harsh light of the interview room.

'We've discovered that Reynolds was the illegitimate son of your brother, who now calls himself Arthur Copeland. That would make him your nephew. He had already tried to exploit the family connection by blackmailing Mr Copeland, some years ago.'

'That's rubbish!' Richards shouted. His voice turned to a sneer. 'My brother can't have children. Infertile. His daughter was adopted.'

Hopkins carried on. He knew he couldn't prove the next part, but wanted to get Richards' reaction.

'What we believe, sir, is that as Reynolds was in a very difficult position, literally a matter of life and death, he once again sought to exploit a family connection and blackmailed you, to try to to save himself. In order to do that, he would need to have something to blackmail you with. We believe that he discovered, through his association with McMahon and Watkins, that you were involved in taking some of the profits from their trading.'

Richards again looked worried, shifting in his seat.

'Well, he might have thought that, but I had no involvement in the running of those properties, or anything to do with drugs. Why would I? I'm a respected businessman, I've done alright for myself, it doesn't make any sense that I would take the risk.'

'Well sir', Reilly broke in. 'Funny you should mention that. We spoke to a member of your former firm in London, about the reasons why you left. He says that you were nearly bankrupt, after a property deal went south, and they forced you to resign. When you got back to Wales, it's very unlikely any bank would have been willing to lend you the money you needed to get started.'

'That's a lie!' shouted Richards, clearly shocked that they knew this.

'Really sir? He's willing to testify', said Reilly, stretching the truth a little.

Hopkins shot him a warning glance.

'Well, I had some financial help from friends. They could see my potential.'

'They must be very good friends, sir. I presume you could give us their names?'

'It's confidential. And a long time ago.'

'Yes, sir. But see it from our point of view. If you couldn't borrow from regular sources, and you can't name the friends who helped you get started, then it looks to us as though you may have had help from criminal sources, to create a front for money-laundering.'

Richards looked as if he might faint, but then Jenkins stepped in.

'Presumptions aren't evidence, not in criminal law, sergeant. Unless you have any proof to back this up, my client won't answer any more questions on this subject.'

'That is his right, Mr Jenkins', Hopkins said. 'But I assume you have explained the words of the caution on arrest to him? If he withholds a legitimate explanation for his actions, which he later provides, that can be taken against him.'

'He has provided you with the explanation, Inspector. We will consider together at the next break whether he wants to give you the names. By the way, when can we take a break? It's been over an hour now, and my client is not a young man.'

'Just a few questions more. Ten minutes maximum.'

Hopkins continued. 'Just over a year ago, at the time when the second septic tank was installed at the lake, we reasoned that there must have been some sort of official communication to members to keep them away on the night in question. However, we struggled to find it, until we found a copy saved on the computer of Kenny Stagg. It had been set to delete automatically after thirty days, but he evidently suspected something and created a copy on his own computer.'

Hopkins passed over a copy of the e-mail that had led to the arrest of Walters.

Immediately, before he could have had time to read it, Richards blurted out,

'But that's from Craig Walters!'

'Is that the first time you've seen this, sir?' asked Hopkins.

'Of course it is! I would never have agreed to this!'

'But you're on the recipient list, sir', Hopkins gently pointed out.

'He must have forged my address somehow! I never saw it!'

'Very well, sir. We will take technical advice on whether that's possible. But I would point out, only you and Mr Walters had administrators' rights over that account.'

'Then it must have been him!'

'That's what we initially thought too, sir. We had him in for questioning and looked at his computer. It showed no activity over that period, as he was away on holiday.'

'Then he used a different computer or a VPN! It's not difficult.'

'No, sir. But we have been unable to establish any connection between him and the drug dealing. You, on the other hand, owned both the properties involved.'

'Coincidence! Just a coincidence.'

'Seem to be a lot of coincidences in this case, don't there?' remarked Reilly, semi-innocently.

'Don't get smart, sergeant' snapped Jenkins. 'You know you've got at best a fifty-fifty chance on this. Clear reasonable doubt. Now, my client wants to take a break.'

'Certainly, sir', said Hopkins. 'Given the time, I'll arrange for a meal for him and refreshments for you.'

He looked at his watch. 'Shall we come back in, say, forty-five minutes? At 8.30pm?'

'Very well, Inspector. But I don't want this to go on too long. As I said before, my client's not a young man.'

At that moment, there was a knock on the door. A young constable passed a note to Reilly. He read it, then looked up and smiled wolfishly at Richards.

'While we've been talking, our technical people have been checking the GPS tracking device on your car. It puts your car in the village of Rhyd yr Afon, at the date and time of the murder. Lots of people who are otherwise good at covering their tracks get caught out by that. Like the crossbow killer up in Anglesey.'

He passed over the copy of the results.

'Something for you to think about during your break.'

...

Hopkins and Reilly were in the Murder Room, hunched over the conference phone, on a call with Madhvani.

'How's it going?', she asked, a note of excitement in her voice, rather than her normal cool, amused tone.

'We've got him on the ropes', said Reilly, 'But like Muhammad Ali, he's just soaking it up. We haven't established any direct evidential link yet that can't be challenged. In some cases, it could only be challenged on flimsy grounds, but it could still be enough to get him off.'

'He looked pretty desperate a few times,' said Hopkins. 'I'm sure it's him. But as John says, he's just about holding it together.'

'We've got the vehicle GPS evidence', reminded Reilly.

'Yes, but that only puts his car near the scene', said Hopkins. 'He might say he, or his wife, had some kind of secret assignation with someone in the village that they wanted to keep quiet for personal reasons.'

'The crossbow killer said he was meeting up with someone in a field for sex', said Reilly. 'Jury didn't believe him on that and convicted.'

'Yes, John, but there was other evidence there too. Like a clear link to the murder weapon. We don't have that here, yet. Doctor, can you give us anything else?'

'Nothing conclusive, I'm afraid. The lab say the fibres do match his jacket. But not necessarily that jacket alone. Others in the same batch could have used the same blend.'

'It's got to be pretty unlikely, that someone else was there, who just happened to own a jacket from the same batch, particularly as it's a prestige brand and they probably don't release too many at once', said Reilly.

'Unlikely, but just about possible. Maybe enough for a reasonable doubt', Madhvani answered.

'What about the other matter?' Hopkins asked.

'The lab's still working on it. I'll push them again.'

'Thanks, Doctor.'

Hopkins ended the call.

'Think the other thing will break him, sir?' asked Reilly.

Hopkins took off his glasses and rubbed his eyes. 'I don't know, John. But I really don't want to have to use it. Have the tech people sent us anything yet?'

Reilly opened his laptop. 'This came in while we were interviewing him.'

He started to read, summarising for Hopkins as he went.

'They tried to reconstruct his back-up profile from that time, using the time and date the e-mail was sent, but either he was smart enough to turn off the automatic updating, or nothing showed because he used a VPN.'

Hopkins' face showed his disappointment. 'Anything else?'

Reilly's face brightened. 'This might be something. They say that activity data is commonly stored in the log files of the computer used. Things like the domain accessed, the date and time, and the length of time the activity continued for.'

'And?'

'The logs on Richards' computer show that he accessed a VPN provider just before the time the e-mail was sent, on the same date. Then he logged off immediately after the time the e-mail was sent.'

'He'll say it's another coincidence.'

'It's a pretty big one, sir. And the coincidences are mounting up. And a good matrix of circumstantial evidence can be enough, if we can convince a jury that there's no realistic chance of all these coincidences happening at the same time.'

'Yes, hopefully that's what they'll have been discussing over the break. Jenkins will know that well enough.'

...

'Interview recommencing at 20:30', intoned Reilly into the recorder.

'Before we start, Inspector, my client has a statement he wishes to make', said Jenkins. 'He wishes me to read it for him.'

Hopkins looked surprised, but said, 'Go ahead.'

A wild hope sprang up – could he be about to confess?

'Usual preamble, name, address, age, profession. We'll add the formal attestation details later.'

Jenkins drew a breath and started to read in a formal voice, as if presenting a case in court.

'I do not admit to having any involvement in drug dealing or money laundering and deny completely all the allegations made in that regard.

However, I do admit that my car was parked in the village of Rhyd yr Afon on the night of the murder. This was because Jason Reynolds, who claimed to be my nephew but is definitely not, due to my brother's infertility, had threatened to blackmail me. The blackmail was in connection with one of my companies' ownership of a property which he knew to be concerned with drug-dealing, but which I did not, i.e. Shadows night club in Bridgend. He threatened to expose my alleged connection if I did not pay him the sum of one hundred thousand pounds.

I agreed to meet him at the lake, Yr Hen Chwarel, at around 11pm. We didn't think anyone else would be there because of the cold weather, but Jason would get there first and if there was someone else fishing, he would call me and we would meet somewhere else. I parked in the village so as not to be observed by the CCTV camera in the industrial estate, and walked across the fields to the entrance to the lake. On the way, I saw Robert Locke, on his way back from pre-baiting the lake for pike fishing the next day, I assumed, as that is what he often did. I managed to avoid him and I do not believe he saw me.

When I got to the lake, Jason Reynolds was there. He had just caught and weighed a fish and was excited, as he thought he might have caught the record Crucian carp that has recently been landed from our lake. However, I told him it was only a common carp, so he released it. He did not seem to know very much about fishing, and it was always a mystery to me why he was so often at the lake at nights. I know now from information provided to me by the police that he was using this as a front for drug-dealing. I did not know this at the time, and I knew nothing of the second septic tank installed, which was used for storing drugs, and which again I now know from information provided by the police.

I confronted him about the blackmail. I denied what he had alleged, and I said I would report him to the police if he did not withdraw it. He flew into a rage and threatened me. I stood firm and said again I would report him to the police. He then drew a knife from his belt. I accept that it was similar to one I own, but there are many such knives on the market. It was not my knife. I did not bring a knife to the lakeside that night.

Reynolds attacked me. I managed to grab his arm. We fought. I was terrified for my life and didn't know what I was doing. In the darkness, I tripped and fell backwards. Reynolds fell on top of me and landed on his own knife. He went still and I managed to push him off me.

I saw that he was dead and I panicked. I thought I would be accused of his murder. I took the sheath off his belt, put the knife back in the sheath, and rolled his body into the water. I took the knife and sheath with me because I knew that they both float.

I went out of the gates and locked them. I stumbled back to my car, still in a panic. I wiped the knife and tried to wipe the sheath, but unsuccessfully as it was dark and my hands were shaking. I accept Reynolds' blood was in the sheath and the partial fingerprint on the knife is mine.

I dropped the knife in a nearby bin. I then drove home.

I never intended to kill Jason Reynolds or cause him serious harm. He attacked me first and the stabbing was a pure accident.'

Jenkins looked up. 'That's it', he said.

Hopkins was the first to find his voice.

'So, is your client admitting to manslaughter?'

'He's admitting to nothing of the kind, Inspector. He will defend all charges on the grounds of reasonable self-defence.'

'Well, he has admitted to obstructing the police, attempting to conceal evidence, failure to report a death, perjury and a few other things I could think of.'

'Maybe so, Inspector. But as he has told you, that was because he was panicked immediately after, and

293

then later worried that he would be wrongly charged with murder. As has proven to be the case. And these are relatively minor matters. I doubt he will even get a custodial sentence, given his previous lack of convictions.'

Reilly broke in furiously. 'You expect a jury to buy that? It's obvious he's just made it all up because he knows we've got enough to get him for murder.'

'Then prove it, sergeant', said Jenkins, with a derisive smirk. 'I don't think you can. And please lower your voice. You're attempting to intimidate my client.'

'It's alright, John', said Hopkins. He turned to Richards. 'Some new evidence has come in. This,' he pushed over several sheets of paper, 'is a forensics lab report that matches the fibres found in the sheath, to those of your tweed jacket.'

Richards opened his mouth, but Jenkins leapt in first.

'Come on, Inspector, you know that's misleading. All that a fibre match shows, is that someone with a similar jacket was there. And he's already accepted he was there anyway.'

'Then how did the fibres get on the knife and inside the sheath?'

'They must have been transferred during the struggle.'

Reilly made a sound of disbelief, but Hopkins stayed calm.

'Very well, We'll discuss it with our pathologist, see whether that is a feasible theory. It's yet another coincidence, though.'

'Moving on', Hopkins said swiftly, not giving Jenkins time to give the predictable response. 'Here is a report from our IT department on your laptop, Mr Richards. It shows that a device with your IP address was used to access a VPN provider just before the time the e-mail closing the lake was sent. You were online for the same time as it took to send the e-mail, and then you logged off immediately after it was sent.'

'It doesn't show I sent it', said Richards. 'Just that I was online at the same time.'

'That's a pretty astonishing coincidence, Mr Richards, given the very narrow time frame.' Hopkins waved his hand at Jenkins. 'I know, I know what you're going to say. Coincidences aren't direct proof. But they do form part of the matrix of circumstantial evidence that is building up around you, Mr Richards. There have been many such coincidences in this case, as Sergeant Reilly has just pointed out. Quite a few of them, you at first denied, and then accepted in your statement, once you saw our evidence. A jury won't like that. But Mr Jenkins has no doubt advised you of that.'

'Don't presume to know what I have advised my client', snapped Jenkins.

Reilly broke in, his voice scornful, his face hard.

'If, as you say, Reynolds fell on top of you, a considerable amount of blood would have fallen on the front of your jacket. But we found no bloodstains. How do you explain that?'

'I soaked it and then had it dry cleaned', said Richards. 'And threw away my shirt.'

Reilly looked incredulous.

Hopkins said, 'It does seem unlikely to the point of impossibility, that ordinary cleaning could have got rid of the amount of blood that must have resulted from a wound to the heart. But we will check that with the pathologist also.'

'We need another break to consider this so-called new evidence', said Jenkins swiftly.

'Be my guest', said Hopkins expansively. 'Interview terminated at 20.55. Back at 9.20?'

In his heart he was praying, but at the same time dreading, that Madhvani had got the final piece of information he had asked for.

Chapter 32

A necessary evil

I think we are in rat's alley
Where the dead men lost their bones
T S Eliot, *The Waste Land*

Reilly and Hopkins called Madhvani again.

'Has he confessed?', she asked eagerly.

'I'm afraid not', said Hopkins gloomily. 'He admits he was there, and that he killed Jason. But he says Jason attacked him, and in the scuffle, they both fell over and Jason fell on his own knife.'

'So we wanted to discuss with you how feasible that theory is', put in Reilly.

'Very improbable, I would say. Given the age and strength difference between them, it would appear very unlikely that Richards could manage to turn a knife through 180 degrees to face Reynolds.'

'But is it a possibility?', pressed Hopkins.

'If I was asked on the stand, I would have to say that it is.'

'Damn. That's sufficient for reasonable doubt.'

'I'm sorry, Inspector. But I have to give my professional view.'

'No, thanks Doctor. We need to know exactly where we stand. Now, what about the angle of the wound?'

'Again, very unlikely it would enter the body in that place and go straight in. If Reynolds did indeed fall on the knife, you would expect it to enter the abdomen at an angle, not straight on into the chest. But again, I can't deny that it is a possibility.'

'With the fibres in the knife handle and the sheath, Richards says they must have got transferred there during the struggle with Reynolds. Is that possible?'

'Extremely unlikely. Some fibres may well have transferred in that way, but given contact between the knife and Richards' clothing would have been fleeting, it's hard to see that amount transferring. The amount we found suggested longer-term contact with the jacket. I'd say it's in the realms of the just about possible, but not really a realistic proposition.'

'Let's hope that the judge directs the jury clearly on the difference between a reasonable possibility, and a remote chance.'

Reilly stepped in.

'And what about blood stains on the jacket? If Reynolds landed on top, you would expect a lot of blood to have fallen on Richards. But so far as we are aware, the lab found no trace of blood on his jacket. He says he soaked it, then had it dry-cleaned. How likely is that to have got rid of all bloodstains?'

'Yes, I can confirm there were no bloodstains at all found, either under UV testing or microscopy. It really is a practical impossibility, particularly with a thick woollen material like that, and the amount of blood that there must have been, that you could remove every trace of blood with normal washing. It might just about be possible to remove it with intensive cleaning, but still very, very unlikely. I'd be happy to say that that is not a reasonable hypothesis.'

'OK', said Hopkins, 'so we've got two things we can say are unlikely to be acceptable as reasonable doubt, thus disproving two key elements of his defence.'

'But if he's desperate', said Reilly, 'He could still put it to the jury, see how it plays out, then plead to manslaughter if it looks like going badly for him.'

'True. And his solicitor will no doubt advise him of that as an option. Doctor, have you got a result on the final test we asked you for?'

'Yes', she said, but now sounding subdued. 'I've just e-mailed it over to you both. It's a match. But I wouldn't want to be the one to tell him.'

...

'Interview recommencing at 21:20', stated Reilly into the recorder.

Jenkins jumped in. 'It's getting late and my client is an elderly man and is getting tired. We want to leave it for tonight.'

'I hear what you say, sir. But we have just a few points to put to you, which may make your client reconsider aspects of his previous statement. First, we are advised by our pathologist, that it is extremely unlikely that the amount of clothing fibres found in the sheath and the point where the blade joins the knife handle, could have got there during a brief struggle, such as your client has described. It is more indicative of prolonged contact over a period of time, such as being worn and used by the owner. She will testify that the level of possibility does not amount to a reasonable doubt, and that therefore, this was clearly your client's knife.'

'And we'll get an expert to say the opposite, and the jury can decide who they believe', said Jenkins. 'Next.'

'What do you have to say, Mr Richards?'

Richards started. 'Er, well, the same as he just said.'

'That doesn't sound very positive. Do you stick to your story that the knife was Jason's, and collected the fibres during the struggle?'

'Er, yes.'

'Thank you. And the next point, Mr Jenkins, I should appreciate if you would let your client answer, rather than jumping in. Although I assume you will make the same point, that it's a matter for expert disagreement.'

Hopkins turned to Richards.

'Mr Richards, regarding the point that Sergeant Reilly here made about the total lack of any bloodstains found on your jacket, the pathologist says that it is not a realistic hypothesis, in her words. It may just be possible with very intensive cleaning, to remove all traces. But not with the normal processes you described. So, if Jason fell on top of you, as you say, and you admit that his blood fell on you, how is it possible that no trace of blood was found?'

'I gave it a really hard scrubbing and soaking! I'm telling the truth!'

'Hmm. We can't see a jury accepting it.'

'But it's my client's right to put that case to a jury, Inspector', put in Jenkins.

'We would also mention', put in Reilly, 'that your statement proves that your wife lied in providing you with a false alibi. That could open her to charges.'

'I hope you're not threatening my client with action against his wife, to induce him to confess?', said Jenkins, angrily.

'Absolutely not, sir. Simply stating that that is a possibility.'

Richards looked troubled.

Hopkins asked, 'So are you sticking to your previous statement, Mr Richards?'

Richards looked sideways at Jenkins, who gave him no indication.

'Er, yes. Yes.'

Hopkins took off his glasses, looked down and rubbed his eyes. When he looked up, Reilly saw an expression of deep sorrow and regret. Yet, when he spoke, there was a note of steely resolve in his voice.

'Very well. I didn't want to have to tell you, Mr Richards, not like this.'

He passed over a single sheet of A4.

'You will remember giving a cheek swab when you were brought into custody. This is a summary by the forensics lab of their analysis of your mitochondrial DNA against that of Jason Reynolds. There is a fifty per cent match between you and him. You were right, Mr Richards. Jason Reynolds was not your nephew. He was your son.'

Richards' face froze. For long moments, he showed no reaction. Then suddenly, he jumped up, screwed up the paper, and threw it across the room.

'You – evil – swine!' he hissed viciously. 'What is this? Some dirty trick to make me confess? Well I won't! I don't believe it!'

'Please sit down, Mr Richards.' Hopkins turned to Jenkins. 'You can of course speak to your own doctor to verify that this is what the report says. Here is another copy.'

He passed one over to Jenkins.

'And how am I supposed to contact a doctor at this hour?'

'Oh, I have no doubt that a man of your long experience has a network of expert contacts you can call on out of hours. But we can wait until morning, if you prefer. We have forty-eight hours to hold Mr Richards, as you know.'

'Well, I want to call a halt to things for tonight. My client's old, and he's had a nasty shock.'

'That's his decision. We'll leave it up to him. But I rather imagine, once he's considered the position, he'll want to get it over with tonight, rather than sitting all night in his cell dwelling on it.'

'Interview terminated at 21:40', said Reilly.

'Call us when you're ready.'

Chapter 33

Endgame

... Our natures do pursue,
Like rats that ravin down their proper bane,
A thirsty evil; and when we drink, we die.
Shakespeare, *Measure for Measure*

Hopkins and Reilly sat, waiting, in the Murder Room. It was ten to ten. Hopkins looked miserable.

'I wish we hadn't had to do that, John. I hated doing it.'

'Come on, sir. If we're right, then he murdered someone in cold blood to protect his name and his business empire, both built on drug dealing and money laundering. If we don't get him to confess, we face a long drawn-out trial where he might get off with manslaughter, might even get off entirely. And Richards would have had to be told, one way or another, once we had the DNA proof.'

'I know, John, but do the ends justify the means?'

'As a philosophical proposition, I'd say not as a general rule, but in this case, absolutely. He's seen the strength of the evidence we have, and he's had every chance to confess. We both know his excuses don't stack up.'

Hopkins breathed out heavily.

'Maybe you're right, John. I'm all in. If he's still holding out when we get back, we'll call it a night.'

Another half hour dragged past, both of them too tired to speak. Reilly stepped outside to call Catrin. Hopkins felt he should call Mair, but he had texted earlier and was too tired to have another discussion about whether he was stretching himself too far.

Just as Reilly stepped back in, the internal phone rang. Reilly picked up. He listened for a moment, then said 'OK.'

He turned to Hopkins.

'They want us back down there.'

...

Weary as a runner at the end of a marathon, Hopkins tried to disguise his fatigue. He knew Jenkins would try to exploit it, if he noticed.

They sat down and Reilly re-started the recording. Jenkins spoke.

'In light of the, er, further information, my client wishes to change his statement.'

He turned to Richards.

'I wish to state, for the record, that what he has indicated he wishes to say, is against my legal advice.'

Coward, thought Hopkins. Covering his own backside. However, he remained silent.

Richards looked up. Both detectives were shocked at the change in him. He was broken, his face collapsed into lines of misery, and he had obviously been weeping. When he spoke, his voice was shaky.

'I don't really know where to begin. I just know there's no point going on. Even if I get away with it, I have to live with this for the rest of my life. And I can't face it all being picked over in court and in the papers, for weeks.'

'Why don't you start with when you returned to Wales from London, Mr Richards?', asked Hopkins in a quiet voice. He hoped getting started on a less painful subject would enable Richards to open up.

'Well, it's true, what you said. I came back with just enough to keep the family afloat for a few months, but knowing I'd go bankrupt if I didn't find something soon. No bank would lend to me, given my lack of funds and collateral. We'd had to sell the house in London as I mortgaged it to help raise money for the land deal. So, I turned to loan sharks to get the money to buy into a local firm, so I could get a regular income, and to finance the first property deal. I'd learned my lesson and bought a pub, a going concern, so as to get an immediate income stream. I didn't realise that, even then, my lenders were pushing me in the direction they wanted me to go.'

'So it went on for a few years. I worked hard, learned all about the grants system, and we bought our first former industrial site, used the grant to part finance the renovation, then sold it on at a good profit. After two or three of those, I was able to get normal bank finance again, so I went to my lenders to talk about starting to repay their initial loan, as the interest was racking up.'

'They said no. They didn't want me to. They had a proposition that they said would make us both more money in the long run. They said they would introduce me to their associates, who would make the next stage of the plan clear.'

Richards shuddered at the memory and a shadow crossed his face.

'The – associates – who had been in the background all along, turned out to be a London drug gang. They were looking for new businesses as ways of laundering money. They suggested that I start trying to take over the accountancy firm in which I was a partner, buy out those who wanted to retire, replace them with people that they recommended. I could pick some of my own, to make it look like a genuine business venture. Then we would continue the property deals, gradually grow that side too, slowly so as not to arouse suspicion. Of course, it was clear to me that the people they would appoint would be specialists in what you might call 'creative accounting', and that the whole thing would be a front for money laundering.'

'I tried to back out. I said I just wanted to pay the loan back. So they showed me the level of interest that had accumulated, and made threats against me and my family if I couldn't pay it back there and then. I had no option.'

'So that's what happened. I started buying the other partners out – there were only twelve of us. They were replaced by people the 'associates' recommended, and in a few cases by people I knew who wanted to leave London and come back to Wales. They're all on the level and know nothing about this. As far as they're concerned, we have a property side and an accountancy side, and they don't get involved in the accountancy side. I used my knowledge of the grants system to get development grants to part-fund developments, with the rest being put in by my associates. Eventually, when I got over 50% of the voting power in the firm, I was able to force the remaining partners out.'

'We then started buying up pubs and clubs across the area. I know now that was a front for more drug-dealing. They were all placed with suitable tenants who knew the score, and set up under separate companies, to provide us with plausible deniability. If one business got busted, we could always say we knew nothing about it.'

'Then Jason got involved. He was a local dealer on a small scale and he got recruited by the London guys. He had the idea of using the fishing club, I gather, although I never spoke to him directly until later. He set up all the logistics of that with Andy McMahon, one of the tenants of Shadows. The London end thought he was a smart boy who was going places.'

'Somehow, Jason found out I was the landlord of Shadows, through the various companies. I think either Andy or Sandra must have moaned about the amount they were paying under the ratchet clause. Jason already knew from my brother about the family connection, but he must have kept it to himself, in case he needed to use it one day.'

'Then Jason got careless and got himself photographed by Kenny, who started blackmailing him. Jason couldn't afford to pay and so he came to me. He threatened to expose me and claimed I was his uncle. Well, I thought that was a lie, like I said before.'

'I told him he didn't know what he was doing, he didn't know how central I was to the whole thing, and if I got brought down, the London guys were going to be after him. He didn't believe me, and I wasn't going to tell him the whole story, and give him an even bigger hold over me. As far as he knew, I was just peripherally involved as the landlord, and taking a share of the drug profits.'

'We had a big row, ended up yelling at each other. I threatened to go to the police, but he just said to go ahead, if my business really was on the level. When I didn't do it, he knew he had me.'

'So, I put him off for several weeks. But there came a point I couldn't avoid him any longer. He suggested meeting at the lake. I took my knife. I didn't really know what I intended doing with it. For protection or to threaten him, maybe.'

'We met at the lake, just after 11. He'd landed and weighed a fish, like I told you, but it was just a small common carp, not the Crucian, so we put it back.'

'He threatened me again, to bring me and my business down, if I didn't pay him. I tried to explain to him again that he was in way over his head, that I was more than just a crooked landlord, and if he brought me down, there would be other people after him. But he didn't believe me, thought I was just bluffing. He called me a stupid old has-been trying to play up my importance, and he laughed at me.'

'I pulled out the knife and said he'd better back down, or I'd use it. He laughed again, and said I didn't have the guts, and to put it away or he'd take it off me. He just carried on laughing, and it sort of got inside my head. I was trapped, I couldn't see any way out for me and my family.'

'My mind went blank and I just lost it, I swear I didn't know what I was doing, and I just lashed out wildly with the knife.'

'I think he was too surprised to get out of the way. He just stood there, and the knife went straight into his chest. I remember thinking, I didn't expect it to go in so easily. He fell to his knees, and then toppled over on his face, on the gravel. I turned him over, and it was obvious he was dead.'

'I just panicked. I shoved the knife back in the sheath without thinking to clean it first. Then I rolled him into the water, to try and hide any evidence.'

'What about the blood, sir?' asked Reilly. 'There must have been quite a lot on the path and on the grass, where you rolled him down.'

'I ran to the container and got a bucket. Threw water everywhere. I knew it wouldn't wash away every trace, but I thought, if it wasn't visible, maybe you wouldn't look too closely there.'

'Thank you, sir. Please carry on.'

'Well, like I say, I was in a panic. I realised I should have wiped the knife first, so I did the best I could with some rags I found in the container, and put them in an old plastic bag. I shoved the bag inside the grassbox of the mower. I meant to go back and dispose of them later, but of course you started searching the site the next day.'

'I took the knife with me, as I knew it would float if I threw it in the water. Then I went back across the fields, threw the knife in the first bin I could find, and drove home. That's it.'

He lowered his head and started weeping again.

Hopkins waited a decent interval, then asked, 'Why didn't you simply tell your associates you were being blackmailed? I'm sure they would have solved the problem for you.'

Richards lifted his head. His voice was even thicker now.

'I didn't want to. I thought it would put me in a bad light with them. And – Jason was the coming man, to them. I couldn't be sure which one of us they might decide to get rid of. I was nearing retirement – they might have thought I'd outlived my usefulness, put one of their guys in my place.'

Hopkins nodded slowly.

Then he said, 'Mr Richards, I know you're still in fear of these people. But it's not just Jason's life – you've helped ruin hundreds, maybe thousands of other lives. I can't begin to imagine how you feel, but it would go some way to atone for what you've done, if you were to co-operate with my colleagues and name these associates of yours. It might also get you a lower recommended jail term from the judge. It will still be life imprisonment, but the term the judge recommends that you serve can vary, depending on your conduct.'

Richards smiled, bitterly.

'Don't make me laugh, Inspector. Given my age, I'm going to die in prison, whatever the term. And if I give you the names, I'd be stabbed in prison pretty quickly, I imagine. My family would be at risk too.'

'We can arrange protection for your family. And, as I say, it would start to make amends for what you've done.'

But Richards just buried his head in his hands and began to sob again.

Jenkins spoke, quietly. All the snide confidence had gone from him.

'Inspector, please leave it for tonight. He's clearly not fit to continue.'

'I agree, Mr Jenkins. We can do the formal charging in the morning. Mr Richards? Please think about it overnight. We can talk again tomorrow, when you're rested.'

Richards showed no sign of having understood. Reilly got up and opened the door, and the custody officer came in to take Richards back to his cell.

The two detectives and Jenkins walked down the corridor to the front desk. Before they left him, to turn up the stairs to the MCIT room, Jenkins gave Hopkins a sad smile and said,

'Well done, Inspector. You got your win.'

Hopkins paused, with one foot on the first stair.

'It doesn't really feel like it. Goodnight, Mr Jenkins.'

Chapter 34

The healing stream

Open now the crystal fountain
  Whence the healing stream doth flow.
  William Williams, *Cwm Rhondda (Guide me, O thou Great Redeemer)*

A few days later, Hopkins came into the MCIT room at his usual time. As soon as he pushed open the door, there was a colossal cheer. All the detectives were on their feet, clapping and grinning.

Hopkins looked bewildered.

'What on earth is going on, John? Have I retired without knowing it?'

'Come and look, sir', said Reilly, steering him over to a whiteboard at the back of the room. The front page of the 'Angling Times' had been printed off and enlarged many times.

'TOP COP COPS CRUCIAN RECORD!', ran the headline.

'Not particularly imaginative', muttered Hopkins, glowing bright red.

The accompanying photo showed him kneeling, in his suit, holding the fish and giving a confused smile.

'Read on, sir', said Reilly, his grin almost splitting his craggy face in two.

'*Top cop Detective Inspector Tomos Hopkins sensationally landed a new British record Crucian* carp at *Yr Hen Chwarel* lake, near Bridgend, South Wales, whilst making an arrest. The fish took a luncheon meat offering, tipped with red maggot, while DI Hopkins and his colleague were arresting a suspect. Being the nearest person to the rod, DI Hopkins was forced to pick it up. Without any previous experience, he managed to land the fish after a thrilling 15-minute battle, with the able assistance of Chief Bailiff Craig Walters.

The catch has been officially verified as a Crucian carp by the British Record Fish Committee and, after calibration of the two weighing devices used, an official weight of five pounds two ounces, comfortably beating the previous record of four pounds fourteen ounces, was recorded.

DI Hopkins was unavailable for comment, but Bailiff Walters said,

'We're very proud that this fish was landed from our club water. We are a long standing private members only club – but it looks as if we may have a couple of vacancies now.'

A local man in his sixties was arrested in connection with the death of Jason Reynolds, another club member, at the water several weeks ago.'

Hopkins shook his head and walked over to his desk. The partition had been adorned with multiple Post-Its, in different colours, cut into the shape of fish. All bore various jokes, mostly on a 'carping on' theme, but one said,

'Was it a knife – or was it poisson?'

Hopkins chuckled embarrassedly. 'That one's almost good.'

313

'That was me, sir', said Reilly.

There was also a printout of a still from Jaws, showing a shocked-looking Chief Brody, and the words, 'Not the first cop who became a fisherman!'

He settled down, weakly, not knowing what to say. The others gathered round, expectantly, and he supposed he should say something. But he hadn't got beyond,

'I really appreciate this, everyone. It means a lot to me', and wondering what the hell he was going to say next, when thankfully he was saved by the appearance of Chief Superintendent Jeffries.

'Could you pop into my office, Tom?'

There was another huge cheer as he exited the room.

As they walked down the corridor to Jeffries' office, the Chief murmured, 'I thought it looked like you could do with an excuse to leave, Tom. I know how embarrassed you get about these things.'

'Thank you, sir', said Hopkins gratefully.

'Sit down, sit down.' Jeffries closed the door behind them, and then sat behind his desk.

'I wanted to update you, confidentially, on where we are with Richards, Tom. As you know, the morning after you and Reilly got the confession, I got the Drugs Team to speak with him instead of you. I thought you were too close to it, and it's their business, they have the know-how in fixing up protection, etc.'

'It's turning out to be even bigger than we imagined. There's a chance to roll up one of the big London gangs that the Met have been after for years. So the Met were able to make a very good offer to look after Richards' family, and I'm pleased to tell you he has accepted. Names, co-operation on accounts, the works. Of course, his family will have to be re-located.'

Hopkins felt a pang of guilt.

'Don't go feeling bad about it, Tom', said Jeffries. 'Richards put them all in danger when he made his pact with the Devil all those years ago. Now, because of what you did, there's a chance for them to be free of the curse he put them under.'

'So, all in all, a great result for us. We've solved a murder and got a confession, wound up a decent-sized drug operation on our patch, and now the Met think they'll be able to roll up a major gang in London, which I have insisted we get joint credit for.'

He looked directly at Hopkins.

'I'm doubly impressed that you managed it with all that's been going on in your personal life.'

'DS Reilly has done a huge amount too, sir. Both in solving this case and helping me get through the personal side.'

'I know. It has been noted, and we'll have our eyes on him for future advancement. But it's you I wanted to talk about. You know one of the Chief Inspector positions has been vacant for six months, since Rhiannon Morgan retired, and we haven't lined up a replacement for her yet. I want to recommend you for the job.'

'But sir, I'm barely coping with the job I have!', protested Hopkins.

'That's because you push yourself too hard, take too much on yourself. As Chief Inspector, you'd be head of a team, so you'd be able to delegate much more. And I need you, to pass on your expertise to the younger staff. You never have any time at the moment, with running from one thing to the next.'

Hopkins looked uncertain.

'Look, at least think about it. Talk it over with Mair.'

Jeffries paused, then looked sharply at Hopkins.

'And speaking of Mair, don't think I haven't noticed you avoiding my invitations to get together for dinner.'

'But sir!', protested Hopkins. 'I haven't been avoiding –'

'No excuses, Tom! I won't have it. I'll get my secretary to make reservations and put it in your diary. We need to celebrate this properly.'

'Yes sir', said Hopkins, weakly.

'Good man. Well, get back out there. I imagine the fuss has died down now. And think about what I said.'

'About the promotion or dinner, sir?'

'Only the first is optional, Tom. Now be off with you.'

Hopkins returned to his desk. Reilly was happily making up a list of invitees to celebratory drinks the following night.

'All of our lot, of course. And the Hanger – he gave us that tip about checking up on Richards' old firm – Nick Goodall from the Drugs Team – PCSO Jones – need to give her a big shout-out.' He paused. 'And Dr Madhvani, I suppose.'

'You're finally getting to like her, then, John?'

'I wouldn't say like, sir. More tolerate. But she really did go the extra mile for us, and much quicker than old Morty would have. And I bet she's a real laugh after a few drinks.'

He grinned innocently up at Hopkins.

'Shame Shadows isn't available, as a venue.'

Hopkins punched him on the shoulder.

...

A few days later, on a Sunday afternoon, Hopkins and Mair drove out to Merthyr Mawr, passing by Ewenny Mill, and turning right just after the turning for Heronston Lane.

Hopkins suppressed a shiver as they passed.

He still hadn't told Mair the full story of what had gone on there, but the details of the dank attic, the smell which he now knew to have been burnt flesh, and McMahon stepping out of the shadows to point that huge black automatic at his head, were burned into his brain. He was glad when they reached the car park, under the dappled shade of the trees, changed into walking boots, and picked up their rucksacks.

They set off down the path through the woods, towards the dunes and the sea. After a few minutes, with mild surprise, he realised that they had naturally slipped into walking hand in hand, like so many years ago.

Emerging from the woods, they reached the sea, and turned left along the high shingle bank, towards the dunes. Happy though he was, Hopkins' sense of foreboding grew. He had told Mair about the offer of promotion, but she had received it non-committally. He had half-heartedly tried to raise it a few times since, but she had avoided discussing it. He sensed though, that she was building up to something. He knew she would prefer it if he took early retirement, that she was worried about the effect on his health.

What if she asked him to give it up? He himself didn't know the answer he would give.

At last, they reached the dunes and started to climb up the path that led along the tops of the highest ones. Hopkins was getting fitter, a product of his lunchtime training sessions with Reilly, and was barely short of breath when they reached the top.

What had been their favourite spot was now overgrown with straggly gorse, so they walked on a little further until they found a secluded spot off the path, under some stunted trees, looking out over the sea.

Mair took the picnic rug out of her rucksack and spread it on the short, rabbit-cropped grass, while Hopkins took out the flask and sandwiches. They sat for a while, munching away and sipping tea.

Suddenly, Mair turned to him and asked,

'So, what have you decided? About the promotion.'

'Well,' he paused. 'I'd like to take it, but only if you think it's a good idea. It should mean more regular hours, and giving more supervision and training. I'll still be able to get involved in the bigger cases. But overall, it should be more regular and less stressful. And I'll have a team to support me.'

She was silent.

'What do you think, *cariad*?', he asked.

She thought. 'Well, at first, I was dead against it, knowing how you are. You'd end up shouldering more and more of the burden – you wouldn't be able to help it. You know I've wanted you to give up for a while, even before the diagnosis.'

She turned to him.

318

'But this time, I think you really mean it. I don't know what it was, but I think something happened to you on this case, that made you think about yourself for once. And about us, and what your life means.'

He looked at her, surprised.

'I could tell, the night after that raid on the mill back there. And you've been taking more care of yourself since. Eating properly at work. Training with John. Even inviting me out for romantic walks, you old fool.'

She carried on. 'And I know what this job means to you, Twm. Even after all these years, after all the terrible things you've seen, you haven't turned all cynical, like a lot of them; you still care. You still want to help people, to make a change. I'd never take that away from you. It's who you are. And it's why I love you.'

Surprised, all he could say was,

'Who's the romantic fool, now?'

She smiled crookedly.

'Thank you for leaving out the 'old'.' But I mean it. I think you should accept, if that's what you want.'

Hopkins thought for a moment.

'I wasn't sure that was what I wanted, not until now. But now I know you're OK with it – I think I will. There's only one problem.'

'And what's that?'

'We've got to go to dinner with Chief Superintendent Jeffries and his wife, next Friday.'

She laughed and slipped an arm around his waist. He put his arm around her shoulder and they sat close together, watching the dancing golden path cast by the sun, across the grey waters of the Hafren.